ANY BETTER THAN THIS

A Summer of Love Story

ERIC SEAN RAWSON

Black Rose Writing | Texas

ISBN: 978-1-68513-067-1
PUBLISHED BY BLACK ROSE WRITING
www.blackrosewriting.com

Printed in the United States of America
Suggested Retail Price (SRP) $20.95

Any Better Than This is printed in Garamond

*As a planet-friendly publisher, Black Rose Writing does its best to eliminate unnecessary waste to reduce paper usage and energy costs, while never compromising the reading experience. As a result, the final word count vs. page count may not meet common expectations.

Praise for Rawson's previous novel,

BANANA REPUBLIC

"Like Quentin Tarantino's *Pulp Fiction,* Eric Rawson's *Banana Republic* incorporates irony, humor, and the lurid and seedy conventions of schlock to create a wonderfully entertaining, unputdownable novel."
–Ron Hansen, author of *The Kid, Desperados,* and *The Assassination of Jesse James by the Coward Robert Ford*

"*Banana Republic* is an absolute delight, as funny as it is apt, as inventive as it is entertaining."
–Amy Meyerson, author of *The Bookshop of Yesterdays* and *The Imperfects*

"A debut novel that sings with polish on every page."
–Aimee Bender, author of *The Particular Sadness of Lemon Cake* and *Willful Creatures*

ANY BETTER THAN THIS

*"An assumption of 'chance' encapsulates
all the inevitable unpredictability of the world."*
–Sir David John Spiegelhalter

PART ONE

Pasadena, May 15, 2020

Nowhere is the mixture of fact and fiction more potent and ineluctable than in episodes of family history, the telling of which necessitates a willingness to embrace the sentimental, the absurd, and the factually false. I don't pretend that the adventure that follows here—this story of murder and miscommunication—is an accurate record of events. It unfolds over three days in 1967, during the Summer of Love, when, as we all know, reality was more elastic than normal—as it is in memory and imagination, where family stories reside.

Hunkered down in the San Gabriel Valley with my seventeen-year-old daughter, Talia, waiting for the pandemic to burn out, I have been thinking a lot about my family and the precariousness of life-as-we-know-it. Fifty-three years ago my parents, a computer engineer and a colorblind marketing executive, married. In 1971, they produced me. My father, Elliot Ames, died of cancer at the beginning of this year, and for the last few weeks I've been going through boxes of his things at my childhood home in Encino, reconstructing a past that might somehow reassure me—of what, I don't know. That I've inherited the right stuff for navigating unstable times? That like my parents' marriage, my own might somehow be salvaged from the ashes of betrayal? That there's a "reason for everything"? (How I hate that phrase.)

I've spent most of the lockdown—between excruciating Zoom meetings—watching Korean soap-operas and conscientiously nurturing my microbiome. I've also done a lot of reading. An inveterate bedtime reader and anxious night owl, I empathize with all those who, on the threshold of dreamland, struggle to calm the heart and engage the mind. Meaning: would these insomniacs appreciate, say, my finishing a novel about a harrowing episode in my parents' lives? A quick survey over toast and orange juice reveals what I already know: Talia prefers audiobooks and doesn't remember what she's recently listened to. If she had to read, *for fun*, she guesses she'd pick up an old Harry Potter book or maybe something with a kick-ass girl who lives in the future.

I doubt this story will capture her interest.

Like me, both my parents had a bedtime reading habit. My father developed his to relieve boredom during an involuntary stint in the Army in the late 1950s, when he was stationed in Germany. He was of the generation of "middlebrow" readers who did not expect to plumb the depths for spiritual meaning or messages of social improvement. He simply liked the experience of reading—invariably a Book of the Month Club selection or a *New York Times* bestseller. When my father finished a book, he made a practice of inking on the flyleaf his name and the date. He shelved the volumes in strict chronological order in an old walnut bookcase. When he died, his modest library, along with his record collection and his audio diary on reel-to-reel tapes, went into the cardboard boxes along with his awards and souvenirs from trips abroad. Last month, when I drove over to Encino to check on the house while my mother shelters in place at her A-frame in Big Bear where she can "get something done for a change," I retrieved the boxes marked *1966* and *1967*, so I have a good idea of what my father was reading immediately prior to my parents' marriage. During these weeks of coronavirus lockdown, I've been working my way through the books, continually surprised, letting other minds shape me and, therefore, the narrative that follows here. For those who are interested, my father read the following: *Cancer Ward, Unsafe at Any Speed, The Naked Ape, S Is for Space, The Ghost in the Machine, The Freelance Pallbearers, Up Above the World, Office Politics, Octopussy & the Living Daylights, In Cold Blood, Wide Sargasso Sea, The Chinese Looking Glass, The Old Man and the Bureaucrats, Paper Lion, The Moon Is a Harsh Mistress, The Last Picture Show, Inside South America, Phyllis Diller's Marriage Manual, The Tolkien Reader, The Art of Memory,* and *Rosemary's Baby.*

In the mid-Sixties, there was a lot in the California air about fate and predestination and synchronicity. Perhaps such thinking helped relieve the anxiety of peak affluence and American global domination, or maybe an Aquarian precession of the equinoxes really was generating psychic skeins of random connections. I suppose such thinking was—and is—valid in the sense that unseen chains of events cross, and occasionally tangle, creating the knots that are the significant moments in our lives. Indeed, the tale I tell here is basically a series of knots of family testimony and allusion, desultory research in the digital archives, and my own imagination.

What follows is a personal entertainment, a fact-based fabrication. But having known my parents well, I imagine that what happened to them in June 1967, when they were young and America had burst its seams and was beginning to fall apart, was something like what I have put down here. Or not. Imagination is not witness.

· · ·

Redondo Beach, June 7, 1967
Everybody knew it didn't get any better than this.

The Peking Palace was packed with engineers and draftsmen, supervisors, and secretaries from Pacifidyne, Inc., the secretaries in skirts and closed-toe shoes, the supervisors in suits and ties, the engineers and draftsmen in short-sleeved white shirts, drab pants, and brow-line eyeglasses. Every day at noon the Research, Development, and Design Division disgorged nineteen hundred of Pacifidyne's thirty thousand employees onto the sun-flattened Southern California landscape for one hour of hysterical conviviality. Although it was only Wednesday, all of them were planning, at the top of their lungs, for a weekend of country clubs and beaches and barbecues, while they drank beer and dipped egg rolls in sweet-and-sour sauce. Gusts of laughter and lascivious comments about Pacifidyne's female employees filled the back room, which was reserved for packs of smart, vaguely patriotic analysts and aerospace engineers, their faces veiled in clouds of cigarette smoke, glistening in the heat, all complacent in the knowledge that their jobs were secure, their wives were the best people on the planet, and that even if their children were going to hell, as was obviously the case, the hell they were going to was provisioned with every luxury of the modern world.

• • • •

Westwood

The large orange tabby cat, wearing a collar with the name *Kismet* tooled on the blue leather, had spent the night patrolling the neighborhood, searching, it might be assumed, for food, water, and a mate. It had been a fine moonlit night, made for adventure, but the day had grown hot, so he returned through a torn window screen to the kitchen of the ground-floor apartment where he lived with the person who provided him with irregular meals. At the moment, this benefactor was seated at the kitchen table, topless, counting twenty-dollar bills into tidy stacks, which she secured with rubber bands. Glancing up at him, she stowed the bundles in a crumpled brown paper bag. Kismet sat on the counter next to a pile of the dirty dishes and watched her with blank green eyes. As she folded the top of the bag, once, twice, a knock sounded on the door. She looked up and gave him a happy smile. Kismet yawned and climbed into the sink to lap water from the dripping faucet.

• • • •

Redondo Beach

Freddy Happ raised his camera and pointed the telephoto lens across the expanse of parking lot at the front of the Peking Palace. The morning marine layer had burned off and the parking lot was scorching. He was a pudgy man with thin hair and a face the color of a basketball, and he was sweating through his shirt. The slump of his shoulders suggested that his birth had been a stroke of bad luck. He sat behind the wheel of a six-year-old white Ford Falcon with carburetor problems and a rear tire that would not hold air for more than twelve hours.

As Elliot Ames crossed the street from Pacifidyne Building C, a charmless edifice faced with phony tan bricks and topped with a complex array of ventilators and air-conditioning units, which occupied two city blocks where once had been St. Clotilde Catholic school—and before that a salt marsh—Happ pressed the shutter. His target, Ames, waited for a refrigerator truck to back into the alley beside the restaurant. Then he walked on rapidly past the neat row of date palms to the front door, where a group of Building C stragglers was trying to enter while a group of early birds was trying to exit. Happ pressed the shutter again and laid the camera on the car seat so that he could pencil a notation on the clipboard that rested on his meaty round thighs.

On the eastern edge of the parking lot, an Econoline delivery van (FRANCO'S—FLOWERS WITH SOUL) reposed in the glaring light. The rear of the van was occupied by F.B.I. Special Agent Bert Armbruster, and the front passenger seat by Special Agent Don Clegg. Both had Koss electrostatic headphones over their ears. It was hot in the van. The agents' suit jackets sagged on wire hangers on the rear door; their ties drooped from their collars.

Armbruster was wearing mirrored aviator glasses to hide the inflamed blood vessels in his eyes, and he was chewing wintergreen gum to kill the smell of alcohol. Clegg, neat and competent even in the heat, raised a camera with a long lens and pointed it through the windshield.

Armbruster snapped his gum. "Whaddya got, Don?"

"Dunno. Same guy we've seen all week."

Clegg twisted the focusing ring, and Freddy Happ's automobile came into sharp relief. The shutter clicked. Clegg thumbed the film-advance lever.

In the back of the van Armbruster leaned toward the bank of electronics and turned a knob the size of a salad plate, tuning in snatches of conversation from the tables in the Peking Palace:

". . . best bladder man in Los Angeles. . . [*break up*]. . . now Reagan's governor he's gonna crack down on these. . . see [*static*] still get three-percent loans in the Valley. . . [*shrieks of laughter*]. . . I told her, baby, you either take that off or [*dissolving in static*]. . . ."

"Goddamn mikes," Armbruster muttered. He twisted another, smaller knob, which had no effect on the signals from the restaurant.

Armbruster leaned over the back of the seat to peer through the windshield. "Where is he?"

"Two o'clock. The white Falcon. It's been here every day. I thought it belonged to one of the restaurant staff, but I can see the guy's got a Nikon with a three-hundred-millimeter lens."

"Not bad."

"Not as good as ours. I'm guessing C.I.A."

"He might be Army intelligence. They could've tumbled onto this place."

"Maybe someone tipped off D.I.A."

"Goddammit." Armbruster snapped his gum. "Who's that guy going in the restaurant? We've seen him too."

"I count about five-hundred guys we've seen."

"The one holding the door. Caucasian, thirty years old, handsome."

"Handsome?"

Armbruster turned his head so that his partner's face was reflected on the twin surfaces of his mirrored shades. "Handsome. Yeah. I said it."

• • •

Elliot Ames was swept through the doorway on a seething wave of techno-whiz energy. The late-arriving engineers dispersed through the room, shouting for their lunchmates, who shouted back, guiding them with frantic heartiness through the steamy restaurant.

Elliot stopped to talk to the man behind the register. "Hey, Percy. What's wrong with the air conditioning?"

Percy Wu grunted. He tugged at the black vest he was wearing. "The compressor always goes out the first hot day of summer."

Elliot jerked his head toward the rear. "Are they back there?"

"What do you think? You come in here every damn day. I don't know why you defense guys are so crazy for Chinese. Go eat a hamburger once in a while, why don'tcha."

• • •

On the western edge of the parking lot, a man known in his organization as Pegasus peered through high-powered Swiss military binoculars. Pegasus—who in ordinary life had appropriated the name Albert Carpenter from a child who had died of polio in 1926—was wearing a golf hat, a golf shirt, plaid trousers, and white soft-soled shoes. His clubs were on the back seat of the Buick. As soon as he finished his business for the day, he planned to hit the links. Along with tacos, mom-and-pop gun stores, and dental anesthesia, year-round golf was one of the things Pegasus liked most about California.

When he had cruised past the rear of the Peking Palace on his regular sweep the week before, looking for the chalk mark that signaled a drop from his anonymous asset in Pacifidyne, he had identified at least two surveillance vehicles. One was a flower-delivery van that did not belong there; the other was a sun-damaged Ford Falcon positioned at the north edge of the lot. The driver, a moon-faced man, had his sausage-like fingers wrapped around an expensive Nikon F2. He was here again, taking photos.

Pegasus laid down the binoculars. The situation was not good. They were watching the restaurant. That meant they had knowledge of the asset in Pacifidyne, a man Pegasus knew only by his designation, Canis Minor. Canis Minor provided a steady stream of classified material—about what Pegasus never knew. The microfilms were sealed when he retrieved them from the dead-drop in Culver City, which he visited whenever he spotted the chalk mark. In turn, he handed the films off to Sagittarius—at least he thought it was Sagittarius—at a dead-drop in San Francisco. From there they went to the consulate in Pacific Heights and into the diplomatic pouch for transport out of the country. He did not know who Canis Minor was, but obviously someone in American intelligence did.

If Pegasus had been a man who trembled, he would have trembled.

Elliot slid into the horseshoe booth. He pulled his wallet, as thick as a paperback, from his pants pocket and laid it on the table. Like the other men in the booth, he had loosened his necktie and was perspiring. A gust of Mennen aftershave blended unpleasantly with the miasma of hair tonic, tobacco, and chow mein.

Unlike Arthur Reuhl and Gordon Blackmon, who were working on their third beers, Elliot Ames was feeling anxious this Wednesday noon, three days before his marriage to an absolutely wonderful, admirably intelligent, physically appealing—he could not emphasize this enough—woman named Constance Campbell. She had been nominated by an IBM 1401 computer at Operation Matchmaker in Cambridge, Massachusetts, as the ideal mate for Elliot, a selection confirmed by Elliot's own after-hours labor on the CDC 6600 supercomputer at Pacifidyne, Inc., RD&D Division. He and Connie had a 92.4 percent compatibility rating and a predicted marital success rate of 88.1 percent, the numerical difference between compatibility and success attributable to the possibility that one or both of the spouses might, in the unknowable future, stumble across someone with a higher match score. That possibility, a statistician would tell you, was negligible. Operation Matchmaker, Eliot had no doubt, was the future of pair-bonding.

"The blushing bridegroom!" Arthur Reuhl cried.

Elliot signaled to the waitress to bring him a beer. Arthur and Gordon had eaten all the eggrolls. Their lips were shiny with cooking oil, their eyes with alcohol.

Elliot rubbed his hands together. He grinned. "I'm going to devour an entire duck, bones and all, that's how hungry I am. I can't tell you what kind of day I've had with the new interface message processors."

"Now we have to hear about it," Gordon said to Arthur.

"Nope," Elliot said. "Not gonna think about *imps*. All I wanna do is eat. This is my last Peking duck for three weeks. At six p.m., I'm wiping my mind clear. Not gonna think about work. Not gonna think about you jokers."

"What are you talking about?" Arthur blew cigarette smoke in Elliot's face. "You can't find a plate of duck in San Francisco?"

"Berkeley, my friend. Then on to Honolulu."

"L.A., Berkeley, Honolulu," Gordon shouted drunkenly. "It's all one party!"

. . .

Berkeley

Constance Campbell held a smoldering, lipstick-stained cigarette in her outstretched right hand. Her left hand was wrapped around a banana-yellow telephone receiver connected to the wall-mount in the kitchen by an extraordinarily long cord. She wore a sleeveless blouse and capri pants, and she was folded onto a chaise longue in the sunroom overlooking the backyard of the Campbell home. Below, the city stretched into the hazy blue distance.

"Honestly, Sheilah," she said in an aggrieved voice, "I don't see anything wrong with hiring a private investigator. You can't be too sure. Look what happened to you and Philip. I'd like to know *before* the wedding is what I'm saying. No surprises."

She took a drag on her cigarette. Her intelligent gray eyes gazed out the window through lashes furred with mascara. In the yard a hairy guy without a shirt slouched on an Adirondack chair, annotating a paperback book (which, if she had had better eyesight, Connie Campbell would have spotted as her copy of *Games People Play*) with a ballpoint pen. He had a patchy, infuriating beard. Her brother, Frank.

"What do you mean—*predictable*? I am not!"

She listened.

"Well, of course, I love Elliot. Who do you think I am?" Connie unfolded into a standing position and, holding her cigarette so that she did not burn a hole in the fabric, pulled at her waistband. She leaned on one hip and shook her leg to get the blood flowing again.

"Sheilah. Sheilah! Let me stop you right there. You know perfectly well I believe trust is the basis of a relationship. It may not be original, but that doesn't make it less valid. But can you really trust a computer to get the details right? It seems so gimmicky. I want to make sure I have a *basis* is all."

She emitted a cloud of smoke, which settled around her blond bob-and-bangs hair.

. . .

Westwood

A wisp of smoke curled from the cone of sandalwood incense smoldering on a porcelain saucer and touched the heaving shadowy forms entwined on the mattress on the floor. Thumbtacked to the wall above the mattress was a promotional poster for *Blow-Up*. The orange tabby cat squatted by the saucer and sniffed delicately. Through the open window came the sound of a garbage truck's hydraulic packer, drowning out the strains of the flamenco guitar someone was playing in the next apartment. The mood was spoiled.

Fortunately, the heaving forms had finished, with a long mutual exhalation, like air hissing from an inner tube. The woman pushed herself off the damp and, now that she noticed it, unwashed body of the man on the mattress, feeling at her groin a familiar stickiness, which she supposed she should rinse off before it became uncomfortable. She crossed her legs and sat back on the mattress.

"What was your name again?" she said.

"Jim." He reached out an arm and felt around on the floor for his underwear.

"Names," she sighed. She ran her hand between the mattress and the wall and pulled out a cloth bag. It was embroidered with explosive red and green mandalas. Uncrossing her legs, she crawled over to the dresser, on which rested two bricks of Afghan Primo hashish sheathed in aluminum foil and Saranwrap. She jumped up and slid the bricks into the bag.

She chuckled. "Thank you for the home delivery, Jim. This will truly be a gift worth giving."

"You're giving that shit away? Five grand of Primo?"

"Why not?"

He stood up and pulled on his underwear and yawned. "Yeah, why not?"

"I'm heading to San Francisco. I'm going to donate these babies to the Grateful Dead as thanks for all the amazing vibes they're putting into the world. I heard they're seriously short of dope."

"Far out. What was your name?"

She stretched her naked arms and tilted her head back and forth. "I've been thinking about it," she said. "I like the sound of Morning Star." The name—bright, slightly mystical, referencing both Venus and the Virgin Mother—promised, she thought, a way of organizing the incoherent pieces of herself into a new person. Her therapist, Dr. Malcolm (Tuesdays and Fridays), had not been much help in that regard. If anything, he might have been taking advantage of her, although she was trying to stop making that kind of judgment.

"Morning Star. That's cool. Did you have fun?"

"Except for the spanking part."

"Oh. Sorry. It seemed like you'd be into it."

Morning Star thought about Dr. Malcolm. "I guess I should be," she said.

Jim pulled on his pants and looked around for his shirt.

"Hey, Jim?"

"Yeah."

"Do you want to crash here while I'm gone? I need someone to take care of Kismet." Morning Star leaned down and swept up the orange tabby and kissed him on the neck. The cat yowled and scratched frantically at her bare shoulders, drawing blood. She dropped him with a cry, and he bolted onto the windowsill and began to lick himself.

Jim hopped on one foot as he pulled on a boot. "When will you be back?"

"Maybe."

"Maybe?"

"Yes."

"Far out." Jim pulled on his other boot.

"He's allergic to milk."

"No problem. I can't stay. I'm allergic to cats," Jim said, wiping his nose with the back of his hand. "I gotta roll, baby."

Morning Star flopped back on the mattress and rubbed her breasts and inhaled the sweet scent of sandalwood. She smiled. "See you in another dream."

. . .

Freddy Happ rewound the exposed film and unlatched the back of the camera. He took out the yellow roll of film and dropped it into its black plastic canister, then maneuvered a fresh roll into place, clumsily fitting the leader onto the take-up spool, and advanced it two turns and closed the camera back. He was drenched in sweat.

Pegasus watched through the Swiss binoculars. He wondered if the operative would develop the film himself or send it directly to Langley and wait for instructions. He was C.I.A. Or, more likely, some kind of freelancer. Maybe D.I.A. He did not look like F.B.I. Those guys maintained a semblance of professionalism. For instance, the guy with the camera in the passenger seat of the flower-delivery van. A necktie? Who was he fooling?

And who was the slender man who had caused both the fat man and the F.B.I. agent to lift their cameras when he approached the restaurant? He was a Pacifidyne engineer, no question about it: white shirt, pocket protector full of pens, healthy. Was he Canis Minor?

Special Agent Clegg, tracking Happ, his eighteen-inch lens resting heavily in his careful hands, wondered why it was that whenever the Bureau opened a domestic surveillance case, every other intelligence agency on the face of the earth piled into the game. But seriously: this sweaty donkey?

. . .

The men fell to their food like wolves on three little lambs. Gordon Blackmon's order was, actually, lamb, with cumin and broccoli. Arthur Reuhl had the egg foo young with shrimp—the second most popular dish at the Peking Palace. Elliot Ames reduced his Peking duck to a heap of bones. Wiping the grease from his fingers with a red paper napkin, he leaned back and drained his beer and groaned.

Arthur pushed away his plate. "So how're you holding up, Elliot?"

"I remain confident in my decision," Elliot declared. "At this point on the timeline, marriage is mandatory. I don't mind telling you guys that I never understood what my life was missing until I met Connie."

"But if you get married now, you'll never know what your alternatives might have been," Arthur objected. "No more dreams."

"Nothing kills romance like marriage, is that it?"

"It's true," Arthur said morosely.

"Half true," Gordon corrected.

"You think everything is half true."

"That's true." Gordon nodded. "Half true."

"Jesus, Gordon," Elliot said, "what kind of engineer are you? I don't want to fly to Hawaii on an airliner that's half true."

"Granted," Gordon said. He belched. "But engineering and—whaddaycallit?—propositions!—propositions about the world are two different beasts. You can't engineer the truth."

"You might be wrong about that."

"You computer guys think you know the mind of God," Arthur said. He meant to amuse, but Gordon nodded solemnly.

"Anyway!" Arthur said brightly. "Gordon and I—"

"And our better-halfs—"

"—Will swoop into Oakland airport on Saturday morning for moral support."

"Halves."

"I see on the news the hippies are swarming San Francisco like some kind of goddamn plague," Arthur said. "Don't get caught up in that."

"No danger. I'm getting off the 101 in San Jose," Elliot said.

"Smart man. What's the itinerary?"

• • •

"First thing when I get there," came the thin sound of a man's voice, "I'm stopping on campus for Knizner's seminar."

Special Agent Armbruster, cursing under his breath and wishing he had a double whiskey sour and a couple of Dexedrines, fiddled with the knobs on the control panel. He had finally found a table mike with a partially intelligible signal, and now it was swallowed in a rush of whining interference.

The man's voice re-emerged: ". . . wasting time with arpurghleshshsh."

"I'm telling you, the key is distributed networks. It's this. . . [*garbled*]. . . in the U.K. . . ."

"Goddammit," Armbruster bellowed. "What's going on?"

Clegg laid down his three-pound hunk of photographic technology and climbed into the back of the van. He finessed one of the dials, his other hand pressing the headphone against his left ear. "Busboy probably poured water on the flowers again. Those artificial displays look too real."

". . .if you can use it to figure the vector sheer, we could. . . "

". . .in any case, that's the theory. How it performs under real-world conditions hasn't been established. . . ."

Armbruster beat his fists on his thighs in frustration. "These've gotta be the most boring guys in the world. This is bullshit."

"It's called surveillance." Clegg used his patient voice. "It's called an investigation."

"Says who?"

"Says whoever figured out that the leak at Pacifidyne was running through this joint. They found signals on the back of the building or something. Jesus, Bert, don't you read the reports?"

"There's gotta be twenty-thousand people work across the street. They don't all show up at noon every day to discuss their spy plans. We're wasting time. Let's get out there and do some work. Rattle the owner and see what falls out."

Clegg frowned. "If you can't shoot something or beat it up, you think you're wasting your life. This is not the time to cowboy it, big guy. We don't want to tip off this son of a bitch, give him a head start."

Armbruster patted his shoulder holster and spoke to his .38 Smith & Wesson: "It's all right, sweetie. He's so silly, isn't he?"

The feed from the table mikes was now nothing but a high-pitched wash of sound. Armbruster snatched off his headphones and threw them to the floor.

"I'm gettin' outta this stinkin' place," he said, lunging toward the rear door.

"Nope!" Clegg's hand shot out and grabbed his partner by the belt. "You blow our cover, and I will sure as shit hunt you down and slice off your virile member."

Armbruster paused. He snapped his gum. Shrugged. "It ain't much, but it's all I got," he said and flopped back on the floor of the van.

. . .

"I'm telling you," Elliot said, "avionics'll be deader'n God as soon as NASA lands a man on the moon. The money'll vanish. The future, my tin-bender friends, is communications."

"Spoken like a static man," Arthur said. "The Signal Corps, for chrissake. That's barely real Army."

"Half true," Elliot said.

The waitress brought three fortune cookies on a lacquered tray with a picture of a man in a robe smoking an opium pipe.

The crowd was thinning.

Arthur tore the cellophane and cracked open the cookie. He read from the slip of paper: "*You will find peace in labor*. Ugh."

"*Expect water and ask for wine*," Gordon read.

"Depressing. Whaddya have?"

Elliot munched his fortune cookie. He held out his hand, and Arthur and Gordon dumped the shards of their own cookies onto his palm, a daily ritual. To the others they tasted like dried glue, but Elliot loved the flavor. He swallowed and read from his slip: "*Keep your soul bright as air*."

"That's wisdom?" Gordon said.

"You dumb missile-head," Arthur said. "You got no poetry."

"I got poetry. Listen: 'There once was a girl from Madras, who had a magnificent ass—'"

While they were talking, the three men had been counting money onto the lacquered tray. Now they slid out of the horseshoe booth, stretching, cracking knuckles, tightening the knots of neckties.

Elliot slipped his paper fortune into his shirt pocket. He picked up his wallet, hefted it, and slid it into his rear pocket.

"Three and a half hours till traffic," Arthur said. "Then I'm in my pool till beddy-bye."

As they headed across the room, Elliot picked up the unopened fortune cookies from the lunchtime ruins on the next table. He pocketed one and cracked open the other, glancing at the paper slip before depositing it in his shirt pocket. He stuffed the cookie in his mouth and crunched noisily.

. . .

Clegg, peering through his lens at the white Ford Falcon, saw Freddy Happ raise his camera and point it at the front door of the restaurant. He swung his own camera around in time to capture an image of the three engineers stepping into the afternoon glare. They were talking animatedly as they moved past the pygmy date palms towards the crosswalk. Clegg wondered why these particular pointy-headed types warranted attention from national intelligence, but he decided not to discuss the matter with Armbruster, who was lying on the floor of the van, whispering to himself. Clegg figured they could go inside as soon as the lunch crowd had vacated the restaurant and check out the microphone situation on the q.t. Maybe have a bite to eat and cool their testicles.

Pegasus watched Freddy Happ lay down his camera, wipe his face with a plaid handkerchief, and lean forward to start the engine. It took several minutes.

As the Falcon moved across the parking lot, Pegasus, too panicked now for nine holes with the club pro, turned the key in the ignition and followed, checking the perimeter for signs of additional surveillance. Just the forlorn delivery van. He cruised slowly by, taking a good look at the individual in the passenger seat with the camera—definitely F.B.I.— and plunged into the traffic on the boulevard.

As he passed through the spic-and-span expanse of Design Room Six, Elliot was thinking about Connie Campbell's muscled, mathematically perfect thighs. Draftsmen on tall stools bent over the islands of their desks. Engineers with pieces of chalk in their hands clustered, arguing, around blackboards. A Muzak version of "Good Vibrations," arranged for strings and vibraphone, wafted through the air.

Elliot passed into the secretarial bullpen. Accompanied by the chattering of Selectric typewriters and the chuffing of a mimeograph machine, he progressed along the ranks of desks, three dozen pairs of eyes following his progress, while three dozen sets of fingers missed not a single keystroke. Elliot Ames was marrying the woman who had occupied the most despised position at Pacifidyne, Inc. As the Assistant to the Head of Personnel, Connie Campbell had been, until a month ago, the secretaries' immediate superior and an all-round pain-in-the-keester, who had established mandatory overtime the last week of each month and banned champagne at birthday parties, despite the fact that she herself drank Tom Collinses on Friday afternoons with the executives in the Wing (into which Elliot now stepped, on his way to the computer lab). Connie Campbell had no well-wishers in the secretarial bullpen; it was a humongous relief to see her go.

Elliot continued down a corridor lined with the glassed offices of mid-level executives, all of whom had telephones glued to their ears, possibly talking to one another. He pushed open the door of his chilly research lab, home of the massive CDC 6600, which Elliot knew for a fact cost in excess of two-and-a-half million dollars. The guys over at Boeing had a 6600, but he suspected they did not understand its full potential. At RAND, they knew what to do with one of these babies. He was not sure about the Air Force—they never shared their research—but he had a pal at Los Alamos who had made some wizardly modifications for them, diagrams of which he sent to Elliot via the unsecured channels of the U.S. mail.

Around the perimeter of the lab, the members of the computer research group were clumped in teams of two or three. As the manager of a classified government project, Elliot made it a point not to fraternize with his men, although he was a friendly enough guy and they were his natural cohort: enthusiastic engineers in their early thirties. Ten years ago, the computing at Pacifidyne had been done by unmarried women using IBM 1620s, but everything had been replaced, in various divisions of the company, by massive electronic brains and the all-male staffs that maintained them. The room was filled with the clamor of punch-card keys, whirring tapes, intense conversation, and high-pitched electronics.

One of the new hires, a twenty-four-year-old Ph.D. from Caltech named Stefan Blicks, was sitting at a console the size of a canoe. Stefan Blicks had one purpose in life: applying his knowledge of network topology to improving the signal-to-noise ratios in long-distance electronic communications. Blicks had extraordinary stamina. He spent eighty hours a week figuring out how to make the mainframe talk to the smaller computer nodes the Pentagon was developing into a system that could withstand the effects of a nuclear attack. Elliot frequently had to battle the urge to jump into the problem. Earlier in the year, he had been at a meeting of principal ARPA investigators at his alma mater in Ann Arbor, where the bones of the network had been sketched out. He loved to climb down in the trenches and tackle complex problems, but he refrained. Delegate the work, he reminded himself; be a good supervisor; let the men do their jobs.

Just inside the doorway of the lab was a bank of telephones without dials. No one had ever heard them ring. Each phone was marked with the words *Restricted Access / Do Not Use* in red. Every time he came into the room, Elliot was tempted to pick up one of the receivers and find out who was on the other end.

He fought down the temptation and crossed to his doorless office: desk, phone, boxes of punch cards, gooseneck lamp, snapshots, memos, and bulletin boards filled with equations on graph paper. Everything was in tip-top order. He pulled his wallet from his back pocket and put it on the desk. Then he fished the fortune-cookie slips from his shirt pocket and pinned them to one of the cork bulletin boards. The board was neatly papered with hundreds of fortune-cookie messages arranged in chronological order. Elliot was not exactly sure why he kept them, and it bothered him that he was not exactly sure, but there was something about the uniformity of the slips, the pattern of repetition, the day-to-day accumulation, that amused and comforted him, as if by pinning the ridiculous scraps of paper to the cork he somehow marshaled the forces of chance—of *fortune*—into an intelligible matrix.

His office chair swiveled and tilted so that he could rest his feet on his desk while he looked at the bulletin boards. As he contemplated the array of fortunes, he reached for the phone and punched a number on the Touch Tone pad. There was a faint ringing on the other end.

"Hello?" came the sound of Connie's somewhat querulous voice.

"Darling!"

"Elliot? What's wrong? Why are you calling long-distance?"

"Nothing's wrong. Why do you assume there's something wrong? I thought I'd save a dime and call from work is all." He glanced over his shoulder at Stefan Blicks working at the console.

"God forbid you run up a phone bill," Connie said.

"Aw, Connie, don't do that. I wanted to let you know I'll be at your folks' place tomorrow by mid-afternoon."

"We won't wait lunch on you." She laughed. "Daddy says not to forget your checkbook. He says you owe him a hundred-and-seventeen thousand dollars for everything he's put into me over the last twenty-five years. I told him—"

The phone line crackled, and the signal broke up. "Hello?" Elliot shouted. "Are you there?"

"... and don't forget to get traveler's checks. Also, don't...."

"I didn't hear what you said. Hello? Hello? There's something wrong with the line."

The phone emitted a metallic wheeze, then a long, low hum.

Elliot cradled the receiver. At the same instant, the CDC supercomputer clattered to life.

Stefan Blicks leaped up and pumped his fists in the air. "Go, baby!"

Normally, Elliot would have gone to see what Blicks had accomplished, but a profound unease had overcome him. The failure of the phone line was disconcerting, and it triggered deeper anxieties. In three days his mother would fly in from Detroit for the gathering in the Campbells' back yard, along with a minister he had never met and several dozen friends he did not realize they had until Connie unearthed their addresses. He and his mate would be joined in holy matrimony—new people, with new responsibilities. In an instant, he would be embarked on an inevitable course of fatherhood, professional advancement, and comfortable middle age, a solid citizen in possession of the American Dream. It was all working out pretty much as he had envisioned. A year earlier, he had purchased a house. Matters, he had felt, were being mastered. Yet. . . .

As he sat in his office, scanning the wall of paper slips above his desk, some shapeless dark force nibbled at the edges of his consciousness. It was not that the unspooling of his future would eventually end, as all futures end, in death, although the unknowableness of death often kept him awake at night. Rather, when he thought about all the unknowable things in the universe, a cold, dark wave of panic washed from the top of his skull, and another sprang from the pit of his stomach. At his heart, they crashed together in a turbulent vortex.

• • • •

Berkeley

The Campbell home was perched on a hilltop, like a turtle on a sunny rock. From this high vantage, Carl Campbell could point his brass telescope at East Bay Ornamentals, the artificial-flower factory he owned in Oakland. East Bay produced arrangements for the church-and-restaurant trade. For some time, Carl had been considering expanding into the mortuary market but faced resistance from the flower-wholesalers consortium. Lately, when he peered through the telescope at the roof of his company many miles away, he thought about funeral homes, and when he thought about funeral homes, he thought about his own cold body lying in a walnut casket with East Bay

Ornamentals products surrounding it, and he had to get up to refill his highball glass.

He admitted he was the last person on earth you would expect to own a flower business—his aesthetics ran to Spanish leatherwork and the paintings of Thomas Hart Benton—but when he had bought the business at a ninety-percent discount in 1942 from a second-generation Japanese family who were being removed to the Topaz camp in Utah, he figured he could always sell it back at a profit when the war ended. In 1941, he had inherited a tidy lump from his father, and he had resolved to be wise about it, especially since his wife was expecting a baby. That was right before he joined the Navy, like everyone else he knew, and was sent to fight in the Pacific. When the war was over, he spent several months in occupied Japan, learning about the ornamentals business he had left back in Oakland in the capable hands of his wife.

Carl was an unpretentious man. Having never coveted the power and wealth that derives from the exploitation of others, he was content to come home to a drink and the evening paper, with an annual trip to Colorado or a Mexican resort. He was not a club-joiner; he lacked interest in politics or cultural affairs. His ambition was to live exactly like everyone else but a little more comfortably.

His one passion was playing board games. This was unfortunate, since he could never find anyone who wanted to play with him. His wife was afraid she would beat him and he would feel diminished. His daughter was too bossy and impatient; she did not take losing well. His son never exerted himself, letting Carl win in a minimal number of moves so that he could get back to whatever he was doing. Frank referred to his father as a semiconscious tool of the imperium. Carl was big enough to consider that it might be true, although he still wanted to play checkers.

At the moment he was lying low in his den, engaged in a solo game of Parcheesi. He wanted to avoid what was happening in the back yard, where some workers were assembling canopies and stacking wooden chairs in anticipation of the Saturday nuptials. The affair was costing him more than he cared to pay. The musicians alone ran two-hundred dollars, not to mention the photographer, the minister, the formalwear, the catering, the cake, the silver service, and the honeymoon. At least the flowers were covered; he could return the artificials to the East Bay Ornamentals warehouse and use the arrangements for next year's trade shows. He liked Connie's fiancé, Elliot, well enough, but these days, let's face it, everyone ended up in divorce court, so why blow the money on a fancy ceremony when he could bank it and leave it to the grandchildren, the inevitable products of a broken home, when he died? He wondered why Connie bothered.

On the other hand, the fact that she was vacating the house for good was perhaps worth the expense. There had been too much moving out and moving back. She had gone to college to earn a worthless degree in English, then to Seattle for a job, then to Los Angeles for a job. Neither job had required advanced knowledge of the language she had grown up speaking. Between events, she had taken months of recovery time, during which she filled the house with cigarette smoke and drank mai tais in the sunroom with her sloe-eyed friend Sheilah, who had been making herself at home since the two girls were nine years old.

At this very moment Sheilah Robinson was waiting in the doorway of the sunroom, watching Connie, in heels and a pale-peach A-line dress, march across the freshly clipped lawn to where her hairy brother was lying on a chair in his shorts, pretending to read a book. Sheilah had taken off early from the travel agency where she worked so that she could drop off Connie's airline tickets and honeymoon reservations at Waikiki. Now they were on their way to the catering company that was servicing both the rehearsal luncheon and the wedding reception; Connie had discovered unacceptably similar items on both menus.

"Frank," Connie said. She crossed her arms and looked down at him.

He squinted up at her. "Frantz. Not Frank—Frantz."

"Frank. Will you please be nice to Elliot when he gets here?"

Frantz sat up and scratched his beard. "I've got nothing against Elliot, except that he's a warmonger."

"You'd call him a warmonger if he donated to the Salvation Army."

"Very funny. Seriously, Connie, why are you wrecking that man's already useless life? Let him build his missiles in peace. If you go distracting guys like Elliot Ames, we'll never achieve total nuclear annihilation."

"He doesn't build missiles, Frank—"

"Frantz."

"He builds computers. I mean," she amended, "he operates them." She uncrossed her arms and shook a cigarette from the pack she had in her hand. "Don't be so dismissive. Elliot's highly respected in his field. He's on an upward trajectory."

"And you're along for the ride."

"Yes, I am."

"Just because by some wretched accident Fascist One stumbles across Fascist Two doesn't mean the two fascists have to get married and produce the next generation of automatons."

"You know perfectly well we didn't just stumble across each other. It was a compatibility survey. You obviously understand nothing about assortative matching."

"Is that a meaningful concept?"

"I think so. Yes." She lit her cigarette and watched the workers putting up the canopy.

"Admit it, Connie, if he didn't have a house and a job with an iron-clad pension, you wouldn't pick up Elliot Ames if you were lost in the desert without a Bloody Mary. All you're going to do is make his life miserable while you slowly collapse into the hollowness of your own being."

"He's a very good-looking man."

"Seriously? So pin his picture over your bed. You don't have to marry him."

"He happens to be a very satisfying lover. He's very disciplined."

"Yuck." Frantz lay back on the lawn chair and opened his—or rather, his sister's—book.

"And he's thoughtful. Just an hour ago he called for no reason except to enjoy my conversation."

"Come on, Connie," Sheilah called from the doorway. "It's getting late. We won't be able to get the dresses."

Connie shot cigarette smoke at Frantz's head. She didn't see why there had to be a brother in the middle of her happy event. "Just be courteous, Frank. He deserves that much."

As she marched back across the grass, her indignant figure caught Carl Campbell's eye through the window of the den. He rested his hands on the card table and wondered if his new son-in-law would be more amenable to playing Parcheesi than his children were. He should have pulled out the game boxes that time when Eliot had come to the house.

• • •

Redondo Beach

In addition to its massive aerodynamic design and production departments, Pacifidyne, Inc. had one hundred and sixteen distinct research-and-development programs scattered across the five buildings on the main campus and at its four satellite locations. There were groups investigating ion propulsion, infrared detectors, electron beams, electro-optic materials, millimeter-wave technology, electron storage tubes, radar, display systems, communications satellites, laser weapons, and networked computers. Every Wednesday afternoon, contractors, subcontractors, and project managers from the various units gathered in Building A and Building B of the Redondo Beach facility to meet with their immediate superiors and hash out schedules, priorities, and solutions to new problems. Like everyone else below the rank of vice-president, Elliot despised these meetings.

"What our internal surveys reveal," a v.p. named Halifax Deane droned, puffing on his pipe, "is the ideal distribution of formal education among the technical staff in order to produce the most efficient operations."

Although Elliot was interested, professionally and personally, in ideal distributions, he disliked Deane, a bald man with a crumpled neck who did not understand the importance of networked computers for doing work that a technical staff could not handle no matter how ideally distributed they were. Deane was a statistician by training; he resented machines that did his job better than he could, and his resentment flowed into the dullest possible channels. His ability to bore his audience verged on the sadistic.

"To wit," Deane went on, "seven percent of the project group should have doctorates, thirty-three percent master's degrees, forty-seven percent bachelor's degrees, and twelve percent engineering degrees."

"What about the other one percent?" Elliot interrupted.

Deane glared at him. "Patience, Ames." He cleared his throat. "The remaining one percent should be self-taught, self-made men, who can contribute natural talent and perseverance to the general welfare of the enterprise. These men, in particular, benefit from our job-rotation program—although, of course, *every* new hire is afforded the opportunity to test his worth on a number of projects. We want our employees to attain job satisfaction within the first eighteen months at Pacifidyne and to maintain that level of satisfaction subsequently. Indeed, employee satisfaction is the reason we contracted with Operation Matchmaker last year. No one can deny that sexual satisfaction is an important component of an orderly life. Having so many vital, young, unattached males—and, uh, females, such as there are—is unhealthy not only for the men—and, uh, women—but also for the organization. In short, our excellence in innovative aerospace and communications technology is severely hampered by our workers' lack of sexual access—within the bounds of convention. We're not running a brothel."

At this point Elliot started thinking about Connie Campbell's thighs again, then about the way she rumpled her hair when she pulled her sweater over her head, then about the lace trim on her bra, then about the floral smell of her breasts as he pressed them to his face and ran his hands over the curve of her buttocks.

As Halifax Deane's relentless voice wore through his daydream, Elliot discovered that he was experiencing significant tumescence. He glanced around the group and realized that several of his colleagues had also been considering the carnal pleasures referenced by Halifax Deane and were now covering their laps with their clipboards or shifting on their chairs in embarrassment. The ion-propulsion guys looked particularly uncomfortable.

Elliot crossed his legs and winced.

Deane had pushed the Operation Matchmaker perk aggressively. The unmarried Pacifidyne employees had each filled out a one-hundred-fifty-question form. The forms were sent to Cambridge, Massachusetts, where the information was entered on punch cards. Three weeks later each employee received a sheet of paper with six names and telephone numbers on it, along with compatibility rankings indicating the probability of marital bliss.

Elliot Ames and Connie Campbell topped each other's list. He heard that several men in the company were matched with partners elsewhere in Southern California; he and Connie were the only two Pacifidyne employees who matched internally. Elliot was not surprised that two highly compatible people would be located in the vastness of the modern aerospace industry. There was a very large, clearly defined sample set, even if the number of females was limited. Still, neither had previously registered on the other's radar. It had taken a computer to sift them from the data.

"In conclusion," Halifax Deane said, tapping his pipe on the table. Elliot glanced at the clock and saw that an hour had passed. "We believe that we know everything we need to know about the composition and maintenance of the ideal workforce. Please have the educational-distribution data for your project groups on my desk on Monday morning. Except for Ames, who is finally getting married," he said, somehow simultaneously approving and disapproving of his decision to wed. "He'll be in Hawaii for a month—"

"Three weeks."

"—while the network-computer group goes to hell."

Elliot was worried about this possibility, especially if Stefan Blicks decided to take things in his own direction, but he did not care for Halifax Deane's public concern. He reminded himself to check in daily from Honolulu.

• • •

Los Angeles

Morning Star—or, as she was known at the registrar's office at UCLA, Mary Ellen McGovern—closed her notebook and felt around at her feet for her bag. It was the last day of spring quarter, and thus the last meeting of Anthro 278: Current Problems in Population Genetics, with Professor T. Larson, who at this moment was pacing the front of the room, slapping his cowboy hat against his thigh to emphasize the important points he was trying to drive into his students' thick skulls so they wouldn't have to cheat on the final exam. He seemed particularly insistent that they understand the Neutral Theory of Molecular Evolution, with an emphasis on the polymorphisms that can coexist within a species.

Morning Star stood up abruptly and, stuffing her notebook inside, swung her bag onto her shoulder. A little blood oozed through her blouse where Kismet had scratched her. She began making her way toward the aisle, bumping the knees of the other students. A couple of guys took the opportunity to squeeze her leg.

"Excuse me!" Professor Larson called. He stopped pacing and fixed her with a penetrating gaze. "Are you ill, Miss McGovern?"

Morning Star stumbled into the aisle.

"Yes, I *am* ill," she said in a loud, defiant voice. "We're all ill. I mean, population genetics? I mean, what the fuck, man?"

· · ·

Berkeley

When Frantz woke from his morning nap in the back yard, the workers were gone. His stomach told him he had a half-hour until lunch. He hoped that meant he had a half-hour until Connie came back from wherever she had gone with Sheilah Robinson. He wanted to get out of the sun, but not if she was hanging around in the house. The paperback book he had been marking lay in the grass at his fingertips. He considered picking it up. Instead, he levered himself to his feet and made his way cautiously through the French doors into the living room.

He sniffed the air but did not detect fresh cigarette smoke. Both his sister and his mother had gone. He would not have to talk to them; he feared being pressed into service for the wedding. It was awful enough that he had to wear his gray suit, in mothballs since his high-school graduation, but he loathed having to stand up for Elliot Ames and face the ranks of every dull, square, reactionary person that Carl, Helen, and Constance Campbell knew. And who could predict what might show up in support of Elliot. Engineers. Warmongers. Creeps. Frantz shuddered. He took a few steps into the dining room and listened. His father might have gone down to East Bay Ornamentals, or he might be doing something in the den. The muted acoustics of the carpeted rooms offered no information.

Now that he was in the house, he could think of nothing to do, so he went down the hall to Connie's room to see if there was anything interesting in there.

The lease on her apartment in Santa Monica had run out at the end of April, so here she was, back home, saving a few bucks before getting hitched. Most of her stuff was in Elliot's garage. She would sort it out, she said, after she discovered what they had received in the way of wedding gifts. There had been no bridal shower to guide her expectations.

The previous summer, he had visited her apartment complex on Pico Boulevard. The trip to L.A. should have been more fun than it was. He had no car, and the bus maps Connie provided were indecipherable, so for five days he had hung around the swimming pool, hoping to meet chicks. But all the women in the complex worked during daylight hours and had boyfriends at night, and most of the time he found himself floating on an inflatable mattress in the heavily chlorinated water. Connie herself went to work at seven-fifteen every morning. When she came home, she spent her evenings running up a phone bill talking to Sheilah Robinson about shoes and books by Helen Gurley Brown. Or she went out with Elliot. They had recently begun dating, and it was only grudgingly that she allowed him, her brother, to accompany them—once—to an Italian restaurant in Santa Monica.

Elliot had been cordial. He expressed interest in Frantz's political-science classes and recommended a computer seminar offered by a professor named Amadeo Knizner. It did not sound like a course Frantz could get his head into, but the professor's name stuck with him. Frantz could tell that Elliot, at that early stage of his relationship with Connie, was eager to demonstrate his bona fides as an in-law. He had skipped work one afternoon to take him sightseeing in Hollywood. They had gone to Grauman's

Chinese Theatre and the Walk of Fame and the Hollywood Bowl, as well as the Sunset Strip, which was swarming with all the chicks he had hoped to find in the swimming pool at the Casa Colada. He had harbored some hope of taking in The Doors or a Doors-like band at the Whiskey or the Troubadour, but Elliot seemed ill at ease with his suggestion. Instead, they had gone to Musso & Frank for martinis. Elliot was a square, but he had paid for the drinks.

The whole trip had induced in Frantz a low-grade depression that had never quite lifted.

Feeling blue, Frantz sat down on Connie's nubbly salmon-colored bedspread and started poking through her nightstand. Cold cream, a horoscope pamphlet, a hairnet, Chapstick, a picture of Dusty Springfield (did Connie admire her?), a mutilated blank pocket calendar, and a "Sorry to See You Go, Boss" card signed by several Pacifidyne employees who, Frantz was sure, were not at all sorry to see her go. Looking at the contents of Connie's nightstand, he felt a brief, unwelcome stab of pity.

He shut the drawer and picked up the book that rested on her pillow. *A Garden of Earthly Delights*. He thumbed through it. He had never heard of Joyce Carol Oates, but the first page looked like she might have something to say. Connie's time at Mount Holyoke must have done her some good. He stood up and stuffed the book into the waistband of his jeans and went back down the hall to the living room. It upset him that his sister, so bossy and greedy, appreciated fine writing. It was the ultimate bourgeois bullshit.

He considered finding his shirt and shoes and driving the VW down to campus for his hideous computer class with Knizner but decided that, having already missed most of the quarter, it was pointless to attend the last meeting. He drifted back through the French doors and across the trim grass, avoiding the stacks of folding chairs and piles of latticework that would be assembled, he assumed, into some sort of arbor for the ceremony, and stretched out on the Adirondack chair. Working Joyce Carol Oates out of his waistband, he wondered what his mother would make for lunch.

· · ·

As she topped the hill at Mulholland Drive in her Dodge Dart, radio blasting, and gazed down the north slope at the panorama of the San Fernando Valley spreading beneath a layer of yellow haze, Morning Star could not help feeling that some sort of revelation was at hand. The shackles that bound her were falling away. She had cast off her classes, her job at the May Company on Wilshire Boulevard, her apartment, her therapist (Tuesdays and Fridays)—all the embarrassing impedimenta of middle-class life. She had severed her attachments to her friends, including two girls she had known since kindergarten (who were unaware that they had been cast off, casualties of the changing times). She had rid herself of five thousand dollars, the cost of two bricks of Afghan hashish destined for the Grateful Dead in San Francisco. Now she was going to visit her father and unload the burden of the automobile.

Beside her on the seat, Kismet thrashed in his carry-cage, expressing his unhappiness with the sharp-winding route up Coldwater Canyon. He had already clawed to shreds the bath towel that lined the bottom of the carrier and urinated through the wire mesh onto the seat. He stopped thrashing and curled into a torus and began to gnaw his toenails.

Morning Star pulled onto the shoulder of the road and got out of the car. The air was filled with the smell of sage and eucalyptus. She came around the car and opened the passenger door and carried Kismet in his cage a few yards into the underbrush, where she unlatched the wire door and poured him onto the dirt. It crossed her mind that a coyote might eat him—if a car didn't run over him first—but she decided to have faith that he would find his way in the world. He was a blessed creature.

He arranged himself and started to groom.

"Goodbye, Kismet," she said. "See you in another dream."

He looked at her with his big blank green eyes and made a faint forlorn sound.

She carried the cage back to the car. As she pulled the door closed, she noticed a joint she happened to have in the ashtray. She fired it up and pulled onto the road. Another link in the chain of obligations had been broken.

As she swooped across Ventura Boulevard, singing at the top of her lungs to Aretha Franklin rattling from the dashboard speaker, she felt as free as a kite. The traffic was dense but moving. Normally an adept, even careful driver—she had been the first in her circle of friends to get her license—today she felt like cutting loose, letting it all happen. Her eyes were half shut, and she did not notice the turn signal flashing on the car in front of her.

The crunch of metal jolted her back to herself; her forehead hit the steering wheel, and the joint flew out the open window. She slammed her foot on the brake. The Dart was struck from behind, sending another jolt through her body.

The driver of the first car, an old white Ford Falcon, looked over his shoulder in terror, as if he saw death itself on his tail. With a gurgling sound, one tire thumping flatly, sparks trailing from the muffler dragging on the street, the Falcon raced off around the corner.

In the side mirror, Morning Star glimpsed the irate visage of the driver who had rear-ended her. He leaned out the window of his Buick and shook his fist at her. She put the car in park and opened the door. The angry driver threw his car into reverse, ripping the bumper from the rear of the Dart. It clattered on the pavement as the Buick lurched into traffic, and tore around the corner after the white Ford.

She looked at the caved-in rear of the car. People yelled as they pulled around the wreck. She picked up the bumper and dragged it to the curb and dropped it. Then she wiped her hands on the grassy verge and got back in the Dart and continued on her way to her father's Chrysler-Dodge dealership.

T.J. McGovern was a former pharmaceutical sales rep who had lost his love of people around the time his brother-in-law, who had built up the dealership, discovered he was dying of cancer. His brother-in-law wanted to keep the business in the family when he was gone and offered T.J. a terrific price. T.J. jumped at the offer, and as a business owner, he had come into his own. As the dealership prospered, he seemed to have grown physically larger. Perhaps it was the pompadour. Or the thick-soled shoes. Or the way he patrolled his domain in his wide-shouldered burgundy sports coat, casting a lordly eye over the showroom floor, the repair bays, the finance department (where, he suspected, he was being robbed blind with every car he sold; he just hadn't figured out what scheme his employees had devised).

As his daughter pulled under the awning at the front of the showroom, T.J., standing at the window, drifting on the anodyne strains of the piped-in music that permeated every enclosed space on the lot, was imagining what Miss Stephens at the reception desk would look like if someone covered her naked body with melted chocolate. And crushed walnuts, why not?

He was eating an egg-salad-and-tomato sandwich he had made himself because his wife, for no good reason, had decided to go back to work as a nurse, and the hospital was punishing her for being old and a mother by putting her on the graveyard shift, just when T.J. had decided to keep the dealership open until midnight during the week to capture the insomniac market. By the time she got home, Joanne was too tired to make him a late dinner, not to mention his lunch for the next day, so it turned out the hospital was punishing T.J. as well. T.J. saw his wife's return to the hospital—they had met there when he was still a pharmaceutical rep—as the first step on the road to divorce, and it terrified him. He was, he knew, incapable of surviving on his own. In his younger years he had managed only because he ate whatever the closest greasy spoon served up and because the pharmaceutical company offered a laundry service to its bachelor salesmen, who clustered together in a four-man apartment. He didn't see how he could live without Joanne's routine care. His egg-salad sandwich was nearly inedible.

Now he noticed that the Dodge Dart he had given his daughter on her twenty-first birthday had suffered significant damage to both front and rear. Frowning, he tossed the remainder of the sandwich in the trash and pushed through the glass double doors.

"Before you start yelling," his daughter said, "it was a hit and run."

T. J. eyed the car skeptically. "A double hit-and-run?"

"That's exactly what it was." She pointed to the lump forming on her forehead.

"Are you high?"

"Oh, Daddy."

"You're still smoking that stuff, aren't you?"

"Really, Daddy, I'm only just getting started."

"Oh my God. If you get your sisters hooked, I'll beat the crap out of them."

T. J. circled the car. He muttered to himself.

"What?"

"I said," T. J. said without taking his eyes from the place where the back bumper should have been, "this is one hell of a way to care for the things that are given to you. Thank God your sisters won't see this. What kind of example are you?"

"I don't want to be any kind of example," Morning Star replied. "I'm not into playing that role. I don't play games anymore. I'm returning the car."

Her father looked at her and cocked his head. "Say that again."

"I'm returning the car. I don't want it anymore."

She stepped over and pushed the keys into the pocket of his burgundy jacket. She hooked her arm around his.

"You don't want the car?"

"It's weighing me down, Daddy. It's everything that's wrong with everything."

T. J. looked out at the half-acre of spanking new automobiles arrayed in the dizzying summer sunshine, at the looky-loo customers trailed by desperate, shiny-faced salesmen in gold blazers, at the sudsy effluence from the carwash where a half-dozen Mexican teenagers were scrubbing cars with hog's hair brushes, at the clamoring repair bays where hard-faced men in greasy clothes inhaled noxious fumes and ruined their hearing, and he feared that he understood what she was driving at. He shook her loose.

"This is unacceptable. It's irresponsible!"

"If you're going to get violent, I'm ending this conversation."

T.J. spoke through tight lips: "How will you get home without a car?"

Morning Star lifted her right hand, thumb up.

"Oh, no, you don't. —Victor! Get over here and drive my daughter to Westwood! Jesus Christ! We're on the brink of chaos." He turned to go into the showroom. Then he turned back and shouted at the man in a gray work shirt who had come out of the carwash office: "And don't let her smoke anything, goddammit. She's turning into a subversive."

Morning Star opened her arms. "Victor! Como estás, amigo!"

"And take a bath," T.J. called after her. "You smell like—."
But he was too embarrassed to finish the sentence.

• • •

Studio City

Pegasus' girlfriend, Susan, would be waiting at the curb in front of Valley Savings and Loan, where she worked as a teller. Usually, she rode home on the bus, but on Wednesdays she got off early, and they had a standing date to go for a late lunch and drinks before visiting the supermarket, a task Pegasus dreaded. Today, given the circumstances at the Peking Palace, the trip was especially inconvenient, but at this juncture any interruption of routine was dangerous.

Susan was an agreeable woman who looked to Pegasus as if she had just stepped off the prairie. She had a hospitable body. Like his neighbors at the Palm Marquis apartments on Burbank Boulevard, she knew him not as Pegasus but as Al Carpenter. He wielded the meat tongs at the Friday night cookouts on the patio by the pool, and he and Susan had friends at the gardening club on Sunday afternoons. Although they were both apartment-dwellers, they anticipated that someday—soon?—they would own a house with a yard.

Even before he had discovered the surveillance at the Chinese restaurant in Redondo Beach, Pegasus had begun to fret about what would happen if the Southern California operation were exposed. He had come to appreciate the fruits of late-industrial capitalism. His life in Los Angeles had gotten progressively better, so that he resented everything that preceded the present and also feared the future that awaited him when he was inevitably recalled or deployed elsewhere. Long ago, he had determined never again to set foot outside the Golden State, where he could look forward to balmy winters and fresh lettuce. He feared living out his days in a damp, dingy room in Moscow without a working television. Even worse, if the F.B.I. could connect him to the problem at Pacifidyne, he might spend the rest of his life in federal detention. Lompoc. Lewisburg. Leavenworth. For years the L-words had haunted his dreams. Cached in a safe-deposit box, his secondary identity papers were ready for use, and he had bank accounts his handlers were unaware of, accumulated from padding the expense account. Pegasus was not sure how Susan would react to a sudden name change when the time came to trade his current life for a new one.

She was willing to marry him if his executive-recruiting agency started producing the level of income it seemed capable of producing. The agency operated primarily as a cover for coordinating the activities of assets and sympathizers in the defense industry. In the seven years since Pegasus had purchased American Executive Management with the ten-thousand dollars he had brought with him when he was reassigned from San Francisco, he had placed scores of legitimate candidates in positions at the electronics and aerospace companies, as well as what he believed were two illegal-resident agents in the South Bay and half a dozen sympathetic individuals with security clearance; by design, he had no way of knowing which of the candidates who passed through A.E.M. were legitimate. Most of the executives who walked through his door seemed like hard-working, alcoholic family men who believed in themselves and their country. He recalled one obnoxiously boring guy named Halifax Deane, whom he had recruited for Pacifidyne in 1960, the first executive he had placed after buying the business. He almost hoped that Deane was Canis Minor; it would be a long-delayed pleasure to kill him. The asset in Pacifidyne might have been recruited by the *rezidentura* in San Francisco, perhaps by Ursa Major himself. Pegasus' job was to take instructions, coordinate pick-ups and payments, and solve problems, not interact with the assets.

Although Pegasus' cover name, Albert Carpenter, was on the business license, he had very little to do with the routine operations of the office. He was hardly ever on site except to shake hands with assistant personnel directors who were thinking about using American Executive Management. This was one reason his two-person staff liked him. Pegasus spent his days driving around Los Angeles County, just as he had spent his days driving around the Bay Area, navigating the ten-thousand smoggy miles of surface streets, access roads, and freeways, using different patterns of travel each day for at least two hours to evade surveillance before beginning his actual route. He ranged from Burbank to Lakewood, Long Beach to Torrance, checking for signals wherever there was an asset at a defense firm. The signals were simple: chalk marks on the backs of nearby restaurants, somewhere the assets would naturally go for lunch or dinner. Sometimes he was the one making the marks on a wall by a row garbage cans. Circles, crosses, parallel lines. Each symbol had a meaning: *radiogram received, order received, delivery deposited, danger—get out!*

He seldom spotted a chalk mark. Many of the assets—Andromeda, Canis Major, Cassiopeia—had not been active for years. But he had to make the rounds every day, sometimes stopping to hobnob, in his role as an executive recruiter, with the personnel directors at the aerospace companies, always intentional, always with a legitimate reason to be where he was.

Now the surveillance at the Peking Palace meant Pacifidyne was burned. There would be arrests, diplomatic expulsions, recalls of illegals such as himself. Seven years of building up the business. Grooming contacts. Writing reports. Making maps. Building a decent life. Seven years. And now this!

He sighed gloomily. Comfort and quiet were all he wanted. Gone were the days when he derived any satisfaction from his job. The biggest thrill of his life had been killing two German infantrymen with one shot in Stalingrad in 1943. Postwar, Pegasus' biggest thrill had been meeting Arnold Palmer by accident at the Brown Derby.

As he pulled across two lanes of traffic and lurched to a stop at the curb, Susan, looking bright and healthy and happy to see him, waved. She jumped into the car: "Darling!"

There was no way he was going to give up Susan and their awful weekly trip to the supermarket.

• • •

West Los Angeles
Elliot lived on a cul-de-sac in an up-and-coming neighborhood lined with sycamores and jacarandas and three-bedroom ranch houses featuring sunken living rooms, mosaic tiles, and floor-to-ceiling fireplaces. In his backyard was an enormous brick barbecue pit and a swimming pool slightly

larger than his kitchen. His neighbors were his co-workers or people very much like his co-workers: engineers and equipment sales reps and soldiers in the trenches of Hollywood who manned the cameras and designed the sets and publicized the talent. Some of the wives worked part time; one owned a shop in Westwood. A sober European television director and his wife and three or four noisy children lived next door.

He pulled his brand-new cream-colored MG convertible with chrome-wire wheels into the carport. The car was a dream. It had a 150 net b.h.p. three-liter engine; the torque was incredible; the four-speed manual gearbox with a non-synchromesh straight-cut first gear and optional overdrive made him feel like he was piloting a spaceship. Or riding a thoroughbred; it had that kind of beauty and grace. When he climbed behind the wheel, he wanted to drive forever. Some evenings on the freeway it felt as though he might have to. He had spent the last forty-five minutes fighting traffic on the 405.

As he shut off the headlights, he was listening to the end of the Dodgers game on the radio. Vin Scully capped it off: "So Lefebvre goes down swinging, and that's going to do it for the Dodgers, who lose this one in Atlanta thirteen to five." Elliot killed the engine. In the sudden silence, he could hear the distant dry chirr of traffic and the comforting quaver of crickets in the hedges. A neighbor's sprinkler hissed on.

A hundred feet down the block in the shadow of a sycamore tree sat a white Ford Falcon with a crushed bumper.

* * *

North Hollywood
Pegasus knew that he should love the temple of abundance that was the supermarket, where claims of American morality were translated into a utopia of consumption, but when he passed through the automatic sliding doors into the chilled aisles of nectarines and tomatoes, cottage cheese and flank steak and t.v. dinners, he was overwhelmed with the burden of choice, crushed by the sheer much-ness of the American food industry. The most obnoxious music he could imagine slithered from hidden speakers. What

secret voices whispered beneath the breezy strings and muted horns, enticing his soul?

"Do you want green peas with carrots or green peas with onions?" Susan lifted one frozen bag and then the other, oblivious to his suffering. She always chose green peas with carrots.

Pegasus touched her shoulder. "Excuse me a minute, hon. I'm gonna wait in the car. I feel queasy."

She turned to him with anxious concern. "Are you getting a headache, Al? I have some aspirin in my purse."

"It's not that bad," he assured her. "What I ate for lunch."

"You eat too much foreign food," she scolded.

He pulled out his wallet and took out a ten-dollar bill. "You know what I like."

"Don't hand me money in public," Susan reproved. "People will think you're trying to buy me for the evening."

He went out into the blood-red twilight and found the Buick. It was hot inside and smelled of Prince Matchabelli perfume. He rolled down the window and turned on the radio, then turned it off and closed his eyes. His head really did hurt, and he felt dizzy.

He closed his eyes and tried to think. In 1965, a radio communication had notified him that one of his assets in the satellite division of a major defense contractor was on the verge of turning himself in to the F.B.I., and Pegasus had had to visit his home in Canoga Park and eliminate him. There were dogs. He had to eliminate them as well, but the exposure of the network was prevented.

It was imperative that he uncover Canis Minor's identity—immediately—and make sure he disappeared before anyone could question him. The operative in the Ford Falcon would be of use if he could get to him. Then there was the problem of recovering any undelivered film Canis might have in his possession. It would be disastrous if the authorities found classified materials in his home or automobile. Pegasus could not set a signal for him at the restaurant in Redondo. Even if he could, there was a seventy-two-hour delay between signal and contact in case the operation had been compromised—which it had—and to allow time for the asset to see the message. He could not wait seventy-two hours for Canis Minor to show up to the dead drop in Culver City, if Canis was even using that location anymore. Pegasus regretted having never lingered at the drop site, contra protocol, to see who this bastard was.

He felt a tremor and for a split second thought the city was experiencing an earthquake, but it was only the back door of the car opening. He heard Susan admonishing the bag boy to be careful with the eggs and to put the bag with the ice cream on the floor. She hoped it wouldn't melt; it was for a very special person. He didn't know how he could hold himself together through dinner.

• • •

West Los Angeles

The first thing Elliot did after buying his house was to furnish the living room with a hi-fi stereo of his own design. The system featured Klipschorn speakers, Altec Lansing amplifiers, and a Dual 1009 turntable, and he liked to crank it up, just loud enough that he could still hear the ice cubes clinking in the cocktail shaker. He was wearing the silver silk pajamas Connie had given him for his last birthday—his thirtieth. Moving in time with the samba music—long quick, short quick, slow—he approached the wet bar in his living room, rattling the shaker over his head.

Across the street, Freddy Happ trained his binoculars on the picture window. Through the loose weave of the drapes, he could make out the figure of someone dancing, waving his arms like a champion prizefighter. He checked his watch and made a notation on his clipboard.

Elliot spun around, passed the shaker behind his back, and poured the contents into a martini glass. He spun around again and set the shaker sharply on the bar, sweeping the glass to his lips in one motion. Perfection.

He moved across the living room, sliding his slippers on the rust-colored carpet, and shocked himself with a massive spark of static electricity when he grazed the wrought-iron railing on the short staircase that led to the hallway.

In the extra bedroom at the end of the hall, he settled on a padded stool at the worktable where he had set up his equipment: Eddystone shortwave receiver, handcrafted glowbug with Hartley transmitter circuits, Teac A-Series tape recorder, and a dozen custom electronic components that allowed him to capture whatever interesting signal he found floating in the ether on a given night. He placed the martini glass away from the electronics and began dialing through his favorite stations, including—for a few moments—one that broadcast a burst of Chinese Muzak. He did this every evening, preparatory to sleep.

In the last year, since meeting Connie, he had found it difficult to achieve unconsciousness. After he had finished reading and switched off the lamp on the nightstand, he tossed and turned until the wee hours. Lying in the dark, he found himself thinking about the unfathomable condition of sleep itself, the apparent purposelessness of nocturnal unconsciousness. Lately—on the eve of his marriage!—visions of nuclear conflagration, ravaging disease, earthquakes, and random murder chased through his mind and sent a malarial shiver through body and soul. The possibility of his extinction before his actuarial date, which should be, according to the current state of medical knowledge and practice, somewhere around 2009, tormented him. He could not sleep. Although he had spent a weekend at the Pacifidyne science library reading the journal research, he had discovered nothing in the literature to help him nod off.

Fortunately, a few months earlier he had discovered something on the airwaves which could lull him into a few brief hours of oblivion. He turned the dial of the Eddystone receiver, zeroing in on a monotone female voice. "Six six seven four. . . one zero one six. . . nine five one six. . . one nine nine four. . . three six zero seven. . . four nine eight three," the voice droned.

Having monitored the airwaves for Army counterintelligence when he was stationed in Germany, he recognized a numbers code when he heard one. This one most likely emanated from Eastern Europe—possibly Cuba—although he had not been able, despite appeals to the global community of ham-radio enthusiasts, to pin the signal to a particular location. The station went on the air every night at nine p.m. Pacific Time with a four-note musical tone, like a doorbell chime—ding DONG ding

DONG—followed by "Ready? Ready?" and the monotonous sequence of numbers. Anyone in the world could access it, but without a key to the code, the flat recitation was as meaningless as a weather report from Antarctica.

Elliot listened, sipping his drink and losing himself in the rhythm of the numbers. He imagined a tired-faced woman in shapeless gray coveralls sitting in a windowless room on a windswept steppe, calling, calling to the diaspora of intelligence agents across the globe, ordering assassinations and sabotage, requesting reports, connecting them, briefly, to their controllers. To home.

· · ·

North Hollywood

"Ready? Ready?" Sitting on his bed at the Palm Marquis, Pegasus listened anxiously to the signal. He had powered up the shortwave receiver he kept behind a false back in the cabinet under the bathroom sink just in time to hear the first reading of the numbers.

His headache had not abated during dinner at Susan's place. He was sorry, honey, but he had to take off, try to get some shuteye. No, he doubted if rubbing tiger balm on his temples would help. She understood, didn't she?

"Good grief, Al, if you don't like the swiss steak, just say so."

"I love the swiss steak," he protested.

"Maybe it's your contact lenses."

"It's stress, that's all."

"Oh, that," she said. She stood up and unzipped her skirt and pulled down her slip.

"No, really, Suze. I'm out of sorts. Forgive me."

She tilted her head. "You really are stressed."

She pulled up her slip and zipped her skirt and began clearing the table.

Now he sat on his bed with the North Hollywood phone directory in his lap, pencil ready to copy down the sequences on a sheet of lined paper as soon as he heard his designation: "two two four two."

It never came.

In the five months since the numbers station had changed its broadcast frequency, he had not been issued a new code key, nor had he heard his designation number. He suspected they were cutting him out, but he had no idea why. When he had filed his recent report via the dead drop in San Francisco, he had received no acknowledgment. Maybe they had recognized the material he had been filing for the last couple of years consisted mainly of passages copied from *Report from Iron Mountain* and brochures he picked up when he went sightseeing with Susan. He followed meticulous evasion protocols, devising labyrinthine routes through the city on his daily rounds, but when it came to writing reports, he was lackadaisical.

"Nine six five one... one two nine eight... four four seven four...."

Even when he had a functioning code key, it distressed him that he could not decipher all the messages broadcast to the four corners of the earth. He understood only the communications meant specifically for him. For all he knew, someone else in Southern California was at that moment decoding the sequence. Maybe Canis Minor had even acquired his own designation. He doubted it. It was not normal for an asset to receive direct instructions. On the other hand, the situation at Pacifidyne was not normal.

Pegasus turned off the receiver and sat on the bed and began to page idly through the phone directory. After a while, he dragged himself up and found a shoebox on the shelf in his closet. He pried up the closet floorboards and gathered into the shoebox the microfilms that had not yet gone to Sagittarius, the secret ink, the detailed maps of Los Angeles he had spent years compiling. Then he went to the kitchen and got a bag of charcoal from the pantry. He found the lighter fluid and matches under the sink and took a steak from the refrigerator. Cracking the door, he peered out at the swimming pool. The floodlit water shimmered in the dark like a radioactive substance. Seeing no one on the deck chairs, he slipped down the stairs and walked quickly to the barbecue pit. He dumped out the charcoal, doused it with lighter fluid, and lit a match. He dropped the shoebox into the fire.

When the steak was done cooking, he carried it back to the apartment and shoved it down the garbage disposal.

．　．　．

West Los Angeles

The lights went out in Elliot Ames's house. Freddy Happ fell asleep.

．　．　．

As was often the case in West Los Angeles, the morning was an astonishing mixture of tender desert breeze, sea salt, and incipient smog. The kids who lived on the block swarmed down the street on their bicycles for the last day of school, animated by the promise of summer vacation. They had fastened playing cards to the forks of their bikes so that the cards slapped against the spokes and made, with some imagination, the sound of motorcycles.

Elliot popped the trunk of the convertible and slid his suitcase inside. Across the suitcase he laid his tuxedo in a zip-up plastic bag. Then he lowered the car top. He was thrilled to take the MG on this first road trip; driving was much more satisfying than flying. As he hopped in, he pulled out his wallet and tossed it on the carpeted console between the seats. He was shaved, showered, brushed, pressed, deodorized, fed, and caffeinated. He felt good.

Backing out of the driveway, he remembered that although he had phoned his cleaning woman, Bianca, to suspend service while he was gone, he had forgotten to notify the post office and the *Los Angeles Times*. He snapped his fingers and braked to a halt in the middle of the street, debating whether it was worth going back inside and making the phone calls. Too early, he decided; they could wait until he got to Berkeley.

He gunned down the street past the white Ford Falcon in which slumbered Freddy Happ, his mouth hanging open, one hand cupped protectively around his genitals.

. . .

Santa Monica

At the intersection of Santa Monica Boulevard and Ocean Avenue, an erratic line of hitchhikers, not altogether savory, squinted into the early-morning sun, waiting for rides. They carried duffel bags and sleeping bags and old army packs, battered suitcases tied with rope and covered with flower stickers, woven bags full of oranges, and paper bags full of bread and sweating cheese. They wore bandanas and blue jeans, leather vests and Civil War-era Hardee hats, motorcycle boots and sandals and moccasins with holes in the toes. Everyone was going to San Francisco.

Elliot's cream-colored roadster rolled to a stop at the intersection. While he waited for the light to change, the motor purring—no, throbbing—smoothly, his foot caressing the accelerator, he leaned over to adjust the radio. Something was wrong with the thing. He could pick up a clear-channel broadcast from Chicago, but he couldn't get a signal from ten miles away.

Without warning, a woman flung herself into the passenger's seat.

Before Elliot could react, she turned and stuffed her duffel bag in the back and, with a thump, dropped an elaborately embroidered shoulder bag on the floor at her feet. Tipping her head to the heavens, she leaned back and stretched her legs.

Elliot looked at her. His mind registered the loose linen blouse, the jeans, the sandals, but he could not comprehend her abrupt appearance in his car. It was as though a genie had popped out of a lamp.

"Hold on there!" he cried stupidly.

She opened her eyes and beamed at him. "Thanks for stopping, man."

"I'm not stopping! I'm waiting for the light to change!"

"Perfect!"

The light turned green. Behind him a horn sounded.

"Get out of my car!" Elliot yelped.

"Don't be a drag, baby."

"What the hell!"

The horn blared again, joined by a raucous chorus.

"You'd better move," she said.

Elliot looked in the rearview mirror and beheld the apoplectic face of a woman in a Mercury. He hit the clutch and, jamming the convertible into gear, shot through the intersection, heading toward the Pacific Coast Highway

"Go, man, go!" his passenger cried.

Elliot was at a loss for words.

As the car rolled onto PCH, he kept glancing over at her, trying to make sense of her presence. She had prominent cheekbones and dilated, murky eyes. There was a distinct red lump on her forehead. An odor of sandalwood and something unwashed, slightly vinegary, emanated from her body. She beamed at him again.

"What the hell," Elliot finally managed. "What're you doing in my car?"

"Traveling, baby."

"You don't even know where I'm going."

"As long as it's north, it's cool. I'm heading to San Francisco."

"*I'm* heading to Berkeley," Elliot said.

"Right on!"

"*You're* getting out the first place I can pull over."

"Don't be like that, baby."

"Stop calling me baby. Elliot. Not baby."

"I like that name. Elliot. I'm Morning Star."

Elliot glanced over again. She had closed her eyes and tilted her head back. The sun shone on her face like the light through a cathedral window. Her hair looked rather oily.

"Morning Star. Is that some kind of pseudonym?"

The woman stretched herself in the summer warmth and murmured, "Sure, why not? It's a beautiful day."

If he had not been focused on this unexpected passenger, Elliot would have noticed that it was, indeed, a beautiful day. The smog had cleared as the highway passed through Pacific Palisades. Traffic was light, and off Malibu surfers rode the glittering waves. The tires sang on the pavement. Overhead, a skywriting airplane inscribed an advertisement on the blue vault of the heavens: TODAY IS A—.

"It's so perfect that you stopped for me," Morning Star said, folding her legs under herself so that she could turn toward him.

"I did not stop for you!"

Morning Star lifted the hem of her loose linen blouse to her chin, exposing her breasts to the Pacific breeze. There were red scratch marks across the top of her chest. "Good morning!" she cried.

Elliot, again, was flabbergasted.

"Don't do that!"

"Why not?" Morning Star said. "I love the experience of my body."

"The rest of the world doesn't need to share your experience," Elliot snapped.

She let the blouse drop. "Don't you want to run naked on the dunes?"

"No!"

Morning Star chuckled. "Don't you want to roll in the sand in the summer sun? Let's do it. We could get to know each other."

"Get to know each other! Oh, boy, that's something. Most people go their whole lives without introducing themselves by rolling naked in the sand."

"Our culture is sick, baby."

"I can agree with that. That's an excellent reason to keep your clothes on."

Morning Star lifted her blouse again.

Elliot groaned.

"Hey, Elliot, let's smoke a joint."

• • •

West Los Angeles

The Assistant Special Agent in Charge of the Los Angeles field office— Muncie by name—looked and, his underlings said, smelled like a slab of raw bacon. He was not a popular man. No one knew about his interest in beekeeping or that he had once given forty dollars to a hurricane-relief fund, because he never brought his personal life into the office. As far as his co-workers knew, he was a simple, dedicated, get-it-done guy who worked with his shirtsleeves rolled up and whose simple, smelly office had none of the trappings of rank. Even his coffee mug had been handed down from the previous A.S.A.C.

Mug in hand, scowl on face, he leaned across his desk and demanded: "How many taxpayer dollars have you two morons wasted this week? And take off those damn glasses!"

Special Agent Armbruster removed his aviator shades, revealing eyes like battlefield casualties.

Muncie blenched. "For Christ's sake! Put 'em back on. You look like hell."

Special Agent Clegg opened a large manila folder and took out a smaller manila folder and passed it to his supervisor. "The name's Elliot Ames. He's been on our radar at the China One location for two weeks. A previously unknown operative's been bird-dogging him. The first photo is from U.S. Army files, 1959. The second picture was taken yesterday. By me." Clegg allowed himself a tiny smile of self-approval.

Muncie slapped the dossier on his desk. "Where did you get all this crap?"

"They do extensive security-clearance checks on these aerospace guys. Federal requirements."

"Give me the highlights," Muncie snapped. At dawn he had been working his beehives; the stings on his wrists and neck prickled and burned and made him irritable.

Clegg cleared his throat. "Thirty years old. Unmarried. Raised in Dearborn, Michigan. His father, deceased, was an engineer at Ford, which explains why the guy drives a foreign car." He offered a dry laugh.

"Act of rebellion," Armbruster explained.

"Got it," Muncie said sourly.

Clegg went on: "Double-majored at the University of Michigan. Graduated 1958, B.S. in mathematics and B.A. in history. Middle-infielder for the Wolverines in '55 and '56."

"Nice. What happened?"

"He hit .158."

"Say no more."

"Unlucky s.o.b. was drafted three months after graduation—by the Army not by a ball club. Sent to Germany, '58. Counterintelligence, something to do with radios. Discharged in 1960 and goes for his Ph.D. at M.I.T. In '63 he goes to work at Pacifidyne Corporation in the Research, Development, and Design Division. He's been there ever since. Works as the head of the computer section, attached to a project for some agency at the Department of Defense. ARPA."

"ARPA," Muncie said. "Never heard of it."

"The Advanced Research Projects Agency. It's classified. Possibly top secret," Clegg added for effect, although he had no evidence to support this claim.

Muncie glanced at the dossier. "Anything else?"

"He's a real all-American type. The kinda guy the boss trusts to play tennis with his wife. Son of a bitch doesn't even have a parking ticket."

"So you think he's K.G.B.? None of their guys ever have a mark on their history, and every last mother-lovin' one of them can beat the shit outta you at individual sports."

"We know he likes Peking duck," Armbruster offered.

Muncie glowered. "That sounds more like C.I.A."

"They deny," Clegg said. "Maybe Defense Intelligence."

"Goddammit!" Muncie growled. "What kind of field agents are you! Could be C.I.A., could be K.G.B., could be local goddamn P.D. Who the hell knows?"

"My money says he's not domestic," Clegg just then decided. He crossed his legs comfortably. "But the bird dog that put us on to him smells like C.I.A. He was driving a Ford Falcon."

"Huh. That sounds right."

Clegg felt a rush of gratification.

"This fella Ames is the pipeline from Pacifidyne to the Soviets," Muncie went on, building the story. "No doubt about it. He's our man. What d'ya have on the bird dog?"

Clegg uncrossed his legs and passed a second manila folder across the desk. "Goes by Frederick Happ. His car's registered to a business in the Valley. Supposedly, he's a private investigator."

"Just the kind of cheesy cover C.I.A. goes for," Armbruster pointed out.

"Agreed," said Muncie. He took a gulp of coffee and made a face. "Why else would he be running surveillance on this Ames character at China One? Get on him, find out what he's doing. Man, I'd love to see how those C.I.A. bastards like it when they find out they're fucking with a Bureau operation."

"What about Ames?"

Muncie leaned back and examined the ceiling. "Wire the house."

"Can we still do that?"

"Jesus, Clegg, how else are we supposed to get these guys? Pull the surveillance off China One and put 'em on Ames. I don't have enough manpower for both. Sooner or later, he'll contact his handler. Hell, he might have a tube fulla weapons plans stashed at his place. That shouldn't be too hard for you apes to handle." He glared at the two of them. "That's not too hard, is it—finding a tube fulla weapons plans?"

"No, sir," Clegg said.

"And Armbruster—buy some Visine. You're giving me the creeps with those mirrored shades. I can see myself while I'm talking."

. . .

Van Nuys

Morning light seeped through the beat-up venetian blinds. At a battered steel desk, pecking on a typewriter that had been new during the Coolidge Administration, sat Freddy Happ. The camera with the expensive telephoto lens, which he was buying on the monthly payment plan, rested next to the machine. On a clothesline strung in the doorway of the bathroom hung several black-and-white photographs of Elliot Ames performing the mundane tasks of a single man. Here he was going to work. Here he was coming home. Here he was on his way to lunch. Much to Freddy Happ's disappointment, after two weeks of surveillance the only interesting thing

Ames had done was to polish his sports car with some kind of motorized buffing device that Happ had never seen.

• • •

Malibu

Elliot pulled onto the shoulder and crunched to a halt. The motor throbbed impatiently. A diesel truck roared past, raising a tornado of debris that swirled around the convertible and settled onto Elliot's hair. Morning Star blew two aromatic tendrils of marijuana smoke from her nostrils and stubbed the joint on the dashboard.

"Out," he said. "I'm sorry, Miss—Morning Star. You'll have to find another ride."

Morning Star smiled placidly. "You're upset."

"Yes! I'm upset! You jump in my car, you strip off your clothes, you start smoking drugs. We haven't even left the county!"

"You need to cool off, Elliot," Morning Star said. "You're hysterical."

"Out!"

"How will I get to San Francisco?"

"Flag down a Greyhound. You'll have a whole busload of guys to roll naked in the dunes with you."

"Don't be so uptight, Elliot. I happen to take an interest in my body."

"Yes, I can see that."

She picked up his wallet from the center console and started looking through it. It was fat with money. He had over six hundred dollars, which he had not had time to convert to American Express travelers cheques for the trip to Hawaii, but she seemed interested only in the photographs.

"You're right," Elliot said, trying to control his voice. "I need to cool off. In a little more than two days, I am going to marry a fabulous woman who would go absolutely out of her mind if she knew I'd picked up a drug-smoking hippie on the highway. She would completely—"

"Is this your old lady?" Morning Star pulled a photograph from one of the plastic sleeves in the wallet.

"As a matter of fact, it is." He grabbed for the picture. "Give me that wallet."

"I'd love to meet her," Morning Star said, scrutinizing the snapshot. "I can tell she's a lustrous person."

"Meet her! You're not getting within three-hundred miles of her. Out!"

"What are you ashamed of?"

"I'm not ashamed! Connie is a terrific woman. Everything about her."

"Like what?"

"You're very intrusive, you know that? But if you must know, our computer profiles happen to have a statistically significant correlation."

She looked at him with a mixture of fascination, sadness, and revulsion. "What's the point?"

"What's the point? The point," Elliot explained, forgetting why he had stopped on the side of the road, "is that if someone's going to make a lifelong commitment to another human being, it behooves that someone to select wisely. We now have the tools we need to improve the odds of marital success. In the past, it was all happenstance or maybe some sort of family arrangement. People got married, people like your parents probably and your grandparents, without a clear understanding of whether they belonged together. In other times, it didn't matter so much. Life was short and so were marriages, but these days people might be married for, what, forty, fifty years? You better be damn sure that's what you want. Otherwise, look out, divorce rate. Wow! Why am I telling you this? Get out of the car!"

Morning Star settled more comfortably on her seat. "You might as well drive," she said.

"What?"

"There's no point in fighting, Elliot."

"We're not fighting. I want you to get out of the car."

"Stop saying that. It sounds unfriendly."

"Do I have to drag you out?"

"You're not going to drag me out."

"And why am I not going to drag you out?" Elliot demanded.

"Because you're responsible."

"I'm not responsible for you."

"Yes, you are. You're the kind of person who takes responsibility. You're saddled with responsibility. It's like doing mescaline."

"I'm positive that being saddled with responsibility is nothing like doing mescaline," Elliot said.

She lifted her blouse.

"Cut that out!"

"Feel the ocean air." She smiled, with a trace of malice.

"Sit up," Elliot commanded, and Morning Star closed her eyes.

He looked at her. She seemed impervious and content.

"Obviously, I can't leave you here. God knows what situation you'd end up in. Dead."

"Or worse," Morning Star replied without opening her eyes. She stroked her midriff.

"Don't make me put the top up," Elliot threatened. He threw the convertible in gear and roared onto the highway, a plume of gravel spraying behind him.

• • •

Van Nuys

A messenger wearing a faded blue uniform and cap stood in front of Freddy Happ's battered desk, surveying the office with a disdainful eye. Although he was a teenager, he had the jaundiced air of a man who had witnessed humanity's manifold attempts to overcome its essential isolation and found them wanting. He yawned.

"Hey!" Happ said. He thrust a manila envelope at the kid. "When you're done casing the joint, maybe you can take what you came for and get the hell gone."

"Sure, man," the kid said and gave him a cynical look that implied that whatever was in the envelope—dirty pictures, records of illegal transactions, whatever—was none of his business, he'd seen it all before.

"Before noon tomorrow, right?"

The kid glanced at the work order on the aluminum clipboard he was holding. "Berkeley? Guaranteed, pops." He winked. "This chick'll get the bad news before lunch."

• • •

San Luis Obispo

Elliot carried a flimsy cardboard box of hamburgers and fries from the takeout window of the High-Fare drive-in back to the convertible. The sun was high and hot, and he thought about making good on his threat to put up the top, although Morning Star had managed to keep her shirt on. She was trying to find a Top Forty station, but all she could locate was an agricultural news show.

"You forgot the Cokes," she said as he climbed in.

"Rats!"

"Also, ketchup works on a lot of things."

Elliot got out of the car and went back to the takeout window.

"I forgot the Cokes," he said to the girl behind the counter. She was wearing a striped paper hat and a smock with the name *Shari* stitched on it in yellow thread.

"What Cokes?" she said.

"The ones I just paid for."

"Can I see your receipt?"

"You didn't give me a receipt."

"I'm sorry, sir. If you do not have a receipt, I cannot give you any merchandise."

"But I just ordered five minutes ago."

"Would you like to order a Coke?"

Elliot stared at her. "Yes, Shari, I'd like to order a Coke. Two Cokes. Large, extra ice. And some extra ketchup."

She wrote on a pad of green paper. "That will be fifty-two cents with tax."

It occurred to Elliot that they did not really need Cokes—he would have preferred water—but when he glanced over at the convertible and saw

Morning Star wolfing down a hamburger, he realized that if a person offered to provide lunch, he should provide the whole thing. He was responsible. He sighed and reached into his pocket and counted out his loose change, leaving him with a single penny.

. . .

Back on the road, Morning Star finished her second burger and tossed the paper wrapper into the wind. "So you're a cog in the corporate machine," she said.

"How do you arrive at that conclusion?"

"It's obvious." She turned the tuning knob on the radio; static poured from the speaker.

Elliot reached between his legs for the sweating cup of Coke. When he picked it up, it left wet spots on his pants and the car seat. "I wouldn't say I'm a cog. No. Or if I am, I'm a well-compensated cog who loves what it does."

"Oh, man."

"Don't be like that. I work at Pacifidyne. I'm privileged to be a part of the most exciting breakthroughs in communications since the invention of the telephone. My team is connecting an array of geographically isolated computers into a kind of resource-sharing network. There are hubs in Boston and Berkeley and Utah. I run the hub in L.A.—Redondo Beach, actually."

Morning Star turned off the radio. "Don't feel bad, Elliot."

"Why should I feel bad?"

"I was working at the May Company store on Wilshire. But it was like, you know."

"A corporate machine?"

"Exactly! They started taking American Express cards! Can you believe it? They had me in the ladies' junior-executive training program while I was going to school. It was nothing but an assembly line for citizen-slaves."

"You were in school?" Elliot was surprised. Morning Star was nothing like the girls he remembered from college. "I'm sorry. I don't mean to sound. . . ."

"Don't worry, baby. UCLA. Junior. Anthropology."

"Oh." It crossed Elliot's mind that she was engaged in some kind of field study. He had read in *Time* magazine about anthropologists who immersed themselves in other cultures, drugging themselves with the local psychedelics and taking up native customs. Maybe Morning Star had organized a research project in San Francisco for some kind of senior thesis on the hippie movement. He glanced at her. She stuffed a clump of french fries into her mouth and wiped her hand on her jeans. She did not strike him as a person who organized things.

"It's going to be beautiful," she said with her mouth full. "Golden Gate Park. Haight-Ashbury. Everybody coming together to cure society. It starts in San Francisco and spreads across the world. I heard George Harrison might show up."

"Has spring quarter ended? Don't you have finals?"

"Final exams are a capitalist sorting-mechanism," she said severely, tossing the empty french-fry bag over her shoulder. "They fail to account for true learning. I'm done with all that. It's dead to me. I had to get out of there and get my head together before I lost my soul. Have you read 'The Structural Analysis of Narratives'?"

"I don't think so," Elliot said. He was sure he had not.

"It's radical. Roland Barthes shows that we're all decoders of the great narrative. Like Freud. The whole world is a dream made available for our interpretation."

"Really?"

"It's all how you choose to understand it. Like I understand that in this dream I'm meant to be right here, right now, riding in the sunshine. With you!"

Elliot was perplexed. "How could you possibly understand that?"

"Why?"

"Why am I asking you a question?"

"Okay."

"Okay what?"

"Don't you believe that there's a reason for everything?"

"No, I don't believe there's a *reason* for everything," Elliot said testily. "I believe there's an *explanation* for everything. There's a difference. There was no predetermined reason for you to jump into this particular car when I stopped at that particular light, but that doesn't mean we can't discover an explanation, however implausible or imbecilic. We can trace the chain of improbable events that led you from wherever you live to a corner in Santa Monica. It can be known. Everything can be known, eventually. Given enough time, energy, and will, everything can be explained if you want to take it all the way."

"How awful!"

"No, it's not," Elliot insisted. Irritation pricked at his scalp. "Happiness, if you can even define what that is, depends on knowledge. Right? If you don't know things, you can't draw comparisons, and if you can't draw comparisons, you can't judge when things are good or when you're feeling better than you might otherwise feel. That's happiness. Don't you want to know things? You're in college. Don't you want to understand the world?"

"Definitely not," Morning Star said.

"You just said that you wanted to decode the great narrative."

"That doesn't mean I want to explain everything, which is an impossibility. I want to experience the dream of the world. If everything could be explained, I wouldn't do anything."

"That's an incoherent philosophy."

"It's not a philosophy. It's a template."

"It's willful ignorance."

"It's faith in life!"

"Okay, fine. What if I were some predator who picks up girls and disembowels them in the desert?"

"You didn't pick me up. I jumped in your car."

"That's worse! You would be the agent of your own doom."

"You might be right about that," Morning Star said placidly. "Whatever will be, will be."

Berkeley

"For Christ's sake, Sheilah, will you listen to me? Listen to me before you start. Listen."

But it was Connie who, for now, had to do the listening. She appreciated her friend's interest in her life, but, honestly, sometimes Sheilah inserted herself too deeply into other people's affairs. Connie shifted the telephone receiver to her other ear and peered out the kitchen window at the gentle curve of Moraga Drive, with its picturesque lampposts and blooming jacarandas, and wondered where the valets were going to put all the cars on Saturday afternoon. She noticed that the gardener had, again, failed to sweep up the purple blossoms on the sidewalk, which he claimed was the city's responsibility. Maybe she could make Frank do it before Saturday.

"I know you know your business," she interrupted, bringing her attention back to the conversation, "but I don't want to spend my honeymoon hiking over volcanoes and eating pineapple or whatever people do on the Big Island. I want sandy beaches, with beautiful men and women on them. The hotel's all set for Waikiki, so please, please, please don't change the reservations. Don't you have other clients to take care of?"

She paused again to let Sheilah talk. Aside from her annoyance at having someone else in charge of her plans, even if that someone was her dear friend, Connie was worried about what she would learn from the report the private investigator had promised. She was convinced, absolutely, that Elliot loved her and was, probably, loyal to her. But her convictions about her future spouse were complicated by the fact that she did not have to make any effort, not even a little, to attract him. To be sure, she was an alluring woman, literate, possessed of an artistic eye and an intricate mind, but it had been too easy. The two of them had slid from introductions to intimacy to impending matrimony without the slightest friction. Whatever she wanted, he wanted. Whatever she said, he agreed with her. Whatever she liked, he supported. If she didn't care for something he did, he stopped doing it. What kind of person did that? How could a confident, successful man-on-the-rise, in charge of budgets and subordinates and multimillion-dollar equipment, be so accommodating?

Despite what she told people, she only partly shared his belief that the two of them, barely aware of each other's existence, had been accurately matched by a machine in Massachusetts. His faith in the power of algorithms was unshakeable. Connie wondered if he had invested so much belief in the infallibility of Operation Matchmaker and that blowhard Halifax Deane, whom he didn't even respect, that he couldn't recognize his own feelings. Maybe he didn't love her, but he didn't know it.

Or worse, he was using Operation Matchmaker as a smokescreen. He wanted a wife and kids—he was thirty years old—and Connie, the fool, had been recruited for duty while he was keeping women on the side. She half-hoped the private investigator had unearthed something. Elliot would be more fascinating if he had a secret life, were a man of mystery, not a brainy work-group manager who spent his nights talking to ham-radio people. Suddenly, she longed for him to arrive and take her riding in his—their—new convertible. The car, at least, was exciting. They could clear the air about what he'd been up to while she wasn't around. He needed to know he was breaking her heart with his devious behavior. He needed to apologize and take her to a good restaurant. The more she thought about his probable infidelities, the more frantic she became.

"No!" she shouted into the receiver. "You retract that statement, Sheilah! This is most certainly not a case of the so-called jitters! Let me tell you: you don't know everything that's going on."

She opened a cupboard and took down a ceramic plate. She pulled the breadboard from its slot under the counter and reached into the silverware drawer for a butter knife.

"I'm sorry, Sheilah. It's just that I'm sick and tired of Mother harping about how dirty Los Angeles is, like it's some kind of recreation room that needs a good sweeping out. And Daddy! He's useless. This very minute I'm making him a bologna sandwich because he can't manage it himself and he won't go out for lunch on business anymore, not even to restaurants that are East Bay customers. I can't believe he was in the Navy. Don't they teach them survival skills, for God's sake? He should be making *me* a sandwich. I mean, this is my special time. And, of course, Frank. All he does is lie in the backyard like some kind of ominous, threadbare ape and write all over my books. He's out there right now, baking himself. He hasn't taken a shower in a week, and I'm certain he's been napping on my bed when I'm not here. I can smell him. If I didn't need him to be nice to Elliot this weekend, I'd kill him."

As she spoke, she opened the refrigerator and began selecting the materials for the sandwich: a loaf of bread in a red, white, and blue plastic bag, a package of lunchmeat, a leaf peeled from a head of lettuce, pickle relish. She put each item on the breadboard. She located the jar of mayonnaise in the rear of the refrigerator and plunked it on the counter and tried to unscrew the lid with one hand. It would not budge. "Hang on a minute, Sheilah."

Connie shouldered the refrigerator door closed and lifted the phone cord over her head and put the receiver on the counter. She eyed the mayonnaise jar. Intolerable. She wanted to scream. In a fit of frustration she attacked the jar and managed, after banging the edge of the lid on the counter, to loosen it enough to twist it off. Task accomplished, she turned to the bread bag. Instead of removing the yellow twist-tie, she lacerated the plastic bag with the butter knife and pulled out two torn slices of bread and slapped them onto the plate.

She picked up the receiver. "Goddammit. Go on."

Squeezing the phone between her left ear and shoulder, Connie began to assemble the sandwich. On one slice of bread she spread a gob of mayonnaise, on the other the horrid pickle relish her father liked. She dropped the knife in the sink and laid two lubricious rounds of bologna, just beginning to go green at the edges, on the bread. She licked her fingers. "Of course, I can find something to fill the time. I have a pretty good map of the future, you know. As soon as the kids can look after themselves, and if Elliot is doing well, which he positively will be, if we're still together, I'll start my own business or take over an existing one. I'm a terrific boss. I could really do something with Daddy's company, sales and advertising-wise. Look at all these hippies. I bet I could unload two gross of artificial daffodils in an afternoon at Golden Gate Park. Why are we talking about this, Sheilah?" she demanded. "I've got enough to worry about right now without planning my middle age."

At this point, there was the sound of the front door opening. Helen Campbell had returned from the beauty parlor, where she had gone to have her hair set for the wedding. She was wearing her imitation pearl necklace, the one she reserved for errands that did not involve special people. She put her purse on the counter, patted her stiff, streaked locks, and surveyed the scene. She smelled of hairspray.

"For Daddy?" she mouthed elaborately and pointed at the sandwich on the ceramic plate.

Connie gave her a curt nod; she wished she would go back outside for ten minutes.

"Let me do that," Helen went on in a stage-whisper, making it obvious that she did not wish to interrupt her daughter's telephone conversation, which was more important than Carl Campbell's lunch.

Connie waved her off.

Helen gathered her purse from the counter and, after plucking exactly two paper napkins from the filigreed brass napkin holder she had purchased at the 1962 Seattle World's Fair, folding them diagonally, and laying them on the serving tray next to the napkin holder, clipped down the hall to the bathroom.

Connie set her jaw and watched her go. She maneuvered a cigarette from the pack lying on the counter and lit it with her thin gold lighter. "Mother's home," she said into the phone, in response to Sheilah's question. "It's time for lunch."

She listened.

"Oh, all right. Call me back when you're done."

She cradled the receiver and stood for a moment, looking at the bologna sandwich on the ceramic plate on the counter. She exhaled a cloud of smoke, watched it dissipate, and stubbed out the cigarette in the middle of the sandwich.

• • •

Near Salinas

When she woke, Morning Star had the sensation of riding a boat across a lagoon. She gazed up at the clouds painted on the wide canvas of the sky and wondered how far away they were. She wiggled her toes in her sandals. She looked out over the countryside and saw fields with crates stacked at the ends of the rows and tiny figures that were vegetable-pickers in straw hats.

Her feet rested on her embroidered bag on the floor of the car. She could feel the bricks of hashish inside. A delicious sunburn had risen on her arms and face. How unbearably humdrum were the halls in the castle of daily life! She had embraced adventure, and her world was getting better and better. Fate had chosen this lovely means of ferrying her to San Francisco, where everything shimmered and glowed.

She stole a glance at Elliot. He was staring grim-faced at the hot strip of pavement slashing through the endless fields. He was, she noted, a good-looking hombre, fit and trim. Smart, apparently. Sane, for whatever that was worth. He smelled like aftershave.

"What's your old lady's name again?" she said.

Elliot started. "Oh, you're awake." He glanced at her. "Connie. Constance. And she's my fiancée."

"Connie. I suppose she's going to take your last name."

"My last name is Ames, and yes, she is."

"Not cool," Morning Star chided. "Surnames are an instrument of oppression. It's like you're colonizing her being."

"You're judging me?"

Morning Star looked horrified. "Oh, my God, I am!"

They drove in silence for several miles.

"The two of you are in love?" Morning Star finally said.

"Of course we are. I told you: it's been ratified." Elliot realized he sounded impersonal. "Yes, we're in love."

"Is she scintillating?"

"Yes," he said. "Very."

"Is every day incomplete without her?"

Elliot could not tell if she was mocking him or was sincerely interested. He had never considered this question. He took his eyes off the road and looked critically at Morning Star. "What about you? Do you have a boyfriend?"

Morning Star stretched herself upright. She furrowed her brow. "I can't take that kind of responsibility for another person. I'd rather share my love and see what happens."

Lately, she had been sharing her love wherever she went, testing the limits of her erotic energy. Her body sent messages to her mind, and she responded to them all. Her sharing had created some problems among the middle-managers at the May Company, which was another good reason to get out of there while she could. A week ago she had been sharing her love on the workbench in the garage of her apartment building. In the middle of the action, the landlord had walked in. There had been yelling. The maintenance man had been sacked on the spot. She suspected that she might be evicted, so she had skipped her June rent payment, but nothing had happened yet.

"I find that attitude lazy and short-sighted," Elliot said. But for some reason, he was pleased to hear that she was single. Then he was baffled by why he cared and quickly resumed talking. "Those no-strings-attached flings might be fine for summers at the lake, but then what do you have? Fond memories? A dose of the clap?"

"I have myself," she said. "I have the pleasure of the moment to carry with me forever."

"But isn't there more to life than the pleasure of the moment?"

"Why do you exist, Elliot?"

The question caught him off guard. "I don't know," he admitted and shifted in his seat. "I have a job to do, things to discover. A family to raise. Probably. Who knows why we exist? You don't have to know why you exist to find meaning in life." He suspected that this statement was not entirely true. "Why do you exist?"

"I exist to keep you company," Morning Star said, "and you exist to give me a ride to San Francisco."

"I find that unpersuasive," Elliot said. "Don't you have a car?"

"Are you going to lecture me about hitchhiking again?"

"No. But you seem like an independent sort of person. Don't you drive?"

"As a matter of fact," Morning Star said, "my father owns a Chrysler-Dodge dealership. He's a genuine kulak."

She told him about the Dodge Dart that T.J. McGovern had given her, and about the double-accident on her way to return it.

"You returned a smashed-up car to your father?"

"It was a *gift* to me," Morning Star said. "It was mine."

"That's even worse! You obviously don't respect your father."

"Everything in life is a gift. A gift economy, without explicit agreements for immediate or future rewards," Morning Star said, drawing on a pool of knowledge she did not realize she had acquired in Anthropology 129, "unsettles market relationships and perturbs ideologies of property-rights in favor of building communities based on reciprocal obligations."

"So you reciprocated the gift your father gave you by smashing it up and then rejecting it."

"It was a burden, man."

"It was placed in your care," he reasoned. "You bear the burden of responsibility, like it or not. You can't give away the trust other people place in you."

"Why do you need to criticize?" Morning Star said. "It's not attractive. And kind of dumb."

"You were irresponsible," Elliot concluded.

"Being irresponsible is one of the perquisites of youth. It's called audacity, baby."

· · ·

Van Nuys
Freddy Happ lay on the filthy linoleum floor of his office. Over him stood a man attired in checkered Dacron golf pants, a Kelly-green polo shirt, a light windbreaker, a golf cap, and golf gloves, pointing a Sig P210 pistol with a custom silencer at his porcine face.

"I swear, I don't know anything about missiles or technology or anything like that," Happ cried through broken teeth. Blood gurgled from his mouth. "I told you, this broad from Berkeley hired me outta the Yellow Pages to watch her boyfriend. Campbell. Constance Campbell. She lives on Moraga Drive."

"Tell me again about the boyfriend," Pegasus said, poking Happ in the belly with the toe of his white golf shoe. Happ quivered and heaved.

"He's just a guy. Elliot Ames. A-M-E-S. He's an engineer, a computer expert. He's at Pacifidyne out in Redondo. I already told you. They're getting married in Berkeley on Saturday. This guy's supposed to go up there today, and then they're going to Hawaii on their honeymoon for, I don't know, a couple weeks, I think. I don't know anything else about it, I swear."

"That," Pegasus said, "is unfortunate."

He fired twice into Freddy Happ's face.

If the man was freelancing for the C.I.A., he had an excellent cover: a hard-luck gumshoe in a sad, crummy office in Van Nuys. No connection back to the Agency.

Pegasus put the pistol in his waistband and began efficiently searching the drawers of the battered steel desk. Nothing but blank paper and an old Colt revolver in the top drawer. He turned to the upright file cabinet, digging through years of faded folders, a palimpsest of Freddy Happ's marginal career as a private investigator: evidence of sleazy divorces, family squabbles, inheritance fights, small-business feuds. Looking at these records, Pegasus could not help thinking about all the evidence that he, despite meticulous care, had left scattered across California, in offices and restaurants, in department stores, at women's apartments, at a half-dozen dead drops—traces of himself that an electronic bloodhound or some future method of surveillance and identification might recuperate, reconstructing him from the minutest specks of information.

At last he found the carbon-paper duplicates of the pages Freddy Happ had typed regarding Elliot Ames. For some reason, the file was in a drawer labeled MISSING PERSONS.

The report did not reveal much about the subject or why the C.I.A. was surveilling him. Perhaps it meant something to Happ's superiors. Pegasus folded the pages lengthwise and pushed them into his waistband beside the pistol. In the bathroom he plucked one of the prints of Elliot Ames from the clothesline. He picked up the strips of 35mm film lying next to the photo enlarger, examined them, put them down. Glancing at the mirror over the sink, he noticed a faint new horizontal crease between his lower lip and chin.

He frowned; the crease deepened, and he frowned some more. He was getting old. Running out of time. He had passed the point where it mattered what he accomplished in life, the point—after forty, before death—when age, which has been creeping up like a thief in the night, smashes down the front door and attacks you where you live.

Pegasus spent much of his personal life examining the ravages that time had visited upon his flesh. He pored over his body like a crime-scene investigator, cataloging the lines around his mouth, the incipient jowls, the age spots as they appeared on the backs of his hands. He noticed an actinic keratosis on his nose and a slight drooping of his left eyelid. When he was in the shower, he fingered his scrotum, noting any change in testicular sagging, and he charted the slightest fluctuation in his daily blood-pressure reading. When the matinal snoring of Susan woke him on the occasions when he stayed at her apartment, the first thing he checked in the dawn light was whether he could touch his toes. Things were getting worse. The laws of entropy and biology were still operating, which meant that the random molecular assaults of a lifetime threatened his California idyll, manifesting in mild arthritis in his hands and the dried-out hair that was receding in two directions, accelerated by the testosterone shots he got from a sympathetic doctor in Glendale, which had done nothing to tighten his sagging pectorals or rejuvenate the pale goose neck that was his penis. Lately, his lips had contracted so that it seemed he had too many teeth in his mouth, and his tongue felt like a leather shoe. He often asked himself why he bothered to avoid alcohol. He was disgusting.

Geez, he whispered, get a grip.

He turned out the lights and stepped cautiously into the corridor, closing the door behind him. He proceeded along the fungous carpet, pausing before the doors of chiropractors and import-export companies to listen for any sign he had been noticed, his mildly arthritic fingers twitching at the pistol in his waistband. He was desperate to find a public bathroom; his bladder was a wreck.

· · ·

Gilroy

For an hour, Elliot had been sunk in a road-trance, floating along the 101 through the vast interstitial landscape of Golden State agriculture. Morning Star dozed. It was only when they stopped for gas that he realized that for the past several miles the stench from the garlic fields and processing factories had been growing. The air seemed murky with the smell.

"That is unpleasant," Elliot said. He wiped his eyes. "Who could breathe that every day?"

Morning Star shook herself awake. Her eyes were watering and red. She inhaled. "I like it. It's like old men in a tent. And soup."

An attendant in khaki coveralls slouched over, mopping his face with a rag, and asked Elliot if he wanted some gas.

"I can't imagine another reason for stopping here," Elliot said. "Give me five dollars' worth."

"Super, regular, or ethyl?"

"There's only one grade for this machine."

"Super?"

"You got it. Check the oil while you're at it."

"Do you want oil?"

"I won't know until you check it."

"What grade?"

"We'll figure it out if it comes to that," Elliot said.

"I'll pump the gas," Morning Star volunteered. She leaned across Elliot's lap to gaze up at the attendant.

"Thatta girl," the attendant said appreciatively. "But the owner'd have my balls."

Elliot took five dollars from the wallet lying on the center console and climbed out of the car and stretched. The day had grown hot. In the distance, shimmering mirages floated over the highway. Blobs of color, wavering, indistinct, appeared. As they drew close, Elliot watched the blobs resolve into cars.

While the gas was pumping, the attendant leaned against the car and chatted with Morning Star.

Elliot turned his gaze from the highway. "The oil?" he said.

"Gimme a minute, sir."

He went inside to pay for the gas and buy a newspaper, but the woman at the counter told him they carried only the local paper and there was nothing in it worth reading. He took a drink from the water fountain.

When he came back, the attendant was still loafing on the fender of the convertible, and Morning Star was sitting in the driver's seat.

Elliot glared at the attendant, who reluctantly pushed himself to his feet and went to service another car that had pulled up to the pumps.

"No," he said to Morning Star. "Move over."

"Let me drive, Elliot. You can enjoy the scenery. This is such a fun car."

"No," Elliot said. He spoke slowly. "This is not a fun car. This is a brilliantly engineered, lovingly crafted precision machine. Believe me. I grew up in Detroit, where we respected our automobiles. Besides, the last time you were behind the wheel, you smashed up your car."

"Did I tell you that?"

"In detail."

Morning Star lifted herself over the center console into the passenger's seat. "You're such a tyrant," she said.

"Did that guy check the oil?"

"I don't think so."

As he eased onto the highway, Elliot regretted, again, having been abrupt with Morning Star. Despite calling him a tyrant, she meant no harm. He glanced at her and asked in a friendly, tolerant voice, "Why are you going to San Francisco, if I may be so bold? Do you have someone waiting for you?"

Morning Star grinned. "Maybe San Francisco is waiting for *me*."

"How's that?" Elliot said.

"I'm very good at procuring and dispensing."

"You should work in aerospace. We do a lot of procuring."

"Actually," she went on. "I'm on a mission. I need to find 710 Ashbury Street."

"You have friends there?"

"Not yet. I hear it's a grand old house." She decided not to tell him about the bricks of Afghan Primo she was transporting for the Grateful Dead and the other undersupplied people of the city. "Everyone is welcome. You'll love it."

"I won't love it. I'm dropping you in Oakland. You can find your way across the bridge."

"Oh, c'mon, Elliot. We'll have fun."

"No."

"Don't be a bastard. Please?"

"Forget it."

"I'm trying to help you, Elliot. Why do you refuse my help? Let me help you, baby."

Elliot exhaled loudly. "Reach under your seat and get the road atlas. If you want to help, you can tell me where to go when we get to San Jose."

Although the Gilroy city limits were far behind and the wind was fresh on their faces, the odor of garlic clung to their hair and clothes. Elliot remarked—and Morning Star agreed—that the smell made him hungry.

• • •

West Los Angeles
At Elliot Ames's ranch house, Special Agents Clegg and Armbruster were supervising a civilian named Hawk Fundy, a nineteen-year-old college dropout who could have made a fortune working at one of the electronics companies but was lending his services to the F.B.I. in exchange for an infinite draft deferral, which pissed off Armbruster, Clegg, Muncie, and everyone else who was not Fundy's uncle, the Special Agent in Charge of the Los Angeles field office. Fundy was in the spare bedroom, disassembling the shortwave equipment to see what kind of circuits the guy had designed, while Clegg and Armbruster sat in the living room, drapes drawn, going through Elliot Ames's mail and enjoying the stereo system. Elliot Ames had a fantastic collection of Latin jazz. Armbruster had found some beer in the refrigerator. He figured Ames would assume the cleaning lady swiped it.

"The man has some taste in music," Clegg remarked.

"Uh huh." Armbruster drained his beer. "This tango-samba Cuban shit is right up your alley."

"Because I'm black, right?"

"Are you black?" Armbruster said blandly.

They felt confident they were on the right track. Ames's array of electronics confirmed their suspicions: he was taking orders from overseas. Fundy had estimated it would take a half-hour to wire the house, but he had dawdled so long in the back bedroom that they began to worry Ames might come home. He might even recognize the FRANCO'S—FLOWERS WITH SOUL delivery van parked around the corner. Maybe they should shut this thing down for the day.

Just as Clegg stood up to investigate what was taking Fundy so long, there was an ungodly squeal of feedback from the back room, and, synchronously, the doorbell rang.

He froze. He looked at Armbruster but could make out nothing behind the aviator shades. "Answer?" he mouthed.

Armbruster shook his head.

Clegg pointed at the stereo, which was blasting a Tito Puente track, and raised his eyebrows.

"Shit." Armbruster propelled himself to his feet, killed the sound, and strode to the door.

On the stoop was a sandy-haired man holding a white gift-box with a gold ribbon and a bow on it. He pulled a photograph from the pocket of his green golf shirt, keeping it carefully turned away, and sneaked a look. He held up the gift-box. "I have a wedding present for Mr. Elliot Ames."

"Nobody here by that name," Armbruster said, looking over the man's shoulder at the Buick parked across the street. The front bumper was mashed.

Clegg came over and peered around Armbruster. "We live here," he added.

Inside the house, the phone began to ring.

Pegasus recognized the F.B.I. agent he had seen in the front of the delivery van at the Peking Palace. His blood ran cold. "I see. Roommates. Maybe one of you is getting married?"

"Sure, that's right," Clegg averred, a note of alarm in his voice. He did not want the man to get the wrong idea about him and Armbruster, separately or together.

"Perhaps this gift is for you. From your boss at Pacifidyne?"

"Nope, sorry," Armbruster said. Sweat ran down his neck. "Don't work there."

Clegg stopped breathing and thought about what Muncie would say if they burned the location.

Pegasus looked at the gift, looked at the men, frowned. He was too late; Canis Minor had left for Berkeley. "Could you tell me how to get on the 405 North?" he said.

"No problem, buddy." Armbruster stepped onto the rectangle of concrete that was the front porch, crowding Pegasus down the steps, and began giving directions which, if Pegasus had followed them, would have sent him to the racetrack in Inglewood.

As Armbruster and Clegg watched the man's car disappear down the street, Hawk Fundy came up behind them. "They called from HQ," he said brightly. "You guys have to get down to the China One location."

Clegg turned to look at him. "How the hell did they know we were here?"

"I phoned in to see if the tap was clicking and left the number."

"Are you finished?"

"Barely started," Fundy said.

"Damn." Clegg peered up and down the block.

"What if that delivery guy mentions to Ames's boss that there are a coupla strangers at his house?" Armbruster said. "We shoulda got his name."

Clegg thought for a moment. "We can trash the place, take a few things to make it look like a burglary in case anyone gets suspicious."

"Dibs on the stereo," Fundy said.

"Negative. Anything that leaves the house stays in our custody."

"I dunno," Armbruster said. "We don't need the local cops poking around."

Clegg scanned the neighborhood. He counted at least four windows in which curious housewives were watching. They all seemed to be talking on the telephone, perhaps with one another. "Okay, nix the burglary. You stay here and finish," he told Fundy. "You can hitch back to the office when you're done."

. . .

Elliot Ames, a.k.a Canis Minor, was burned. Pegasus' suspicions were confirmed the moment he passed the FRANCO'S—FLOWERS WITH SOUL van parked around the corner. He could not imagine that Canis would keep classified documents near him, but other items—micro-photography equipment, dead-drop locations, a cache of money, maybe even a shortwave—might be on the premises. It was only a matter of time before the F.B.I. dropped the net on him. Did he know what was happening at his house? Based on what the dead freelancer in Van Nuys had told him, Pegasus assumed that he did not. He had left for his wedding. That was one bright spot. Pegasus might reach Canis Minor before they picked him up in Berkeley. He pointed the car toward the freeway and hit the gas.

. . .

San Francisco
From the outside, the Astro Auto Body shop resembled every other cinderblock building in the neighborhood. Along the street stood a vacant warehouse, several enterprises whose dirt-grimed windows obscured interiors full of crates and machinery, and two bars—a lesbian dive called Maeve's Place, and a nameless Hells Angels hangout. Astro Auto Body had a steady flow of clients referred by lawyers who specialized in collision fraud, but the bulk of its business consisted of chopping up stolen vehicles for the resale market.

The shop was owned by an ex-con named Bobby Dobell, who had a long reputation for violence. Since his fortieth birthday, Dobell, as his associates noted, had become even more unhinged than usual. The stress of raising his three teenaged daughters as a single parent in this crazy city affected him to such a degree that, like Rumpelstiltskin hearing his name revealed, he seemed perpetually on the verge of tearing himself in twain. The outlaw bikers from the bar next door studied him as a model of chaos.

So no one seemed surprised that he and his number-one man, a former demolition-derby champ called Rowdy Gomez, were taking turns smacking around a hippie tied to an old library chair in the middle of the oil-stained concrete floor. Bloody head, broken teeth, soiled pants. The victim had lost consciousness, but Dobell landed a hard one on his temple anyway. The hippie was known on the streets as Little Pete; he sold drugs.

In one bay, two Hells Angels were disassembling a Corvette. The sparks flew as an electric tool bit into the rear quarter panel. The other biker pulled the alternator from the engine and lowered it into a cardboard box, like a surgeon disposing of a lung. Both of them wore tattered Levis and scurfy denim jackets that appeared to have been dipped in dung and left to dry on a spiny cactus. A third Angel pounded the Coca-Cola machine, trying to dislodge a bottle.

In the other bay sat a '66 Chevy Impala, dark red with custom white pinstripes. Dobell rested for a moment against the fender to recover his breath.

"We lost him, Bobby," Rowdy Gomez panted. "He's zonked."

Dobell gulped a lungful of air and stamped around the library chair, his fists clenched in frustration and rage. "Shit! Is there nobody in this cocksucking city knows where Stanley Stokely went? What the fuck!"

"He's slippery," Gomez agreed.

Dobell kicked Little Pete in the shins. "Goddammit. He doesn't know anything. Go ahead and untie his ass."

Gomez flicked open his blade and sliced the ropes, and Little Pete slid off the chair onto the concrete and lay as limp as a scarecrow. Bobby Dobell looked as if he wanted to spit on him, but instead he swung around and glared through the grimy window, wondering who else out there could tell him where the soon-to-be-dead Stanley Stokely had spirited his beautiful daughters. The whole city seemed to be crawling with teenaged runaways and unsupervised high-school chicks. Was he the only concerned parent left in this fucked-up world?

As he glared out the window, a brand-new cream-colored MG roadster sped past. A young woman was hanging over the side so that the wind caught her hair. She reminded him of his girls—same hair, same clothing—and he swung around and stamped his boot on the unconscious hippie's arm.

"Put twenty bucks in his pocket," he told Gomez. "And this." He went to the workbench and found a business card on the dirty bulletin board and handed it to his sidekick. "Name of my dentist. He did my bridge." His mouth gaped open. "Eh?" he said in a strangled voice. "Nice work, huh?"

. . .

Elliot turned at the end of the street and headed into the Haight. The crowds that filled the sidewalks had been descending on the city for three months. He had seen the black-and-white photographs in the pages of *Life* and *Newsweek*, but he was astonished by the multi-colored actuality of the summer afternoon. Everywhere he looked he saw feathers, beads, stripes, stars, beards, boots, flowers, turtlenecks, macramé, waistcoats, bare feet, ankle bracelets, kaftans, serapes, shawls, fringes, floppy hats, fur hats, skull caps, bowler hats, astrakhan hats, motorcycle jackets, ponchos, scarves, happi coats, fishermen's sweaters, plastic sunglasses, guitars, flutes, violins, djembes, maracas, glockenspiels, and day-glo face paint.

Morning Star leaned over the side of the car, calling out to everyone they passed.

She flopped back on her seat. "Wow, look at all the people. Feel the energy! It's a carnival."

Despite her childish enthusiasm, Elliot thought, she had an air of self-possession—not the Connie Campbell sort, which manifested in a peremptory command of her environment, but a sense of herself as an agent of adventure. She was a smart cookie: she'd managed to get him to drive her to Golden Gate Park. When he had entrusted her with the road atlas in Gilroy he had, in essence, agreed to deliver her to her destination. He knew it. They both knew it.

But knowing it did nothing to soothe his exasperation with himself. The fact that he was deep in the heart of San Francisco rather than making small talk over avocado dip with his future in-laws was nobody's fault but his own. He did not think of himself as a person who made this kind of poor decision. Or maybe, he thought with a stab of panic, he *was* a person who did that. Maybe, below the level of conscious decision-making, he had been committing errors for who knew how long.

Elliot looked at her. "I don't know what's going to happen to you," he said crankily.

She chuckled.

• • •

Redondo Beach

The parking lot of the Peking Palace was full of cop cars. Across the street, faces pressed against the windows of Pacifidyne Building C. Two Los Angeles County Coroner's attendants were lifting a body bag into an ambulance parked in the alley as Armbruster and Clegg muscled their way onto the crime scene, cursing A.S.A.C. Muncie for having ordered them to pull the surveillance from the restaurant.

A uniformed cop blocked their progress. "Off limits, gentlemen. Please step away."

Armbruster flashed his badge. "Who's in charge?"

The cop, looking unhappy, nodded towards the building. "Inside."

Clegg yanked open the steel door that led from the alley to the kitchen, and someone in a dull green suit stepped out. He had lank black hair and oily skin. "Who the hell are you?" His voice was like scrap metal.

Armbruster snapped his gum and held up his badge.

"Figures. I'm Senzatela, Redondo P.D. Whaddya want?"

"This is a hot scene, detective," Clegg told him.

"Lieutenant."

"I don't care," Clegg said grimly. "National security. We're taking it from here."

"Hell you are." Lieutenant Senzatela opened his hand. On his palm lay a clump of electronics. Clegg recognized the 375 MHz covert-listening devices Hawk Fundy had hidden in the promotional artificial-flower arrangements from Franco's Flowers with Soul.

Armbruster's mirrored shades flashed as he swiveled from the bugs to Clegg and back. "Deny," he barked. "To our knowledge no surveillance electronics have been used by the Bureau at this or any other location without a warrant. Who's the dead man?"

Senzatela shook his head. "You people want everything handed to you on a platter. Stick-up man. Evidently, he surprised the owner, a guy named Percy Wu, when he opened the restaurant for the prep crew. Wu shot him five times in the chest."

"So it's a robbery gone wrong?"

"You want more, talk to the D.A. He's gonna have questions about these doodads. Hell, the Justice Department's gonna have questions. You feds make me puke, you know that? Bugging a Chinese joint. That's some kind of racial discrimination right there." He shook the bugs in Armbruster's face.

Clegg reached inside his suit jacket and took out a pen and a flip-top notepad. "How do you spell your name, buddy?" he said to Senzatela.

"E-A-T-S-H-I-T," Senzatela said.

• • •

Studio City

Pegasus tried to relax onto the slippery Naugahyde sofa in the lobby of Valley Savings and Loan. Several hopeful applicants were sitting on the armchairs, checking their paperwork and waiting for their interviews with a loan officer. Customers approached the teller windows, chatted in low voices, laughed, left looking pleased about their transactions. Soft orchestral strings saturated the air. Pegasus scanned the ceiling. He wondered when the banks would wise up and install video-surveillance systems. It made sense. After all, he had a gun in his pocket. It was no challenge to rob the place.

As the minutes passed, Pegasus thought about Canis Minor and felt his future slipping away. He wondered if he had time to find a restroom; he had to urinate all the time. Squelching the urge, he leaned toward the coffee table in front of the sofa and selected the most recent issue of *Sunset* from the collection of magazines. He tried to read a story about landscaping with bricks. Then he tried to read one about the otters in Monterey Bay. He remembered that he had a dental appointment coming up on Monday; he was developing plaque.

At last, Susan, spruce and tall, carrying a Styrofoam cup of coffee, came into the lobby. He tossed the magazine on the table and stood and forced a smile. In his impatience, it seemed that she moved in slow motion across the carpeted expanse.

Smoothing her skirt, she sat on the chair next to the sofa and glanced around. "I only have five minutes. Mike doesn't like the girls talking to people we're personal with. Are you going to the golf course?"

"What?" He sat down on the edge of the sofa.

"Your shirt, honey. Are you hitting the links?"

"Listen, Susan," he said urgently. He glanced at the loan applicants and lowered his voice. "I have to go out of town on business. I need you to do something for me."

"Aw," she said. "Why do you have to go now? You'll miss the rose show. Everyone will wonder where you are."

"I'll be back by Sunday," Pegasus said impatiently. "Dear," he added.

"Okay, then."

"But if anyone asks about me, I want you to tell them I've gone to Guadalajara for a couple of days."

"You're going to Mexico!"

"If anyone asks."

"Why on earth would anyone ask about that?"

"I'm going to call you tomorrow. If anyone has questioned you by then, say, 'How's the water south of the border?' You got it?"

"Aw, honey, that sounds crazy."

"Just say it, please."

She cocked her head and frowned. "How's the water south of the border?"

Pegasus got to his feet. Susan stood up. He tried to embrace her, but she pushed him off, protesting, "Not here, Al. Too many nosy Nellies."

"I'll bring you something," Pegasus said.

"As long as you're back by one p.m. on Sunday," she said.

. . .

San Francisco

Elliot nosed the convertible along the crowded street and pulled to the curb next to a fire hydrant. The engine sputtered briefly before dying with a warm sigh.

A man and a woman in Chippewa ceremonial tunics were hauling a crate of cantaloupes down the sidewalk, followed by a clutch of hungry adolescents with sores on their arms and the glistering eyes of feral cats. At the corner, the ragged procession made a detour around a wild-haired man hawking copies of the *San Francisco Oracle*, the cover of which featured a green-and-purple portrait of an actual Chippewa warrior.

In the Panhandle—that grassy finger of Golden Gate Park along the top of Haight-Ashbury—thousands of people had congealed into clans around individuals playing autoharps or denouncing the Johnson administration or leading Hindu chants. Along the edges of the park, police officers from the station on Waller Street surveyed the throng. They slapped their batons against their palms and adjusted their uniforms self-consciously, looking, in their exclusion from the festivities, a little hurt.

Twenty yards from Elliot's car, a dozen adults and almost as many dirty children had formed into a loose drum-circle on the grass. A little girl wearing a crocheted cape was creating huge soap bubbles with a loop of hanger wire and a bucket of sudsy water. The bubbles shimmered and shook as they rose over the crowd. An ice cream vendor drove a lurid blue donkey-cart along the sidewalk.

Everywhere, hippies sprawled on the grass, smoking and watching the world pass by. A person decked out in striped pants, a sheepskin vest, and a purple velvet top hat with a gold letter *S* embossed on the crown was strolling through the throng, accompanied by three girls who looked so exactly alike they could only be triplets. The man had long rusty sideburns and a goatee and liquid eyes. He carried a walking stick with a silver knob shaped like a bird. The girls, barefoot, beaded, peachy-skinned and ruby-lipped, appeared barely old enough to drive. They wore very short cut-off jeans and peasant blouses. Morning Star spotted them right away. She jumped out of the convertible and retrieved her duffel bag from behind the seat. Then she hoisted the embroidered bag full of hashish onto her shoulder. Resting her hands on the car door, she leaned over so Elliot could see down the front of her blouse, "Thanks for the lift, you lovely, fucked-up person. It was a trip. Too bad you're going to miss the solstice."

"I'm pretty sure the solstice is a global phenomenon," Elliot said, glancing at his wristwatch. "Listen, I'm already an hour late, so good luck with...." He gestured vaguely at the park.

"Goodbye, Elliot." Morning Star started off. She turned and waved. "See you in another dream!"

She was absorbed into the swirl of humanity.

When Elliot turned the key in the ignition, nothing happened. He tried again. Nothing.

He consulted the dashboard, his faith in modern engineering for a moment wavering, and thought: We'll never put a man on the moon.

* * *

Berkeley

From the back Helen Campbell could be mistaken for her daughter. Same radiant hair, same dress tailored to show off her slim shoulders, upright posture, and tight buttocks. She took pride in her resemblance to Connie. She wondered if it had something to do with this genetics thing she had seen on educational television. She tried to watch one educational show per week; it kept her young. On Mondays, Wednesdays, and Fridays she turned on *The Jack LaLanne Show* and did calisthenics.

Stirring a pitcher of iced tea at the kitchen counter while Connie sat in the breakfast nook, smoking cigarettes and checking off items on a pad of lined paper while she talked on the telephone, Helen wondered if it was wise for her future grandchildren to be raised in Los Angeles. The air was so dirty; it might cause brain damage or, she thought triumphantly, pulling the term from recent memory, genetic mutations. She supposed that Elliot was not likely to give up his job, although she could not see how playing with computers held much promise for the future. Was he prepared to be a husband and a father, a lifelong breadwinner? She supposed Connie would make him do whatever he needed to do. She was proud of the way her savvy, quarrelsome daughter always got what she wanted. She, Helen, had once had that ability, back during the war when she ran East Bay Ornamentals while Carl was killing people in the Pacific.

"You're a darling," Connie said into the phone. "Ciao."

She hung up and addressed her mother. "Sheilah says the dresses will be ready this afternoon. She's going to pick them up."

Helen put the pitcher of iced tea on a tray with a sugar bowl and four glasses. "I've confirmed the valets for ten o'clock Saturday. Reverend Ross will arrive at noon for the rehearsal luncheon. Everything is going perfectly, perfectly well." She glanced at the clock over the sink. "All we need is the groom," she said, turning to carry the tray to the sunroom, where Frantz was sprawled in his shorts on the floor with a bowl of Grape Nuts balanced on his stomach and Carl was reading the newspaper.

"Oh, you know Elliot," Connie said, following her. "He probably heard a rattle in his car and stopped to tinker. Still, I'm not inclined to give him more than an hour. After that, there's hell to pay."

"Don't say 'tinker,' Connie. It sounds dirty."

Connie lit a fresh cigarette.

"Do you have an extra pack, dear?" Helen said. "I don't want to go out."

"In my purse."

Frantz rolled himself upright. He put the uneaten bowl of cereal on the rattan table in front of the sunroom sofa and scratched his chest. "I'm gonna drift down to campus and see what's happening. I'll probably truck over to the city and stay the night."

Helen shot him a disapproving look. "You'll catch a disease."

"Those hippies!" Connie complained. "They come from God knows where. Hitchhikers mostly. The girls are all whores and acid freaks. It's revolting!"

Frantz folded his hands in prayer and lifted his eyes to the heavens. "God willing," he said.

• • •

San Francisco

From atop a ramshackle Victorian house on the border of the Panhandle, Special Agents Russ Bogosian and Ed Grassmick peered through matching high-powered binoculars. The sound of drums and transistor radios floated from the park. Someone was playing a tambourine. The agents had stripped off their suit coats and rolled up their sleeves. Their trousers were thin, and the composition roofing bit into their knees as they kneeled behind the parapet.

"Got him. Right across Oak," Bogosian said raspily, sounding uncannily like Bert Armbruster in the Los Angeles field office. Grassmick had known Armbruster at Quantico. The guy drank too much, and people suspected he was hooked on amphetamines. Listening to Bogosian talk, Grassmick wondered how two people could sound so much alike.

He swung his binoculars to the right and caught, among the crush of runaways and musicians, the purple-topped cluster of flesh that was their target: Stanley Stokely and his entourage of teenaged triplets. "Man, oh man! He's got his harem with him."

"Holy smoke, look at those asses," Bogosian whispered. "Don't you wanna peel 'em and take a big bite? Fucking Stokely. It's not fair!"

In a surfeit of envy and lust, Grassmick pressed his incisors against his lower lip until he could taste blood. He wondered how Stokely had lured such nubile females into his orbit. The girls looked awfully young—as young as his own daughters. For all he knew, his girls were parading around the city with their own Stanley Stokely while some dirty old men made salacious comments about their derrieres. He felt a rush of shame and glanced over at Bogosian with sudden distaste.

Grassmick returned his attention to Stokely's purple top hat. As they watched, a girl wearing a loose linen blouse and carrying a duffel over one shoulder and an embroidered bag over the other approached Stokely and pressed something into his hand. The triplets gathered around, obscuring the transaction. After a moment, Stokely swept off his top hat and lowered it carefully onto the newcomer's head. It was hard to ignore his high, noble brow; he looked like an eighteenth-century portrait in oils. Then he and the triplets moved off and were absorbed into the mob.

"You see that, Russ?"

"Get on the box," Bogosian said. "We need someone on the female. What'd she give him?"

Grassmick laid his binoculars on the shingles and pulled out his two-way radio. When he pushed a button, it emitted a metallic squawk.

"This is Lost in Space. Over."

The radio squealed. Grassmick turned a knob.

"Come in, Gilligan's Island. Over."

Static. Then a burst of Top Forty radio.

"Goddammit! Japanese crap! What's wrong with this country we can't make our own walkie-talkies?" He slammed the two-way radio on the roof in frustration.

"That's a Raytheon product," Bogosian pointed out without removing the binoculars from his eyes.

"Yeah, Raytheon. Made in Japan, smart guy. Read the manual."

"Forget it," Bogosian said. He peered through the binoculars. "I'll stay on Stokely. You get down there and find the female. See how she figures in this. It shouldn't be hard to track her in that hat."

"One'll get you ten she's his connection to the radical underground," Grassmick declared. There had been a lot of talk around the office about the radical underground, and he was pleased to deploy the term in conversation.

· · ·

Elliot tapped the engine of the convertible with the screwdriver from the toolkit that came with the car. He assumed the starter was defunct, but he knew not to jump to conclusions. It could be the battery. But he knew it was the starter. He had to find a phone and call the Auto Club and arrange a tow to a repair shop and then call Connie to let her know what had happened.

He slammed the hood and leaned in to retrieve his wallet from the center console.

Gone.

He patted his pants.

He climbed into the car and went through the glove compartment, searched under the seats, felt frantically around in the back.

"Oh, boy. Oh, boy," he muttered. "That bitch."

He sprang out of the car and, half-walking, half-running, cut across the drum circle. A giant soap bubble floated onto his face. Wiping his stinging eyes, he stumbled over a man with a harmonium on his lap and crashed onto the sprawling hippies, who, rather ungraciously, pushed him upright. As he regained his feet, he spotted Morning Star. She was wearing a purple hat and moseying across the grass, arm in arm with someone who looked as if he had just come down from a mountain.

"Morning Star!" Elliot waved his arms. "Come back here!"

She moved through the crowd.

"Morning Star!"

She glanced over her shoulder. When she saw who it was, she waved and shouted, "Elliot! You came!"

Her companion looked consternated.

Elliot sprinted over. He rested his hands on his knees, trying to catch his breath. "You—took—my wallet," he panted.

Detaching herself from the mountain man, Morning Star laid a hand on his back. "Of course I did."

Elliot straightened up. "What do you mean, of course you did?"

"Don't you feel happier? You're not weighed down by money and identity and that whole scene."

"Right on," the mountain man said.

"Who are you, pal?" Elliot demanded.

"Hey, man, I'm just diggin' the chick. We don't need your harsh attitude."

"Give it back," he ordered Morning Star.

"Elliot. I released you."

"No thanks," he said grimly. "Give me my wallet. I have to pay someone to tow my damn car, which is stalled in this—." He swept his arm in a semi-circle. "*This,* because I was stupid enough to drive you here instead of dropping you on Market Street."

"Elliot, you're flipping out."

"Give it!"

"Hey, man," said her companion, who had begun shifting aggressively from foot to foot and flexing his shoulder muscles, "you're bumming me out with this authority trip."

Elliot turned and pointed at him. "You shut up!" He swung back to Morning Star. "And you—hand it over, or I'll call the cops."

"I'm sorry you feel this way, Elliot," Morning Star said. "I gave your wallet to that lanky cat over there." She pointed across the park, where Stanley Stokely and the Dobell triplets had just exited down a side street.

"You gave away my wallet?"

"He looked like a man who knew how to spend the bread. He wouldn't get all hung up on it. You know what I mean? I've liberated you from your crass desire for consumer experience."

Elliot gawped at her. "You gave my wallet to a lanky cat. I had six hundred bucks in there! That was my honeymoon money."

"He gifted me with his hat!" Morning Star exclaimed, touching the purple velvet brim. "And he told me the Grateful Dead are in the city. Let's go there right now, Elliot, and present the bricks."

"The bricks?"

"The bricks of Afghan Primo." She patted her bag. "Hashish, baby."

Elliot suddenly needed to sit. As he dropped to the grass, he felt something uncomfortable in his front pants pocket and pulled out one of the fortune cookies he had plucked from the empty table at the Peking Palace the previous noon. The cookie was a mass of fragments. He tore open the wrapper with his teeth and pulled out the message, glanced at it, and read it aloud: "*Know when you have finished it.*"

He laughed bitterly and tossed the shards of cookie in the air.

"Hey, brother, you shouldn't litter," the mountain man said.

Elliot reached up from where he was sitting and grabbed a handful of shirt. With a strength born of frustration he pulled himself upright. "You've got three seconds to get the hell away from me, or I'm going to get very, very angry with you."

The mountain man shook himself free. "All right, man, you don't need to go Neanderthal. I was just diggin' the chick. You don't have to wig out."

Muttering, he drifted off, casting wistful glances over his shoulder at Morning Star.

While Elliot had been chasing across the park after his wallet, a City of San Francisco tow-truck driver was setting the hook on the MG convertible. Now Elliot caught sight of the tow truck. It took him a moment to recognize what was happening.

He sprinted across the grass, flailing his arms.

"Hey! You there!" He reached the curb, out of breath for the second time. "That's my car, fella."

The patch on the fella's gray work shirt identified him as Eli.

"Not any more it ain't," Eli said haughtily, patting the fender of the convertible. "You parked by a hydrant. Now this vehicle belongs to the City of San Francisco, leastways till you pay the impound."

"I didn't technically park by a hydrant," Elliot protested. "I stopped, and then I couldn't get the engine started again."

Moving in an oily-jointed, hips-forward way, as if he were strolling down a country road, Eli ambled to the cab and climbed in.

"Wait!" Elliot cried. "I'm on my way to my wedding!"

Eli leaned out the window. "That's tough luck, man."

"But I don't have any money. And my suitcase is in the trunk. Can I at least get my things?"

"Shit in the car goes with the car," Eli said. He ground the gears and pulled forward a few feet, the MG dangling from the boom. He leaned out the window again and grinned at Elliot. "Peace, brother."

The truck pulled away and was gone.

Morning Star glided up. Elliot turned to face her. "You! You!" he sputtered. He could not squeeze out any more words. He sank to the curb and wrapped his arms around his knees. His head dropped. People passed on the sidewalk. His shoulders began to shake with laughter. "Oh my God," he said in a muffled voice, "Connie's going to kill me. In the span of fifteen minutes, I've lost my car, my suitcase, my tux, my driver's license, my money. I don't even have a dime for a payphone. I gave all my change to the girl at the hamburger stand when we stopped for lunch."

Morning Star kneeled in the gutter and wrapped her arms around him. "You poor man," she said soothingly. "You're like a new baby with nothing in the world."

She clasped his head to her breast and kissed his hair.

"Hello, little baby," she cooed.

PART TWO

Pasadena, June 7, 2020

By the time I was old enough to remember family gatherings, the Story of the Wallet had acquired an aura of legend. Every holiday meal or milestone event occasioned a retelling of how the free-spirited Mary Ellen McGovern relieved the strait-laced Elliot Ames of the burden of money, the story passed around the table, refined and polished by whoever picked up the narrative. It never seemed to yield a moral, but I suppose that was the point—the story was meant to be savored, not used as a guide to good living.

Unlike Elliot's and Morning Star's tale, my Story of the Pandemic (already the phrase sounds stale) will lack everything that makes for a good adventure: strange people, strange places, emotional excess, crises, turning points and reversals, mortal danger. It's not that we live in quieter times. Last night Talia and I ventured out of the condo and walked over to Pasadena City Hall, water bottles in hand (for the tear gas that never came), where the people were gathered to demand a reckoning and reformation. City Hall is situated kitty-corner from the police station, so the cops did not have to travel to meet their protestors face to riot-geared face. Although Talia is not a "fan" of large crowds, we agree that now isn't the time to sit in our bubble playing with the cat. We put on our surgical masks and joined the throng, trying to be good allies in the fight for racial justice, but I admit that I'm no more comfortable in crowds than Talia is, no matter how righteous the cause. A stadium or a concert hall gives me a panic attack; the Rose Parade leaves me dizzy; even a nightclub on television makes me a little queasy. I'm no good for any gathering larger than a game-night quartet.

What happens inside my head and heart translates with difficulty to the social world and vice versa. My parents, featured here, loved picnics, beaches, bridge tournaments, parties, live sports, and theater. I, on the other hand, am happiest sitting on a rock in Eaton Canyon or hiding at the back of a noodle house with a magazine. Colleagues, Talia, my mother—they all tell me I used to be friendlier, before the separation knocked the wind out of me. Perhaps. I concede that the discovery that my soulmate might be better off with someone else came as a shock and has soured me not only on romance but on relationships in general. Of course, I've never trusted relationships to live up to their promise, so my surprise is entirely unearned.

Anyway. On with the story.

. . .

Van Nuys, June 8, 1967

A fly buzzed against the glass behind the venetian blinds. Traffic mumbled on Victory Boulevard. Special Agents Armbruster and Clegg stood over the body of Freddy Happ. Where Happ's left eye had been there was a ragged hole, and there was another hole in the middle of his forehead.

Armbruster snapped his gum and exhaled a gust of whiskey and wintergreen. He was feeling saggy. Lately, he needed a Nembutal just to climb into bed next to his wife; mornings found him groggy and deflated.

"That seals it," he muttered. "He's C.I.A."

Clegg nodded. "If he is, this place'll be as clean as a hospital room by suppertime."

"So call L.A.P.D.?"

"Yep."

Clegg began moving methodically around the office, his delicate fingers picking through the folders in the file cabinet, fondling the items on the desk. He found the old Colt revolver in the top drawer and stood looking at it for a while. It was exactly the kind of gun someone with the guy's cover would have. Then he lifted the wall calendar to see what was hidden behind it. Nothing was hidden behind it.

Armbruster emptied the wastebasket onto the floor. On his hands and knees he began picking through wads of paper and the remains of several meals.

Clegg flipped open the typewriter case on the desk and peered at the ribbon. Using a pencil, he lifted the spools and held the ribbon over the desk lamp before tossing it aside.

"Don, take a look at this." Armbruster held up some wrinkled sheets of carbon paper. "Some kinda report."

Clegg came over and leaned on his shoulder. "My, my," he murmured. "So he had a file on our man."

. . .

San Francisco

While Morning Star sat on her duffel bag and smiled at some kids who were drawing cartoons on the sidewalk with colored chalk, Elliot urinated behind a bush. On the other side of the bush, a girl was strumming an acoustic guitar and singing "The Battle Hymn of the Republic." The collective energy of the afternoon was beginning to subside into a stoned lethargy. A police siren started up and cut off.

"I can't believe this!" Elliot said, zipping up. "Look at me. This morning I was on my way to a resort in Hawaii. Now I'm pissing in the park while Joan Baez works on material for her next album."

"Isn't it great!" Morning Star jumped up.

"Don't you have to pee?"

"I have a powerful bladder," she said. "I do exercises."

Down the street Elliot spied a policeman sitting on a motorized tricycle. "If you'll excuse me," he said to Morning Star, "I need to report the theft of my wallet."

"The cops don't care about you, Elliot. Why bother them?"

Elliot started down the street, jostling through the pedestrians. Morning Star shouldered her duffel and her embroidered bag and skipped along behind him. "Besides, you don't want me to get busted with all this hash, do you? If you think about it, you're the one who transported it from L.A."

He halted. "Oh my God."

"That's right, baby."

"I need to find a telephone," he said, mostly to himself. "Connie's going to be pulling her hair out." He turned abruptly. "Give me a dime."

"You need more than a dime to call Berkeley, Elliot. It costs at least a quarter. Anyway, I told you we're free of the burden of money. Your old lady will understand."

"Perfect," Elliot muttered. He grabbed a scraggly passerby. "Hey, buddy, can you spare a quarter? No?" His hand shot out for the next pedestrian. "How about you? You have any money? No?" He began to walk in a tight circle. "Look at me!" he cried. "I'm begging panhandlers for loose change!"

He accosted a kid wearing a suede turtleneck. "How about you? Wanna buy some marijuana?"

The kid looked interested. "How much?"

"Two bits, my friend. Morning Star, give this man a marijuana cigarette. A joint! Give this man a joint. Come on, let's go! Relieve yourself of the burden of possessions. You've got a bag full of the stuff."

The kid turned eagerly toward Morning Star.

"I don't have any more grass, Elliot, and I can't sell him hash!"

"Why not? I need a quarter. You gave away all my money. Ergo—"

"I'm not into selling stuff anymore. I left that all behind."

"Trade it then. Trade some hashish for a quarter so I can make a goddamn phone call. Here—" He pulled off his wristwatch. "Take my watch, kid. I'll trade you for a quarter."

"Hey, man, be cool," the kid said, plucking the wristwatch from Elliot's fingers. "You look kinda shaky. Why don't you just call collect?"

Elliot blinked at him. The kid was a genius. He loved the turtleneck. He nodded calmly. "Yes, why don't I?"

The kid continued down the street, twirling Elliot's wristwatch on his index finger. Elliot turned on his heel and set his sights on the PacTel phone booth on the corner.

There was litter piled against the skirting, and the glass was foggy and scratched. When he jammed himself inside, the stench of a public toilet assailed his nostrils. He pulled the door closed. Outside, Morning Star dropped her duffel bag and stood with her back against the dirty pane.

Somewhat to Elliot's surprise, the telephone was working.

"Yes, Operator, I want to place a collect call to Berkeley," he spoke into the receiver. He gave her the Campbells' number and his name and waited for the connection.

A tall black woman carrying a wooden box containing a dozen open jars of paint stopped to chat with Morning Star.

Elliot tapped his foot impatiently. Busy signal. "Goddammit! Hang up, Connie."

The operator came on the line. "The number is busy, sir. You'll have to try back."

"Can you break in? This is an emergency."

"I'm sorry, sir, I can't do that."

"But—oh, never mind."

He dropped the receiver on the hook. Outside the booth, the woman was painting Morning Star's face with a pointed sable brush.

Elliot lifted the first of three phone directories in stiff covers hinged to the steel ledge below the phone. San Francisco. He let it drop. The next directory was for Oakland and vicinity. He thumbed through it, looking for the U.C. Berkeley campus listings. Someone had torn out the pages. People were always tearing pages out of phone books for their personal use. Their selfishness infuriated him.

He picked up the receiver and dialed zero.

"Operator."

"I need to make a collect call to Dr. Amadeo Knizner at the University of California, Berkeley campus," Elliot said.

"Number please."

"I don't have the number. I need you to connect me."

"One moment. . . . I show a Professor A. Knizner in the College of Engineering."

"That's right."

"Ringing now."

Outside, Morning Star had lifted her blouse, and the black woman was painting bright designs on her breasts. Elliot rapped on the glass of the phone booth, trying to shoo them away.

"There's no answer, sir," came the operator's voice. "You can try again later."

Elliot replaced the receiver and slumped against the side of the booth.

Morning Star turned around, holding up her shirt to display her torso, which was decorated with obscure symbols in several colors of the rainbow. She beamed.

• • •

Berkeley

At the Computer Center, Professor Amadeo Knizner, dragging his bad foot behind him, paced as he lectured the attentive students in his Linear Sequential Circuits seminar. Knizner was deep into middle age, afflicted by gout and plantar warts, but he was proud to say he could relate to the eager disciples who flocked to his lab. He understood their youthful enthusiasms and desires. He knew their minds. He wore a black mock-turtleneck and a black beret.

The large room was dominated by a CDC 6400 computer. Cartons full of punch cards were stacked on the floor. Knizner was supposed to assist students in processing data, but in reality he allowed no one, for any reason, to use the machine. The 6400 was part of a network created by the Advanced Research Projects Agency, and he was not going to waste resources helping undergrads test their error-ridden Fortran codes when he had ARPA security problems to solve.

The students at the long seminar table scribbled furiously while Dr. Knizner spoke, the faintest trace of a Mitteleuropean accent coloring his syllables. He paused now and then to scrawl equations on the blackboard. At the end of the session, he planned to collect their notes, written in the requisite blue test books, in lieu of a final exam, which was scheduled to take place in a week's time. He did not like to waste his energy creating exams.

The students either understood the material they copied down or they didn't, and it made no difference to him one way or the other.

The room was permeated by a great deal of noise. The phone on his desk rang without cease, and beside the phone was an ancient, loudly ticking alarm clock, set to end the lecture at precisely three-forty p.m. Through the open window came the chants of protestors and the pulsing of traffic on Hearst Avenue. Adding to the commotion was Knizner's habit of punctuating the end of each sentence with a loud, staccato clearing of his throat. "The initial idea," he told the young men bent over their exam books, "was to design a communication system that could survive a nuclear war with the Soviets [*ahem*]. However, it quickly became apparent to me and to my colleagues around the country that a distributed network of computers could provide other benefits, such as enhanced resource-sharing and universal real-time communication [*ahem*]. Until now, data communications have depended on circuit switching, as in the traditional telephone-network design, wherein each telephone call is allocated a point-to-point connection [*ahem*]."

While he was talking, he glanced out the window and was startled to see a bearded young man in a denim shirt crouching in the bushes. The young man peered over the windowsill, trying to see into the lab. Knizner recognized him as a student who had not attended since the first week of the quarter. Campbell was his name. Franklin Campbell. A political-science major who registered for the seminar to learn about applying computers to social issues. What a memory! Knizner mentally patted himself on the back. He took off his eyeglasses and squinted at the window.

Everyone turned to look, just as Frantz, caught out, reeled back through the bushes and stumbled out of sight.

"Soon," Knizner went on, replacing his eyeglasses and resuming his pacing, dragging his bad foot behind him while the phone on his desk rang hopelessly, "we will be able to deploy systems that use a single link to communicate with more than one machine [*ahem*]. This will be accomplished by collecting information into packets and transmitting them via a shared network connection, in the same way that a single postal box can be used to send letters to different destinations [*ahem*]. Each packet can be replicated and routed independent of the others, ensuring, through redundancy, that the message is received by the other nodes in the network [*ahem*]."

The alarm clock shrieked. The students bolted to their feet.

Knizner dragged his bad foot next to his good one and stood watching the young men lunge for their book bags and briefcases. They piled their blue exam books in the middle of the table. He wondered if any of them might join him for dinner. He was not choosy; anyone would do. He did not want to stop talking.

· · ·

San Francisco

Elliot cradled the receiver and admitted defeat. Connie was not going to get off the line at the Campbell house, and Amadeo Knizner was not going to answer the phone at the Computer Center.

He considered calling Arthur Reuhl and asking him to wire money to the Western Union office, but it would be a day before Arthur could send it.

He pushed out of the fetid phone booth and gulped a lungful of clean air. The shadows were lengthening, and the afternoon had a chill in it. The black woman with the paint box had moved on. Morning Star fanned her blouse to dry the artwork on her abdomen.

Across the street, Agent Ed Grassmick pointed his binoculars out through the window of a head shop, as inconspicuous among the shelves of hookahs, totems, joss sticks, and herbal remedies as a camel in the Sistine Chapel. The owner of the head shop sat on a stool at the register, grinding his teeth. Everybody who opened the door spotted Grassmick for a nark and split, but there was nothing the proprietor could do about it except phone around to try to raise some protestors. So far, no luck.

"Settle down there, pretty boy," Grassmick said without turning around. "I'll be out of your hair in a few minutes, and you can carry on destroying the brains of America's youth."

"Hey, man, why don't you shut up?" the owner snarled. "I've got a business license. All I want to do is help people stay high."

"And I've got a field office full of shitkickers who haven't trashed a hippie joint in a month. They're getting antsy," Grassmick said. "So cool it. And turn off that damn radio."

"That's KPFA, man. Alan Watts is on. You got a problem with him?"

"We should've shut that commie joint down ten years ago. What a lot of claptrap." Grassmick was about to launch into a complaint about the politics of Pacifica Radio, which he considered an affront to everything he cherished about federal law enforcement and American values in general, but the female target was on the move. He shut his mouth and focused his binoculars.

The target had tried to disguise herself by adorning her face with an elaborate pattern of flowers and stars, but the purple velvet top hat gave her away. Now she linked arms with a citizen who had been using the phone booth. The man shook her off and began striding down the street, the girl matching him step for step.

"Come on, Elliot," Morning Star said. "I'm hungry."

"Well, that's just great. We have no money, so how do you propose to feed yourself?"

"The Diggers will feed us."

"The Diggers."

"The Diggers, baby. 'Do your own thing'? 'Today is the first day of the rest of your life'? The Free Store?"

"Those words mean nothing to me."

"They serve dinner in the park every afternoon at four o'clock."

"A picnic," Elliot said crossly. "Terrific."

Over in the head shop, Grassmick lowered his binoculars. He scooped up his two-way radio from among the glass bongs on the counter and helped himself to a cellophane bag of granola from the display by the register.

"You gonna pay for that?" the proprietor demanded.

"Tell you what," Grassmick said. "I'll eat this sack of hippie turds, and you can—"

He could not think of a way to end the sentence. He flipped him a quarter.

．．．

Berkeley

Although the air had turned chilly, students lounged on the steps of Sproul Hall. On the leaflet-littered plaza, stalls had been set up, occupied by activists and agitators of every stripe: Black Panthers, tense with historic ire, handing out literature; Maoists in t-shirts enviously eying the Panthers; pipe-smoking Trotskyists glaring at the Maoists; old-school Marxist-Leninists hurling insults at the Trotskyists; war protestors maintaining a silent vigil; anarchists tearing up the pages of their own literature; a New Left vanguard full of programmatic zeal; a grizzled longshoreman from the I.W.W. at a neglected card table; S.D.S. reps trying to lead a teach-in drowned out by a group of placard-waving women who objected to their raging male chauvinism; and a freaky Christian group giving away cups of lemonade and copies of *Good News for Modern Man*.

A roving troupe of Latin percussionists, accompanied by an accordion, played a jittering merengue. The players wore porkpie hats, and their shirts were unbuttoned to their navels. Oblivious to the students elbowing around her, a blond girl in a baggy white sweater danced to the music. Along the edges of the plaza stood a phalanx of handsome Berkeley cops wearing riot helmets and clutching truncheons. Interspersed among them were representatives of the campus police, the Alameda County Sheriff's Office, and the California Highway Patrol, all keeping an eye on one another, waiting for cues. Scattered through the crowd, shifty-eyed and awkward, were several F.B.I. informants who were paid $150 a month to report on subversive activity on campus and, now that summer break was imminent, in the surrounding community. The informants mostly reported on the activities of infiltrators, who were actual F.B.I. agents, some of whom manned a table on the plaza, thinly disguised as representatives of the left-wing response to the John Birch Society but whose real goal was to disrupt the Black Panthers and undermine *Ramparts* magazine.

There were no hippies; they had all moved to the Haight.

As he drifted across the plaza, transistor radio pressed against his left ear, Frantz raised his fist in a salute: the Panthers deserved admiration for the depth of their commitment. They, in turn, glowered at him with a stark intensity usually reserved for state senators, cops, and racist shopkeepers. Frantz moved on. He brushed palms with a passing acquaintance. He gave the finger to the Maoists and a knowing smile to the Trotskyists.

Before he reached the edge of the plaza, he spotted one of the students in Amadeo Knizner's Linear Sequential Circuits seminar. The student was a cricketish youth who went by the moniker Jojo. He sported wire-rimmed eyeglasses and a mustache that drooped around the corners of his mouth. At the moment he was pulling a copy of the 1950 translation of the *I Ching* by Wilhelm and Baynes from his water-stained messenger bag. If he could find a quiet spot, he planned to do some reading.

Frantz hailed him: "Jojo! Hola, hombre!"

"What's happening, my brother? Lay it on me." Jojo swept off his eyeglasses and offered a mock-formal bow.

"Hangin' loose," Frantz said, bouncing the transistor radio on his palm. "I'm gonna cut out, maybe slide over to Hashbury, see what's going down. The scene around here is broken. Hey, man, can you hook me up with some Stokely product?"

Jojo settled his glasses back onto the bridge of his nose. "His shit's all over town, but that sucker hasn't answered his phone for like two weeks. He needs to hire a crew."

His shit was a spectacularly potent, bright-orange formulation of lysergic acid diethylamide which he manufactured in a rented house on Russian Hill. When California outlawed LSD in 1966, Stanley Stokely had responded with creative fervor and entrepreneurial perspicacity, showering the Bay Areas with doses of pure bliss, and collecting a premium for the new risk of long-term incarceration. Until he had thrown it all over to feed the heads of the flower-children, Stokely had been a chemistry professor. But it was not his acid that had attracted the attention of the F.B.I. What captured the Bureau's interest was the way his name kept popping up in conversations among the militant groups they were surveilling. The Bureau assumed he had graduated from cooking up psychedelics to manufacturing powerful new explosives. Why else would these subversives keep talking about him? The revolutionary vanguard did not have leisure, the reasoning went, to get high. Thus far, no one had been able to hang a case on him, and he was free to roam the streets of San Francisco with his entourage of lissome teenagers.

The roving Latin percussionists drew closer. Timbales clanged; congas and tamboras pounded out a syncopated beat. The blond girl spun wildly, her hair fanning around her, hands fluttering like birds. Jojo pulled a glassine envelope from between the pages of the *I Ching*. "I don't know where the man is, but I've acquired a small reserve of his product from that cat, what's his name, Little Pete."

"Yeah, I know that cat."

Jojo pressed the glassine envelope into Frantz's hand. "Take it, man. It'll blow your mind. You can owe me one."

"Outta sight! Muchas gracias, my brother." He dropped the slang. "Hey, how did you come out spring quarter?"

Jojo grimaced. "B-minuses mostly, unless I ace the finals. You?"

"Looks like incompletes. I still gotta knock out three papers."

"I saw you hanging around outside Knizner's lab."

"Why was everybody writing in blue-books?"

"That was the final, man. All you had to do was take notes and turn them in."

"I shouldn't have signed up for that course, but it was the only thing open in the afternoon that my advisor would okay. Morning classes were killing me."

"You better bust those books, Frankie. First thing you know, they'll kick you out of school, and Uncle Sam'll get you."

"I know, I know. Gotta play the game."

"Six months from now you'll be belly-down in a rice paddy."

The percussionists had been tightening in a circle around Frantz and Jojo, gradually drowning out their conversation. Somberly considering the reality of the military draft, they shook hands and parted.

Frantz, after downing a cupful of Christian lemonade, continued toward Telegraph Avenue, where just then Bobby Dobell's customized dark-red Chevy Impala with white pinstripes was cruising past, huffing like a dragon. Dobell's henchman, Rowdy Gomez, scanned the plaza with binoculars. A sawed-off shotgun rested on his lap.

"I don't see anything, Bobby. The guy's not in Berkeley, or your girls neither. They might be trippin' up in Sausalito."

"Look for that stupid fucking purple hat." The muscles of Dobell's face twitched. His foot danced over the accelerator, threatening to send the car tearing into the crowd. "We'll try fucking North Beach again."

"I don't know, Bobby. The guy's slippery."

Dobell gunned the car into a squealing u-turn and was met by a squall of indignant horns. The phalanx of handsome cops along the plaza swiveled their heads but did not budge from their positions. If they weren't allowed to bust the Panthers, they certainly weren't going to chase down reckless drivers.

The car rocketed down the street. Rowdy Gomez, former demolition-derby champion, clung to the seat in terror.

"That man's days are fucking numbered," Dobell screamed over the roar of the engine. "I'll stuff his hat up his stinkin' ass."

· · ·

San Francisco

Lost in a mob of hungry hippies, speedfreaks, acidheads, runaways, junkies, streetwalkers, mystics, musicians, hookers, cowboy-angels, street artists, and winos—a sodality of the dispossessed—Elliot and Morning Star waited for the Diggers' daily feeding in the Panhandle. The smell of soiled clothing and palo santo incense made him want to vomit. Two rail-thin men with matted hair were smoking cigarettes and supervising two aggrieved-looking women who hoisted a steaming steel milk-can onto a trestle table. Another woman, square-jawed, wearing a plaid hunting jacket, began to ladle the contents into old tin cans, which the first two women passed through a giant yellow picture frame bolted to the front of the table. An elf-like individual standing next to her was improvising on a flute.

"You realize," Elliot said to Morning Star, "that right now, at this very hour, I should be having cocktails with my future father-in-law and finalizing plans for *my wedding*."

She chuckled. "Isn't it a relief not to organize everything according to schedules?"

"I don't seem to be reaching you," Elliot said. "I *like* schedules. My work depends on them. My life depends on them."

"Nothing opens the heavens like a dog with a timetable," the man in the line behind them intoned.

Elliot turned around. "Stop listening to us."

The man unleashed a crazy laugh.

Morning Star laid a hand on his trembling arm. "You are so right," she said, and he looked at her with luminous tearful eyes.

They reached the table, and Elliot accepted a bent spoon and a can. Inside was a lump of mulligan stew the color of clay.

"Furthermore," he said to Morning Star, "I don't like eating my dinner from a bean can with half the human flotsam that washes up on the West Coast! —No offense," he said to the woman in the plaid jacket. "This is very kind of you folks."

"Hey, do your own thing, brother," she said. She handed Morning Star a spoon and a can with a faded picture of sliced peaches on it.

"This is lovely," Morning Star said.

She hurried after Elliot.

From the lowest branch of a nearby spreading oak, his shiny black oxfords dangling free, Special Agent Ed Grassmick peered through his binoculars. He located the female target in the purple hat. She was just sitting down on the curb beside the male citizen who had been in the phone booth. Grassmick was confident she would lead them to the cadre that Stokely was supplying.

He wished he had his long-range microphone. If he had, he would have heard the following:

MORNING STAR (*tucking into her stew*): During the day they collect whatever the restaurants and grocery stores throw out the night before. They feed the people with society's waste.

ELLIOT: Terrific. I'm eating garbage soup.

MORNING STAR: It has carrots.

ELLIOT: How the hell did I end up in the middle of this unholy accident?

MORNING STAR: Nothing is accidental, Elliot. You said there were explanations for every event, no matter how implausible or imbecilic.

ELLIOT: Plenty of things are accidental. People have accidents all the time. There may be explanations for events, but they can still be unexpected.

MORNING STAR: You'll feel better after we take a bath. I'll scrub your back.

ELLIOT: Scrub my back!

MORNING STAR: There must be a public faucet around here. After that, we can go down to the Avalon Ballroom. Those three sisters I met told me that Moby Grape is playing tonight. Maybe the Grateful Dead will make the scene, and I can share the wealth (*tapping her shoulder bag*). Bob Weir seems like he might be there.

ELLIOT: Number one, we don't have money to go to the Avalon Ballroom. Remember? Number two, I am heading to Berkeley or anywhere that's not here as soon as I can get someone to answer the damn telephone.

He jumped to his feet. With his free hand, he brushed the twigs and gum wrappers from the seat of his pants. He noticed that his clothes had acquired a thin coating of street grime.

"If you go to Berkeley, you'll miss Moby Grape," Morning Star said with concern.

"Let me be clear: I will not miss Moby Grape, not in the slightest. Whatever Moby Grape is, I will never spend a moment of my life dwelling on the opportunity I squandered by not going to the Avalon Ballroom."

"What if no one answers the phone?"

"Then I will walk."

Still clutching the can of mulligan stew, he strode off.

Morning Star, leaving her duffel bag and peach can on the curb, grabbed her shoulder bag and jumped up. She hurried to catch up with him. "It's too far to walk, Elliot. When the sun goes down, you'll be cold. You don't have a coat."

Elliot stopped in his tracks and turned a wild stare on her. Through gritted teeth he said, "Then I will hitchhike. Everybody's doing it."

He dropped the can and thrust out his arm with his thumb extended.

Immediately, a dark-red Chevy Impala squealed to a halt.

Elliot looked at his thumb in astonishment. "Wow."

"Cosmic!" Morning Star chimed.

As Special Agent Grassmick watched from the branches of the spreading oak, a stocky character with slicked-back hair erupted from the passenger side of the Impala and yanked open the rear door. A moment later the target and the citizen were serially seized and stuffed into the car. The door slammed. The stocky character, who, Grassmick noted, was brandishing a sawed-off shotgun, leaped back into the car, and the car tore off.

Using the sidewalk when he needed to, Bobby Dobell bullied his way along the street. Storefronts flashed by. The startled faces of pedestrians registered briefly in Elliot's peripheral vision.

"Now look here—" he protested, recovering from his shock.

Gomez pointed the shotgun over the back of his seat. "Shut up! Where's Stokely?"

"Listen, friend, you have the wrong—."

"I said shut up!" Gomez screamed. He turned to Dobell. "What should we do with this creep, Bobby?"

"I'll take care of him," Dobell said in a perilous voice.

Gomez pointed the shotgun at Morning Star. "Spill it, bitch. Where's Stokely?"

Morning Star had no response. She picked up the purple velvet top hat from the floor of the car and put it on and wrapped her arms around her embroidered shoulder bag.

Steering with one hand, Dobell craned over the seat. "Stokely! Where is he?" he demanded. "Spill!"

"I don't know who that is," Morning Star said.

"You're wearing his fucking hat! Where is he? I'm gonna tie that motherfucking prick to the train tracks and watch the slow freight chop off his fucking head." He hit the accelerator.

"She's telling the truth," Elliot interjected. "A lanky cat in the park gave her the hat."

"See that fucking 'S'?" Dobell shrieked, turning around in his seat as he barreled along. "That ain't a dollar sign. That's 'S' for fucking Stanley Stokely, motherfucker."

Excitement broke over Morning Star's face. "Stanley Stokely? Do you mean the saint?"

"I mean Stanley Stokely the fucking dead man."

"Stanley Stokely!" Morning Star exhaled. She turned eagerly to Elliot. "He's a legend. He makes the cleanest acid on the West Coast. It's ambrosia." She swept off the top hat and kissed it. "He gave me his hat. Stanley Stokely! I wish we'd had a conversation. I feel like I could learn so much from him."

Doubt began to gather in Rowdy Gomez's eyes. He lowered the shotgun to his lap. "Boss, I don't think this chick knows Stokely."

"That's what I'm trying to tell you," Elliot said.

Dobell leaned over the seat and screamed, "Shut up, motherfucker!"

The Impala screeched to a halt in front of Astro Auto Body. Several itchy-looking Hells Angels were reclining on their choppers outside the bar next door. One of the Angels got up and lumbered over and lifted the rolling steel door. The shop was empty, the workday done.

The car pulled inside, and the steel door rumbled down and hit the concrete with a terrific crash.

Dobell and Gomez jumped out and yanked open the rear doors of the Impala. Dobell grabbed Elliot by the shirt and dragged him out; Gomez did the same with Morning Star, bending her arm behind her back and stuffing a rag into her mouth. Her shoulder bag thumped to the floor, and Gomez kicked it under the workbench. He punched her hard in the temple, sending the top hat flying and buckling her knees.

"Hold on there!" Elliot objected.

Dobell shoved an oily rag in his mouth, spun him around, and kicked him in the back. Elliot's head struck an overturned library chair, and his cheek stung as he hit the floor, which was layered with razor-sharp metal shavings. Dobell kicked him in the ribs.

"Tie 'em up," he commanded. "We'll keep 'em till we find out what's going on with motherfucking Stokely."

• • •

Shafts of golden sunshine pierced the front window of Sacerdotal Rainbow and illuminated the chrome-and-glass cases full of enameled bracelets and donkey-bead necklaces, the pigmented leather purses hanging like ripe fruit from metal racks fashioned to look like dead trees, the blank faces of mannequins dressed in rayon jungle prints and demi-skirts tied with tribal knots.

At the rear of the boutique, Alice Dobell brushed back the fitting-room curtains and sashayed into the little parlor where her sisters, Astrid and Angela, perched on yellow vinyl wing chairs, flanking Stanley Stokely, who leaned back and crossed his legs. Alice was bedizened in a paisley miniskirt, a knobby gold necklace, and knee-high red boots. She dipped and turned.

"That dress *deserves* your body, my dear," Stokely drawled. He stroked his goatee and tapped his silver-knobbed walking stick on the floor and regarded her benevolently. "Mmm. Very nice. That is an amusing scrap of cloth."

Angela pulled on Stokely's arm. She pointed at a fringed buckskin jacket. "Can I have that one?"

"Anything you want, my darlings, anything at all. Papa has been gifted with funds." He slipped a wallet from his sheepskin vest and held it between his thumb and forefinger. Smiling slyly, he opened it and riffled the sheaf of cash inside. "Not that Papa needs it," he said and added, with sudden paranoia, "but if I don't make a point of frittering it away on you darlings, the taxman's going to seize his share. He's been peering into my investments."

He looked around cautiously.

From the front seat of a Ford sedan backed diagonally into a space across the street, Special Agent Russ Bogosian watched through binoculars as Stanley Stokely unfolded his long frame and began to meander around the shop, the girls shimmying and twirling around him, rubbing together like cats. Bogosian felt the blood surge in his loins. His heart hammered against his ribs. His hands twitched. He hated himself. He was disgusted by his loathsome urges, needed to tell someone before he was reduced to slavering imbecility. He wished Grassmick were here.

He tossed the binoculars on the seat and got on the radio. "This is Lost In Space calling Green Acres. Over."

Static. Then a faint, incoherent warble.

"This is Lost In Space. Over."

"Shrr bral carnopg."

"Goddammit, Grassmick, can't you keep your gear in order?" Bogosian howled and hurled the handset to the floor.

• • •

Burbank
As he drove toward the Burbank Airport, eyes stinging from the acidic air in the eastern San Fernando Valley, following streets that stretched for a dozen miles through regions of warehouses, office buildings, parking lots, hamburger stands, bank branches, dry cleaners, supermarkets, travel

agencies, bowling alleys, real-estate offices, veterinary facilities, motels, appliance stores, hair salons, carwashes, six-unit apartment buildings, and two-bedroom crackerboxes with skinny hopeless trees in the yards, Pegasus reflected that he had lived so long and so contentedly in California that he had forgotten that the American way of life was decadent and doomed. Of course, it was decadent and doomed, just look around. He did not want to give it up.

. . .

Berkeley

Except for Jojo, the Computer Center was free of students. He and Professor Amadeo Knizner were seated at the seminar table, on which Knizner had arranged several sheets of wide pale-striped computer paper, a black marker, a hexagram chart, and an open copy of the Wilhelm and Baynes translation of the *I Ching*. He leaned over it meditatively. What, he wondered, had prompted this young man to evince an unexpected curiosity about his work just as the semester was ending?

"So you have developed an interest in the ancient Book of Changes [*ahem*]," Knizner said. "As you are aware, I have been making it my special study [*ahem*]. You know, of course, that in 1703, in his explanation of binary mathematics, Liebnitz divined in the sixty-four hexagrams of the *I Ching* the basis for a universal binary numbering system [*ahem*]. This classification of binary sequences demonstrates knowledge of the convergence of certain linear recurrence sequences of particular interest to the computer engineer [*ahem*]."

Knizner picked up three brass oracle coins with square holes punched in the centers and bounced them on his palm. His pupil watched him with rapt attention, which encouraged Knizner to continue unfolding what had lately developed into a mystical disquisition on ancient algorithms in the electronic age.

"Far out," Jojo murmured.

The CDC 6400 made a lifelike noise.

"All I'm saying, Sheilah, is that he could have the decency to call!"

Connie Campbell stamped out her cigarette in an ashtray piled high with lipstick-stained butts. She was sitting very erect on a stool at the kitchen counter. From the living room came the incoherent sound of the evening news. Since April, when a windstorm had knocked the aerial on the roof askew, the television had received only two channels, one of which was educational. Her father had been badgering Frank to fetch the ladder and realign the aerial, but so far Frank had failed to act. Carl Campbell had taken no further action; he did not want to strain his back climbing onto the roof, and he felt uneasy about asking the gardener to do aerial work. In any case, he had no special fondness for television. His wife, however, missed her shows.

Having grown bored with the ABC newscast, Carl came into the kitchen and began poking around in the refrigerator.

Connie turned her body away from him and lowered her voice. "You don't think he's with another woman, do you? That son of a bitch!"

• • •

San Francisco

In the dim auto-body shop, Elliot and Morning Star, rags in their mouths, faced each other, helpless. Their wrists were tied behind their backs. Their legs were bound to the library chairs, and the chairs were tied together. Elliot's head throbbed. He could not make sense of how they had ended up here. When he looked into Morning Star's murky, bloodshot eyes, barely visible in the gloom, he felt angry at her, and he felt ashamed of his helplessness.

By pressing his feet on the floor and jerking his weight backward, sending a stab of pain along his ribs, he tried to move the chairs across the floor. Morning Star, her voice muffled by the rag, cried out. Sensing his intention to inch the chairs towards the tools on the workbench, she leaned forward as he pushed backward. The chairs jerked and scraped on the concrete, the two of them engaged in a rough dance, but they could make no progress.

. . .

Berkeley

"In imperial China the *I Ching* had two distinct functions [*ahem*]. The first was that of a compendium of ancient cosmic principles [*ahem*]. The second was that of a divination text [*ahem*]. According to the *Great Commentary*, the experience of the *I Ching* leads to a deeper understanding of the universe [*ahem*]."

. . .

San Francisco

Swept along in the stream of traffic crossing the Bay Bridge was the orange Volkswagen Beetle that Frantz Campbell had acquired from a pessimistic pal who had been inducted into the Army and did not expect to return from Vietnam. As he drove, Frantz ate a messy taco in a thin paper sleeve and read the letters to the editor in the latest issue of the *Berkeley Barb*:

Dear Editors: The city of San Francisco, not content with tormenting us with their narks and their fuzz, has now deliberately taken to asphalting Haight Street. I understand they plan to do this regularly, except for the scheduled weekend busts throughout the summer. I know of at least one couple, who, chased out of several condemned co-ops, hounded out of the park by the latest fascist city council no-screwing-in-the-park ordinance, had planned to test the unconstitutional no-love-in-the-streets statute but were unable to because of a small hangup on the part of the girl about the asphalt. Join together to pile feathers into the fresh tar so that we may cry out aloud, "Streets are for loving!"

As he swooped off the bridge into the city, so engrossed was Frantz in the citizen's complaint that he did not notice the dark-red Impala that slashed across his right-of-way and vanished around a corner with a fretful revving of the engine, the occupants cursing the driver of the ridiculous orange Beetle.

•   •   •

Berkeley

"As a mode of divination, the *I Ching* belonged to the marketplace fortune-teller, the roadside oracle, catering to those who believed in a future governed by implacable fate [*ahem*]. The educated elite were of an entirely different disposition [*ahem*]. For them, the future was a function of one's personal actions [*ahem*]."

•   •   •

Oakland

Attired in a fresh set of golf clothes and carrying a trim black attaché case and an overnight bag, Pegasus crossed in front of several buses disgorging military personnel on their way to Southeast Asia and walked briskly through the airport parking lot. His head was bare, and his thin blondish hair gleamed in the twilight. He had made a stop at the airport restroom to empty his bladder, and he felt ready to meet the world, except for the faint ache in his temples, which, he speculated, heralded an undiagnosable neurological disorder on top of his other problems. There would be time, he reminded himself, to worry about his condition when he had taken care of business.

He checked the license plates on the rental cars against the number on the plastic fob of the ignition key until he found the one he wanted. A gray coupe. He put the overnight bag and attaché case in the back of the car, but not before removing his Sig P210 from the bag. It was shocking that U.S. airlines never checked the passengers for weapons. No wonder there were so many hijackings.

Since he did not trust car-rental companies, he made a careful survey of the exterior, including the engine compartment and the undercarriage, before inspecting the trunk, the back seat, the front seat, the door panels, the ceiling panel, the lights, and the dashboard. Finally, having attracted no attention during the fifteen minutes it took to complete the inspection—another great thing about America: if you dressed for the country club, people rarely noticed your suspicious behavior—he settled on the driver's seat and pulled down the visor and adjusted the rearview mirror, satisfied that all was in order.

• • •

Berkeley

Professor Knizner rattled the oracle coins in his hands and dropped them on the tabletop.

"Heads or tails [*ahem*]. Yin or yang [*ahem*]. Binaries [*ahem*]. Like a computer code [*ahem*]. A man's fate—his transformation—as a function of a random-chance algorithm [*ahem*]."

He picked up the coins and shook them again. Tossed them on the tabletop and counted the values of the heads and tails. He drew two short lines with a marker on a sheet of computer paper, constructing the hexagram. Again, he tossed the coins and drew a single line above the two short lines, continuing until he had tossed the coins six times and had drawn six lines, solid or broken, on the paper. Next, he drew a bracket to indicate the division of the hexagram into trigrams. He referred to the chart to obtain the names of the trigrams, using their intersection to identify the appropriate entry.

He went to the *I Ching* book. "*Zhong fu*—an ancient message for a new consciousness [*ahem*]. These days anything goes, am I right? [*ahem*]."

He stared deep into Jojo's eyes, longing for the young man to understand, truly understand, where he was coming from.

• • •

Connie, Carl, and Helen Campbell were assembled around an enameled poppy-red fondue pot. A blue alcohol flame quivered beneath it. The electric candles in the dining-room chandelier had been dimmed, and in the living room the hi-fi reproduced the soporific soughing of the Mantovani Orchestra. Next to his plate—the table was set with the summer china—Carl had placed his portable radio. He was eager to listen to the Giants, who were playing in Cincinnati, but Helen had rules about distractions at dinner. Connie stabbed a chunk of French bread on a long-handled fork into the cheese bubbling in the pot.

"Calm down, honey," Carl said. "It's cold feet, plain and simple. The man has cold feet. It will turn out fine."

"I'm going to kill him!" Connie lifted the fork from the pot and jabbed the air for emphasis, splattering hot cheese on the tablecloth. "Not even a phone call! Sheilah says it's typical. Typical. Exactly what happened with her and Philip. The first night he didn't come home was the last night." She pulled the bread off the fork with her teeth.

"Can't really blame Philip, though, can we?" Carl murmured.

"Daddy," Helen warned. She adjusted her eyeglasses and studied the fondue pot.

Carl frowned. "I was offering an assessment of Sheilah's marital problems. Former marital problems. I suppose now she has something else to occupy herself."

"We're not talking about Sheilah," Connie said crossly.

"Then why does her name always come up? In any case, I'm sure Elliot's sitting in a bar, savoring his last hours of freedom and planning for a lifetime with, er. . . ."

He trailed off as his daughter peevishly speared another chunk of bread.

The doorbell chimed a four-note melody—ding DONG ding DONG. Connie flung her fork on the table and jumped up. "He's here!"

She hurried through the living room to the vestibule, straightening her dress, patting her hair, and pulled open the front door. "Darling!"

The disappointment that passed over her features turned quickly to puzzlement. On the front step stood a genial-looking stranger wearing a windbreaker and holding an attaché case.

"Oh, I'm sorry!" Connie exclaimed, her hand flying to her mouth. "I didn't mean to call you 'darling.' I thought you were someone else. May I help you?"

The stranger smiled tightly. "Is this the Campbell residence?"

"Yes, it is."

"Is Mr. Elliot Ames available, please?"

"Elliot? We're waiting for him actually."

"So he's expected?"

"Who did you say you were?"

Connie's embarrassment had abated, and she examined him up and down in the porchlight, from receding hairline to soft-soled shoes. Were those golf gloves? He looked, she thought, like anyone she had ever seen.

"My apologies, Miss Campbell. I work with Elliot at the Pacifidyne Corporation." He patted the attaché case. "I have urgent materials to review with him. The matter cannot wait."

Connie narrowed her eyes. As the former Assistant to the Head of Personnel, she had a complete mental list of the people with whom her fiancé had worked during the past year. "I wonder if we've met," she said. "I was at Pacifidyne until a month ago."

"It's a rather large operation, is it not? In any case, until recently I worked at Lockheed."

Connie bit her lip. The man sounded plausible. He knew that Elliot was expected. He looked vaguely familiar. "I'm sorry. I'm a little frazzled. Elliot and I are getting married," she explained. "We're going to Hawaii. Of course you know that! Why else would you come all this way for—was it signatures?"

"Yes. I apologize again. I don't mean to intrude, but it's rather urgent."

Connie invited him in. "Elliot should be here any minute. We're just finishing dinner."

With a soft "thank you," Pegasus stepped across the threshold and closed the door.

"Oooh, that Elliot," Connie said, relaxed enough now to let off steam. "It's just like him to have someone deliver work, for God's sake, when he's on vacation."

While she was talking, she escorted the stranger through the living room, "Some Enchanted Evening" swelling on the stereo.

"Are you involved in computers too, Mr.—? You never told me your name." Connie glanced over her shoulder.

"Carpenter."

"Are you sure we didn't meet at the personnel office?"

They came into the dining room, and Carl Campbell reluctantly turned off the radio he had just turned on. (It was the top of the ninth, a detail he would later recall.) Helen took off her eyeglasses and smiled waxily, baring her incisors. "And who's this?"

"Mr. Carpenter has some papers for Elliot to sign before we leave for Hawaii. He's from work."

"Do join us," Helen said graciously. "Do you care for fondue?"

Pegasus looked at the bubbling pot. "I've never tried," he said.

"You don't play cribbage, by any chance?" Carl asked eagerly. "Or Chinese checkers?"

• • •

San Francisco

As Frantz ambled along Haight Street, head bobbing, fingers snapping, transistor radio to his ear, wondering if he should grab some coffee at the Blue Unicorn, he kept an eye out for a girl who looked like she might split a tab of the Stokely acid with him. Maybe build a bonfire in Golden Gate Park. Burn some stuff.

He was slouching across an intersection, lost in thought, when the dark-red Chevy Impala that had nearly taken out the Beetle barreled in front of him.

"Watch it, jackass!" he screamed and jabbed a middle finger in the air.

The Impala's brake lights flashed; tires squealed.

Bobby Dobell, shotgun in hand, leaped out and raced around the car, snarling like a beast.

Frantz dropped the radio and bolted down the street.

In a restaurant at the end of the block, Stanley Stokely and the Dobell triplets—Astrid, Angela, and Alice—sat at the window, enjoying a candlelight dinner. The three girls were attired in expensive new threads.

"You see my dears," Stokely murmured, luxuriating in pubescent adoration, "by the time Papa got his head together and stopped doing research for the academic-industrial pigs that support the pharmaceutical industry, he had realized how damaging the corporate-sponsored diet is to the human omnivore. Likewise, the so-called macrobiotic diet is suspect on the grounds of ideology. I have determined that a repast of seaweed, jerked chicken, rye bread, and chamomile tea," indicating the repast spread before them, "is the key to health and longevity. Naturally, they don't want such information to circulate among the public. One must gain the knowledge first-hand, directly from the source—for example, from me. I am my own best authority. That is why I maintain, with the exception of one or two dear friends, solitude in my laboratory on Russian Hill, without the drivel of lesser minds to muddy the intellectual and creative waters."

The girls, fiddling with their forks, gazed at him with fascination.

If they had glanced through the window, they would have caught a glimpse of Frantz Campbell as he streaked by, their father pounding a half-dozen lengths behind. Frantz dodged around an elderly man with a cane, but Dobell crashed into the frail old fellow, and they collapsed in a heap. He scrambled up, screaming after Frantz. "You cocksucker hippie freak mother-raper! I'll tear your fucking head off, you rat bastard, you hear me!"

Frantz came to an alley, feinted left, dashed right, and lobbed himself through an open window, while Dobell sprinted down the dark street and disappeared around the corner.

Frantz poked his head above the windowsill. Seeing no sign of the lunatic with the shotgun, he stood up and surveyed the room. A family was sitting at their dinner. The father was in his undershirt; the mother had curlers in her hair. The kids' eyes bulged. A television cast a lambent blue light over the scene and issued news of Soviet warships interfering with the Sixth Fleet on maneuvers in the Mediterranean.

Frantz sniffed the air. "Do I smell corned beef and cabbage? Far out!"

The auto-body shop smelled, Morning Star thought, dire. The odor of solvents, scorched metal, and corrosive fluxes made her head swim. The rag in her mouth tasted like dirt. The bruise on her forehead was throbbing. But it was Elliot that concerned her. After failing to maneuver their yoked chairs towards the workbench, they had strained and writhed in an attempt to free their arms from the ropes that bound them. Their efforts were in vain. Elliot stared into her eyes and made a snorting sound as he tried to dislodge the rag in his mouth. His legs, tightly tied to her own, were taut with the strain.

As she gazed over his shoulder into the dim cobwebby space, taking in the metal storage lockers, the cutting torches, the derelict trolleys, the industrial paint sprayer, she could not help thinking of the repair shop at her father's car dealership in Van Nuys. Then she could not help thinking about the angry, disappointed look on her father's face when she had returned the damaged Dodge Dart. The memory of the car accident reminded her of Kismet and his piteous small cry when she had left the orange cat to fend for himself in the hills. She wondered if the universe was punishing her for her inconstancy.

Now that she was thinking along these lines, she realized she had been neglectful of the friends and coworkers and teachers and siblings with whom she had been gifted, abandoning them in her enthusiasm for the pleasures of the moment. A line from Cicero sprang—improbably, given the circumstances—to mind: *Non nobis solum nati sumus.* "Not for ourselves alone are we born." In Latin class at Notre Dame High School, she had sort of believed it. She accepted that her obligations extended to the wide sphere of humanity. On the other hand, people could be a drag. Was there no way, Morning Star puzzled, of resolving the conflict between living for others and living for yourself? The present detour on the path of freedom afforded an opportunity to dig into this heavy question. If they could get the rags out of their mouths, they could have a meaningful conversation.

She was brought back to the moment by the guttural sound of a truck idling outside the shop. The steel door rumbled up. A wash of sallow streetlight illuminated the concrete floor, and the sound of a jukebox and women's laughter came from somewhere nearby. Closer, a motorcycle revved. A tow truck with a brand-new Mustang dangling from the hook backed noisily into the shop. The engine died with a catarrhal cough, and the driver climbed out. The steel door crashed against the concrete. The overhead lights came on.

As he activated the boom winch to lower the Mustang, Eli Tarr caught sight of the two people gagged and bound to the old library chairs, face to face, as if in intense consultation.

"What the fuck!" He leaped back and dropped the wrench he was holding.

Recovering himself—and the wrench—he approached Elliot and Morning Star. He looked down at them, trying to reconstruct the sequence of events that had led to this situation.

He pointed the wrench at Elliot. "I know you, man!"

Elliot and Morning Star made strangled sounds and rattled their chairs.

"That's right," Eli continued, stroking his chin. "I hooked your MG up at the Panhandle. Parked by a hydrant." He gave Elliot a disapproving look and pulled the rag out of his mouth. "Why's there blood all over your face?"

Elliot gasped and choked.

"The chick too," Eli said, his eyes lighting on her. "Hey, baby. How's it going?"

He worked the rag out of Morning Star's mouth and examined her face paint and the eggplant-colored bruise on her forehead. He pointed. "Somebody hit you. That don't look right."

"Oh," she gasped. "Thank you! Thank you so much. That's from a car accident."

Eli stepped back and surveyed them. "What the hell you doing in here?"

"What the hell do you think?" Elliot said. "We're prisoners!" He was not altogether happy to see Eli again, but he was glad enough to have been discovered at all. "How about untying us?"

Eli prowled around the shop until he found a mangled wire cafe chair and dragged it over. He turned it around and sat, his arms dangling over the back.

"Let's not get hasty," he said judiciously. "Whatever Bobby Dobell's got going with you ain't none a my business."

"I take it that Bobby Dobell is one of the men who brought us to this—where are we exactly?" Elliot said.

Eli lit a cigarette. He blew a smoke-ring and watched it rise lazily toward the overhead light. "We haven't even established the basic facts of the situation. How do you expect me to cut you loose if I don't know the basic facts?"

"It's karma," Morning Star declared.

"How you figure that, missy?"

"This afternoon you did a bad deed and towed Elliot's car," she explained. "Now in order to balance your karma you must do a good deed and liberate us."

"Looks to me like you got in trouble without my karma involved one way or the other. Maybe you're the ones did something they shouldn't, and this here's *your* karma."

"Ignore her," Elliot said. "I'm asking you, one gentleman to another—Eli, right?—to untie us. We'll walk away and never look back at this whole—this whole—."

"Scene," Morning Star provided.

"This whole scene. Whatever part you play in the big picture is of no concern to us."

"I don't play any part in this shit," Eli declared. "None. It seems to me that I benefit most if I go on about my business and let Bobby and that demolition man of his do whatever they want with you all."

"Okay, yes," Elliot conceded. "Logic suggests that you leave well enough alone. But—what time is it? Some kid walked off with my watch."

Eli looked at his wristwatch. "It's getting towards ten o'clock."

"In roughly forty-three hours," Elliot calculated, "I'm scheduled for my wedding in the Berkeley hills. I'm begging you to be a good guy and free us."

Eli looked surprised. He pointed at Morning Star. "You're marrying Miss Intergalactic?"

"No, no, no. God no. I picked her up hitchhiking."

"Ah, one a those things."

"No!"

"Can I say something?" Morning Star said. "This man who's tied to me has a worthwhile soul if you get to know him."

Elliot pressed on: "The bare-bones, bottom-line fact of the matter is that tomorrow morning they'll be fishing us out of San Francisco Bay if this Bobby Dobell and his—his henchman—come back without having found someone named Stanley Stokely, who I hope to God can tell them we have no connection to him whatsoever."

Eli dropped his cigarette and leaped up. "What's that about Stanley Stokely?"

"This Dobell fellow thinks we know where he is."

"Man, Bobby's gonna wring that cat's neck," Eli said. "His three little daughters run off with that cat. . . . So hold on, man. You know where Stokely's at or not?"

Elliot shook his head. "I never heard the name until a few hours ago."

"He gave me his hat," Morning Star offered. "It's over there on the floor."

Eli got up and ambled over to study the vivid purple top hat with the gold letter on it. "That is the cat's hat," he declared. "So you know him."

"It was pure happenstance," Elliot said.

Eli started pacing around the shop in his loose-jointed, hips-forward way. "I'm in a damn predicament now. Ever since the State a California outlawed lysergic acid-d, I've had a little side business sending Stokely's shit down to some friends in L.A. and Orange County and what not. This enterprise will suffer if Stokely thinks I put Bobby Dobell on his ass, which I did, 'cause his girls never woulda met the cat except for me bringing them around his house on Russian Hill when I was s'posed to be driving them home from school in the truck."

Morning Star chuckled. "See? Karma."

Eli fell silent and scratched his neck. "Maybe you're right. This thing seems poised to snap back on my ass, that's for sure."

He whipped out a massive bone-handled pocketknife and snicked open the blade. As he cut the ropes around Morning Star's wrists, he exhorted her to flee and not look back.

She began to massage her arms.

Eli went to work on Elliot's ropes. "You, too, man. You better hightail it outta here."

"I wholeheartedly agree," Elliot said. "Before we go, do you suppose I could use the phone?"

"You plan to call the cops, huh?"

Now that Eli mentioned it, Elliot realized that, in addition to calling Connie, of course he planned to call the cops.

Eli, going down on one knee to cut the ropes that bound their legs, continued: "Not wise, man. That could put me in some serious shit. I'd have to do something to you that you and your lady would not like."

Morning Star stood up and stretched luxuriously. Her linen top lifted to expose her psychedelic midriff. "I'm with Eli," she said. "Let's keep the fuzz out of our hair."

"That's the right attitude," Eli said. He stood up and folded the knife blade into the handle.

Morning Star retrieved her shoulder bag from under the workbench and began poking through the metal lockers along the cinderblock wall; the clashing of metal doors echoed through the room.

It occurred to Elliot that a police inquiry would eat up several hours when he could be—should be—in Berkeley. The authorities might even require him to remain in the area. Connie would be furious if they weren't lying on the beach in Waikiki come Sunday afternoon.

"Fine," he said, bending over to pull up his socks. "We won't call the cops. Maybe this Bobby Dobell will find this guy Stokely. They don't know who we are, so I can't imagine we'll see any of them again." He pointed at a battered black telephone sitting on the workbench in a litter of work orders and paper cups. "I still need to use the phone."

"Seriously, man?" Eli said. "If I was you, I'd be ass in the wind."

"If I don't call my fiancée, I'll be ass in a sling."

Eli hesitated. "All right," he said reluctantly. "I've been there, man. I'm gonna be right in your ear, though, understood?"

"Understood." Elliot rubbed his rope-burned wrists to restore the circulation. He went over to the workbench.

With Eli hovering at his shoulder, he dialed a familiar number.

· · ·

Berkeley

The color television in the Campbells' living room was tuned to one of the two functioning channels. Carl, Helen, and Pegasus sat in a row on the sofa, watching *Bewitched*. On the wall behind the sofa was an extensive painting of musical instruments rendered as geometrical shapes in sticky shades of blue and green. The record-player/television console, topped with a birds-of-paradise floral arrangement from East Bay Ornamentals, dominated the opposite side of the room.

Connie roamed restlessly around the house, standing in the doorway, hip jutted, for a few minutes to watch the commercials, then marching to the kitchen to see if the telephone would ring for her, then going to her bedroom to stand with her arms folded, staring into the dark.

"Does that actress remind you of Connie?" Carl said. He pointed his chin at the television screen.

Helen tapped her cigarette in a brown glass ashtray on the coffee table. "Are you saying our daughter is a witch?"

"Not at all. But if she were a little friendlier, she would bear a striking resemblance to that witch."

"Women nowadays are finding their power," Pegasus observed.

"I like the drapes in their living room," Helen said. "She has good taste."

"Anyway, Al," Carl said, picking up an earlier conversation. "When the program's over, what say we set up the card table?"

"Sounds good, Carl."

"Do you prefer Cluedo or Aggravation?"

"Whatever you like. A game's a game."

"I agree, insofar as—"

The kitchen telephone interrupted their discussion. Pegasus jumped to his feet.

Helen and Carl looked at him, startled.

"I'll be right back," he said.

Pulling his pistol from under his windbreaker, he arrived in the kitchen just as Connie was saying, in a not-happy voice, "Elliot! We've been waiting all night!"

Pegasus grabbed her from behind and pressed the barrel of the gun against her neck.

She gasped.

"Be calm. I don't want to hurt you. Do you understand?"

No reply.

He moved the gun so that she could see it, then pressed it against her neck again. "Find out where he is," he whispered in her ear. "Do you understand?"

She made a sputtering sound and began to thrash. He had not expected her to resist.

Pegasus tightened his arm across her chest. "Calm. Calm. This will only take a minute." He shifted so that he could put his ear against the receiver.

"Connie? Are you all right, sweetheart?" said the voice on the phone. "What's going on there?"

Pegasus jabbed the pistol against her neck.

"I'm fine," Connie said, her voice tight with adrenaline.

"I've been trying to call you all afternoon. Listen, sweetheart, I'll explain later but I need you to come over to San Francisco and pick me up."

Pegasus tightened his hold and gave her a shake.

"Where are you?"

"I'm not sure. Wait a minute."

He must have turned his mouth from the receiver, for his voice sounded distant and hollow: "Where are we? My fiancée can pick us up."

A new voice—a man's—joined the conversation at a short distance. "Uh uh. Not here, no way."

Another voice—a woman's—said, "Ask her if she knows where the Avalon Ballroom is."

"Yeah," said the man's voice. "I can drop you all."

"Connie?" Elliot said into the mouthpiece. "Do you know where the Avalon Ballroom is?"

"Corner a Sutter and Van Ness," said the man's voice in the background.

"It's at the corner of Sutter and Van Ness," repeated Elliot.

"Who's with you, Elliot?"

"No one. I mean, no one you know."

Pegasus jabbed her neck.

"I can find it," Connie said, rather defiantly, Elliot thought.

"That's so good to hear! That's the best thing I've heard all day. We'll meet you there in one hour. I love—."

But Pegasus had cut the connection.

• • •

San Francisco

Elliot replaced the receiver. "Boy, oh boy, she cut me off. She is not happy."

Morning Star floated over and laid a calming hand on his shoulder. She acted as if they had never been abducted, manhandled, and tied up in a desolate dark garage. "You look cold, Elliot. You're shivering."

Eli was raising the Mustang on the boom. "We best skedaddle before the man comes back," he said loudly over the grinding noise. "I'm gonna have to drive around with this vehicle for a few hours. I can't leave it here, or Bobby'll know it was me cut you free. So let's get moving."

"Does that soda machine work?" Morning Star said.

"Never tried it," Eli said.

"I'm thirsty. Would you buy me a bottle of Coke?"

• • •

Berkeley

Without alerting Helen and Carl Campbell, Pegasus, the gun to the small of her back, forced Connie to remove the sheets from her bed, tear them into long strips, and soak them under the bathtub faucet. When they returned to the living room, Carl looked up from the sofa at his wet, angry daughter. "Was that the bridegroom on the phone?"

At gunpoint, Pegasus ordered Carl to tie and gag his wife and daughter with the wet strips. Then he slugged him with the pistol, and Carl crumpled. Pegasus bound him with the remaining strips. He left the three of them lying on their sides on the living-room carpet with the television turned on for company.

• • •

San Francisco

Twenty or thirty people who could not afford tickets for the show had accumulated around the door of the Avalon Ballroom with jugs of communal burgundy, which passed from hand to hand, mouth to mouth, along with a couple of joints that did not move so freely. The crowd appeared to be mustering for an assault on the doorman. He was a ropy guy in Army fatigues and wooden beads who looked as if he might be easily overcome. Above them, the marquee cast a dreggy light. The crooked letters announced that, contrary to Morning Star's information, the headliner for the evening was Big Brother & the Holding Company. According to a poster next to the entrance, Moby Grape had played on Tuesday.

A block down the street Frantz Campbell's Volkswagen Beetle was parked at the curb. Several people, including Frantz, were leaning on the car, drinking beer and sounding each other out about possible crash pads. Frantz was not thrilled with the male-to-female ratio; in fact, all the good chicks had gone to the ballroom.

Elliot climbed down from the tow truck and offered his hand to Morning Star. She jumped down, and he slammed the door. His wrists were painful and raw, and he was favoring his left foot.

Eli slid over and stuck his head through the open passenger window. "So you gonna put in a good word for Eli Tarr soon as you see Stokely, right?"

"I promise," Elliot told him. "If we ever see Stokely, we will definitely put in a good word for Eli Tarr."

Eli disappeared into the cab. A moment later his head popped out again, and he tossed Elliot a rain poncho. "Put that on, man. It's chilly on the damn corner. I got one for your girlfriend, too."

"No need, Eli," Morning Star called. "My body runs hot."

Elliot unfolded the poncho. He was suddenly aware of how cold and tired he was. Exhausted. Wrung out. It seemed like days since, filled with anticipation and good cheer, he had been heading for the Pacific Coast Highway in Santa Monica. Now, only a few hours after arriving in San Francisco, he stood shivering on a dark, sketchy street, flat broke, body battered, with a painted woman who ate garbage in the park and shrugged off kidnappings as if they were part of the normal flow of life.

Eli revved the engine, and Morning Star waved. "Goodbye, Eli! See you in another dream!"

With a snorting of gears, the city tow truck, dragging the Mustang behind it, juddered down the street.

Elliot pulled the poncho over his head. He shook his shoulders to square it and took a long look at his companion. "So, Morning Star, you made it to the Avalon after all."

"I know! I hope the Dead can come." She patted her bag.

"Too bad you can't buy a ticket. You gave away all my money."

Morning Star chuckled. She held up a wallet. "I found this in a locker at the garage."

Elliot goggled. "What is wrong with you? It's one thing to take *my* wallet—I'm just a guy. You can't go around stealing from criminals!"

"Money wants to be free, Elliot." Morning Star pulled out some bills. "This money is tainted by greed and pain. I'm cleansing it."

"Oh my God."

"Come on, Elliot. Let's go in and dig the band."

He looked at her in weary amazement. "Is there some kind of faulty wiring in your head? I'm waiting for my fiancée to pick me up!"

"She can come too."

"Oh my God," he said again.

A pair of eagle-eyed youths in Buffalo Bill jackets had spotted the cash and detached themselves from the crowd under the marquee.

"Let me give you a status report," Elliot went on. "My car is gone, my money is gone, my watch is gone, my clothes are gone. I have no identification to prove I'm even me. I'm missing a patch of skin on my face. I think one of my ribs is broken. A madman wants to kill me. I'm under a life-obligation to a degenerate tow-truck driver to send his regards to somebody named Stokely, a drug dealer, yet another criminal I've somehow attracted into my orbit. I'm hungry, and I desperately need to use the toilet. The only thing I have to cling to is the hope that the extremely pissed-off love of my life will pick me up and spirit me away from this freak show!"

One of the guys in the Buffalo Bill jackets put his face up to Elliot's. "That's heavy, man. You know Stokely?"

Elliot stepped back and stuck out his arm to ward him off. "Get away from me!"

"I could use a taste of that sunshine," the guy said hungrily. "Or maybe some tar. I really gotta fix."

"Get away!" Elliot flapped his arms inside the poncho until the two guys fell back into the scrum outside the ballroom.

Morning Star had been handing out money to the hippies milling around. She showed Elliot the wallet. "It's all gone, except for one lovely twenty-dollar bill." She dropped the wallet on the sidewalk and waved the bill enticingly in front of his eyes. She pulled on his hand. "Let's go in. It'll be a gas."

Elliot tilted his head toward the heavens. "She's out of her gourd."

"Just half an hour, Elliot. It's only time. By the way, why don't you want to get it on with me?"

Elliot was nonplussed by the turn of the conversation. "Get it—what?" he stammered.

"Do you deny that while we were tied up, communicating with our eyes, our legs bound together, you weren't thinking about getting it on with me?" she said.

"Yes, I deny it! The two of us should never have met in the first place." He looked at her painted face, trying to fathom what motivated her. "Although you are a desirable woman," he allowed.

"Don't give me that shit," she said. "Are you coming in or not?"

He glanced along the ill-lit street. The guys in the Buffalo Bill jackets were watching him with a predatory look in their eyes. "I'll come in for fifteen minutes," he said. "I don't want to wait for Connie out here."

The cavernous ballroom roiled with fulgurous spinning crystals and day-glo strobes. Amoebic blobs of light writhed on the walls. The crowd was turbulent. On the stage, the band was working its way through a blistering, electric-guitar jam, the towers of amplifiers producing a maelstrom of sonic distortion. Elliot had never heard anything so loud in his life. His eardrums collapsed; the top of his head felt like it had been sheared off.

Rising on her tiptoes, Morning Star shouted into his ear.

"I can't hear you!" he mouthed.

Morning Star patted his chest and plunged into the crowd, marooning Elliot in a sea of writhing flesh. He tried to push through the mass of bodies. Although he could see Morning Star's velvet top hat bobbing across the flashing expanse, he could make no progress toward her. She leaned over to shout into the ear of a drooping girl in a peasant dress, who pointed vaguely to her right. Morning Star was swallowed again into the orgiastic mass of gyrating bodies.

She made her way toward a wiry dude with two bruised eyes and a crushed nose. One arm was in a sling. When Morning Star touched his shoulder, he lit up like a roman candle.

"Are you Little Pete?"

"Urgh?" The wires holding his jaws together made it hard to understand him.

"I heard you were holding."

Through a combination of sign language, shouting, and rubbing herself against him, she managed to propose trading her remaining fifteen dollars for four tabs of Stokely acid. She couldn't stick around, sorry, you're a beautiful person, maybe in another dream.

Having whipped the ballroom into a frenzy, the music morphed into a slow blues. The guitar buzzed like a hornet; the bass loped along hypnotically in time with the sloshing hihat. Elliot, dazed and deafened, panic rising, edged toward the fire exit. He needed air. Connie would be waiting for him, getting madder by the minute.

Before he reached the door, Morning Star emerged from the mob. Pinning him against the wall, she slipped the tabs of acid into her mouth and pulled his head down and forced her tongue between his teeth, sealing their mouths, letting the tabs dissolve. The music crashed through their bodies. Elliot's hands found their way to her waist.

For twenty minutes they remained locked together. Everything was throbbing and elastic.

Outside, Pegasus cruised the street, looking for somewhere to park. As he passed the Avalon, he caught sight of a tall, courtly man dressed in a sheepskin vest and striped pants and carrying a walking stick, accompanied by three identical hip-twitching girls with their arms around one another's shoulders as they swung along the sidewalk. The sight of the triplets struck Pegasus as a bad omen.

• • •

Afterward, Elliot, casting about for words to describe what happened after Morning Star's kiss, could only say that it was "like dissolving into a pool of liquid sunlight." He experienced none of the psychosis, paranoia, and panic he had read about in *The Bulletin of Atomic Scientists* regarding Russian plans to douse American reservoirs with LSD. Instead, every dark knot in his being had begun to dissolve, and a voluptuous peace had filled his body. The music, which had seemed a distorted roar of pain, separated into phosphorescent threads of sound that wove into intricate new patterns he could trace through the volume of air between himself and the stage. He perceived that the circuits in the amplifiers were not overloaded; they were fulfilled. He could hear the whispered love-conversations of a thousand people whose hair sparkled with fire-jewels and whose flesh glowed with the light of a harvest moon. He examined his hands and saw that they were electric. He peered into his mind and found safety in numbers.

He understood why Morning Star had taken his money. Everything that mattered was free, connected in an infinite and infinitely fascinating network of creation and destruction and recreation, a relay system of thought and feeling in which all things were available at some primordial level of being, at no cost whatsoever.

Pegasus pushed into the ballroom. The strobe lights flashed. His eyes swept the crowd, searching for someone who resembled the man in the photograph he had purloined from Frederick Happ's office. And there he was, Canis Minor, leaning against the fire door, wearing an expression of utter astonishment as he gazed at the turbulent mob.

Before he could move toward his target, Pegasus was surrounded. People began spinning him around, smothering him in a pulsating love-pile. He chopped a woman across the windpipe, and she fell, gagging, to the floor. He sprang to his left and rabbit-punched someone in the nose.

On stage, the band crashed into "Ball and Chain." The crowd swooned in a collective violent spasm. At the foot of the stage, Morning Star danced like a dervish. Pegasus fought his way through the crowd, following the dancing figure as she began to snake toward his quarry. The band howled and wailed; the singer belted the lyrics in a voice hoarse and powerful, as if she were shouting across a Mississippi cottonfield. Once again, Pegasus was swarmed and immobilized.

He broke free in time to see the woman with the painted face slide her bag off her shoulder and hang it around Canis Minor's neck. She kissed him deeply and began dancing in a half-circle around him, flinging back her head, thrusting her pelvis. She kissed him again, then whirled away into the crowd. The electric guitar screamed. The crowd surged.

Morning Star was swept away, her top hat tossing like a buoy on rough waters. Elliot tried to follow but was spun around and flung by centrifugal force at the fire door, which fell open, sending him tumbling into the night.

By the time Pegasus reached the fire door and pushed into the alley, Canis Minor was gone.

Ears ringing, Pegasus hurried to the street and scanned the collection of stragglers and panhandlers. He sprinted to the front of the building, slowing to a stiff-kneed walk as he approached the entrance.

"I want to go back inside," he told the doorman.

"Ticket, man."

Pegasus extended his palm, and when the doorman reached for it, he pulled him off balance and grabbed him by the throat with his other hand.

"Be cool, man, be cool," the doorman gurgled.

Pegasus thrust him to the ground. The thread of wooden beads around his neck broke, and the beads rattled on the sidewalk. The stragglers, keen for action, converged on the entrance, hooting and heckling.

Pegasus darted inside. This time he penetrated the mob and made his way directly to the stage. He climbed up on the left riser to get a better view.

It took only a few seconds to pick out the purple-hatted figure of Morning Star, face paint aglow, ecstatic, whirling, oblivious.

• • •

"Hey, Bobby, do you think Stokely's, uh, you know. . . ."

"Do I think Stokely's what?"

"Do you think him and your girls are, you know. . . ."

"What the hell are you talking about?" Bobby Dobell said. His jaw was as rigid as a clutch plate. He gripped the steering wheel with white-knuckled hands as they prowled through North Beach, hunting for the gangly chemist. In the dark it was hard to distinguish the newly arrived hippies, in whose ranks Dobell placed Stokely, from the old-time beatniks and vagrants.

"I mean, you think they've been getting it on?" Rowdy Gomez clarified. He shifted the shotgun on his lap. "Like, all together at once."

Dobell slammed on the brakes, and the car bounced to a halt in the middle of Broadway in front of a topless shoeshine parlor. A caterwauling of horns started up. "What the hell, Rowdy! Why the fuck you think I want to cut off that motherfucker's dick and shove it down his fucking throat? Jesus!"

Gomez, abashed, looked out the window at some girls building a campfire on the sidewalk. "Don't wig out, man," he muttered. "I just want to make sure what we're doing."

"I'm the one who makes sure what we're doing!" Dobell shouted. "So get that shit outta your head and keep your hands on that pump-action. The only thing you need to think about is blowing that motherfucking purple hat off his motherfucking skull."

At the end of this sentence, Dobell took a deep breath. "Give me the shotgun. You drive. I'm a wreck."

. . .

Everything was intricate. There was meaning beyond imagining. No simple otherness. No theory of being. Her senses separated from her body and wandered the streets of the city, detecting the mulch of the nineteenth century, the sounds of insects at play, the taste of shipwrecks in the bay, the edges of the earth. She touched the words that butterflied from her mouth. *Me. That. Kismet.* The words, stitched with pinpoints of white and blue light, became sparking circles of meaning. Her clothing rippled and shredded into confetti. On the street, benign creatures with moon-bright eyes snuffled and pawed. A taxi passed and left behind it a long train of red light. She followed it into the sky. Everything appeared in italics. Everything was illuminated. Vanishing from her body, she peered through the liquid city at the mirror of the sky.

She was the morning star.

Gradually, she became aware that something had captured her soul and was cramming it back into her body. Although she was suspended still in an impossibly complicated matrix of associations, a vague sense of catastrophe came upon her. She could detect none of the familiar landmarks of her interior landscape. Her body felt wooden. It would not move. Dark. Damp. Smell of saltwater and weatherworn hemp. Indecipherable scrabbling on the ceiling. Scribbling on the ceiling. Was that a ceiling? Everything swayed.

Time passed; it vanished like a breeze.

Time passed.

A door opened. A man loomed in an oblong of thick blue light.

"Where am I?"

"Shut up."

"Why am I here?"

No reply.

"Why?"

"You don't need to know."

PART THREE

Pasadena, July 6, 2020

On Friday morning (legal Independence Day this year), Talia and I took the opportunity to drive the holiday-empty lanes of Sherman Way from Burbank Airport through the San Fernando Valley to West Hills, where after fifteen miles the street runs out of room. Talia, at age seventeen, is learning to drive. After spending the pre-covid years ridesharing her way around the city for school and shopping, she has resolved to master the automobile, now, just when there is nowhere to go. Since March, when the lockdown began, we have not crossed the Pasadena city line, except for a visit to the Home Depot in Alhambra, a couple of runs to Encino, and a jaunt to Big Bear to deliver—masked, at a safe distance, under the pines—the bulk of my mother's wardrobe and a box of files from her home office. She has elected to remain indefinitely at the A-frame.

I piloted the car from the condo building to a sparsely populated neighborhood near the airport before offering Talia the wheel. As she buckled up, tensely, I noticed that she was damp with sweat. Since I did not want to distract her with conversation, we drove in silence along the sun-scoured boulevard, while I meditated on the suburban geography that Pegasus had navigated in 1967 on his way to catch a flight to Oakland. A half-century later, the arid, low-slung cityscape of the Valley strikes me as fundamentally unchanged: stucco and glass interspersed with stubborn greenery. By the time the real-estate people finished filling with subdivisions the spaces formerly occupied by truck farms and groves of oranges ("the talismanic fruit," Joan Didion calls it), the texture of post-war life in the

Valley was established, and it has survived into the new century. There are fewer hamburger stands and more Thai restaurants now, fewer stand-alone businesses and more strip malls, fewer two-bedroom ranch homes with bicycles on the front lawns and more McMansions. There are no more Thrifty drugstores or cafeterias or telephone booths. The smog has lessened (thank you, E.P.A.). But the Valley is essentially unchanged, beaten by the relentless California sunshine into the graceless homogeneity one remembers from midcentury photographs and eight-millimeter film clips. Even as a child in Encino, I felt the flat consistency, the paralysis, of the built environment.

When we reached the place where Sherman Way, unwilling to expire, veers south and becomes Platt Avenue, we turned around in the empty parking lot of Bollywood Dance Lessons for Boys, Girls, and Adults. Talia demanded a high-five for a job well done. She felt ready to take the licensing test, although the current threat-level means the DMV won't be offering behind-the-wheel assessments anytime soon.

I took over the driving. On the return trip (via the freeway), I mentioned my reflections on the Valley's suburban immutability, the Thai restaurants (should we grab some lunch?), Pegasus' trip to the airport, and so on. Since she has been picking at the manuscript as it develops, Talia felt free to point out that Pegasus, a.k.a. Al Carpenter, was not, in fact, a "real person" in the way my parents or the Campbell family were real people, with verifiable histories connected to a host of personal memories. In other words, how in the world did I know what was going through the head of some guy I never met while he drove to Burbank Airport? And did all that really happen anyway? And those F.B.I. dicks—you have transcripts of the meetings, do you? I mean, come on, dude. Her successful drive had made her giddy.

After venting about a number of unrelated issues stirred up by her criticism, I finally responded thus: I'm sure it happened something like the way I've constructed it. There are tapes, Talia, as you will discover at some point in the story. Besides, in keeping with the spirit of those times, don't you value the imagination? Give yourself over to the story; that's how it works. Either you inhabit the improbable or you don't.

Although I didn't turn to look, I'm sure she offered her skeptical face. I see a lot of it these days.

• • •

Berkeley, June 9, 1967

A car pulled into the driveway of the Campbells' hilltop home. Sheilah Robinson killed the headlights. Dawn was an hour away, but she had a list of errands as long as her arm before she went to work.

From the back seat, she retrieved three satin dresses on hangers, wrapped in clingy plastic. Then she stepped briskly up the front walk and unlocked the door and went inside without knocking, very much at home.

• • •

Los Angeles

Fridays depressed Special Agent Don Clegg. He was the kind of person who liked to tie up matters in tidy packages, had been like that all his life. Finish a project. Deliver a report. Accept a commendation. Feel good. But for the last few months, Friday meant the end of another week in which nothing had been resolved. All he and Armbruster ever did was continue surveillance. He was beginning to understand his partner's lust for action.

He sighed. It was nearly seven a.m., and he and Armbruster, whose face this morning looked like an open wound, were sitting exactly where they had been sitting the previous morning, in the office of the Assistant Special Agent in Charge.

A.S.A.C. Muncie hunched over the mug on his desk. "Let's have it," he barked.

"At approximately 11:45 a.m. yesterday, Agent Armbruster and myself arrived on scene at the China One location. Owner, Percy Wu, had shot and killed a stick-up man identified as Herman Aguilar, a convicted felon. The Redondo P.D. had discovered our electronics. Consider the location burned."

"Goddammit," Muncie said. "Now the D.A.'s gonna be on our ass."

"We could point him at the C.I.A.," Armbruster croaked. "Those guys'll squelch it."

Muncie saw his reflection in Armbruster's mirrored shades and narrowed his eyes. "Wrong. Aguilar was D.I.A. Made sloppy work searching the location. Should have gone in before daylight."

"Agreed," Clegg said. "Maybe C.I.A."

Muncie glowered at him.

"Probably D.I.A.," Clegg said.

"We've wired the engineer's house," Armbruster continued, scraping the words from his throat, "but nothing so far. He hasn't come home. The mailman came, so Ames must've left in a hurry without putting a hold on delivery."

"He could be playing us," Clegg suggested.

"Nope. He got wind of the China One situation and went to ground," Muncie decided. "What about this snooper, what's his name? Happ."

"Dead."

"No kidding?"

"Two in the face. We found him on the floor of his office."

"Connected to the D.I.A. guy at China One?"

"Happ was C.I.A."

"Damn." Muncie thought for a moment. "What about L.A.P.D.?"

"An anonymous caller reported it." Clegg nodded toward Armbruster, who snapped his chewing gum. "Got it on the record, just in case someone decided to clean it up, without tipping our hand."

"Good man," Muncie said gruffly.

Clegg smiled tentatively. "This is where it gets interesting. We found the carbons of a report Happ was typing. Dates, places, activities. Elliot Ames was the target, no question about it."

He passed the wrinkled carbon papers across the desk.

Muncie perused them, moving his lips as he read and running his hand across his crewcut. He became aware that his underwear was riding up on him, but he could not think of a good excuse for thrusting his hand into his pants and correcting the problem. "You think this Constance Campbell is in this thing?"

"Without a doubt."

"Abso-fuckin-lutely without a doubt," Muncie declared.

"This thing's got C.I.A. written all over it," Armbruster said.

"D.I.A.," Muncie snapped.

"Right. Maybe Army intelligence. Hell, the damn Post Office could be running an operation."

"Or N.S.A.," Clegg stuck in. "Everybody wants a piece of the action."

"Not the Post Office," Armbruster amended after reflection.

"Why can't they let us handle the domestic cases?" Muncie complained. "Goddamn creeps. They've got the whole world to screw around in, but they're always sticking their noses in our business." He glared at them. "All right. I'll have Frisco send someone to pay this Constance Campbell a visit over in Berkeley, casual, let her know she's on the radar, see if we can get on the same wavelength for once."

• • •

San Francisco

For the past decade, the F.B.I. field office in San Francisco had been having an incredible run. They worked espionage, domestic security, and major-crime cases as if they were the only law-enforcement agency holding the line between American democracy and the forces of Satan. The Bay Area was a bottomless pit of subversion, narcotics distribution, high-tech trade theft, and radical terrorist cells. With a little effort, any one of the two-hundred and seventy agents in the office could make his career in two, three years.

If there was anything the agents at the San Francisco office hated, it was sharing credit for operations, especially if the operations involved Los Angeles. So the Assistant Special Agent in Charge, Henry Fagerberg, Jr., left his counterpart in Southern California hanging on the line while he finished his early-morning briefing with Special Agents Bogosian and Grassmick, who were seated on uncomfortable chairs in an arrangement identical to the one in A.S.A.C. Muncie's office in L.A.

Bogosian passed a file folder across the desk, leaning close enough to smell Fagerberg's warm, breakfasty breath and catch a closeup of his rosacea.

"At exactly 3:05 p.m. yesterday, June eight, Agent Grassmick and myself observed the subject, Stanley Stokely, make public contact with a hitherto unknown female at the Rainbow One location."

Fagerberg flipped through the folder. "Very good, very good," he murmured. "On the other hand. . . ." He paused speculatively. "The fact that he made public contact with a cut-out tells me he's leading us on a wild-goose chase."

"Yes, sir," Bogosian said obligatorily. "He might definitely not be on the up and up. He's a known subversive. Anyway, during the course of surveillance, at approximately 4:30 p.m., we recovered the female's duffel bag at a second location in Panhandle Park. It was full of clothes and LPs and some pills."

"Pills?"

"Birth control, sir. It's in the report."

"I see." Fagerberg leaned back and made a temple of his fingers.

"Anyway, we've determined that the female is Mary Ellen McGovern. Twenty-one years old. Enrolled UCLA. Grassmick remembered her name from last week's Cointelpro memo. It looks like she took off with five thousand dollars from a May Company store in Los Angeles. Left a note— said she was liberating the money."

"Some kind of radical, huh? Funneling cash."

"Exactly. That's why it went to us instead of L.A.P.D. Apparently, no one down there has followed up."

The men pondered the incompetence of the Los Angeles field office.

A.S.A.C. Fagerberg, suspicion budding, bit his lip. "I wonder why they haven't acted," he mused. "Do you think Muncie knew she planned to come up here, and now he's screwing with us?"

"How?" Bogosian asked.

"Who the hell knows what goes on down there," Fagerberg said. "Stop worrying about other people and do your own job."

Grassmick sat up straighter; he was prepared to contribute. "At approximately 4:25 p.m., while maintaining my surveillance position in the park, I observed the female and an unknown male enter a garnet-colored car."

"Garnet-colored?"

"Burgundy. Deep red. They entered a deep-red Chevrolet Impala, registration unknown."

Fagerberg made an unpleasant sound. "You didn't get a plate?"

"The heap was a long way off," Grassmick said lamely.

"I didn't witness the incident, sir," Bogosian said.

"So the girl gets into an unknown automobile." Fagerberg picked up the story. "What's the connection to Stokely? I'm guessing he's branching out. He's running guns, boom-boom sticks, that sort of thing, maybe for these Negro agitators—"

"Black Panthers, sir," Grassmick said. "And she didn't exactly enter the car of her own accord."

"Don't interrupt me. Jesus." He shook his head to settle his thoughts. "As I see it, if these radical elements lay their hands on high-grade explosives, we're all screwed. There goes the whole goddamn thing. First on the agenda: blow up government buildings—including this one. It's sedition, pure and simple, with a lot of free-love and booze mixed in. That's where the girl figures in the story."

"The Black Panthers are more serious than that," Bogosian ventured.

"It makes no difference. Stanley Stokely's a pervert and a menace. He's supplying the firepower."

"He's a crackerjack chemist," Grassmick said unnecessarily.

"You got that right. He's capable of manufacturing what we say he is. He gets his kicks from messing with the system. For Christ's sake, the man was a professor."

"We've got guys on the ground in Berkeley," Bogosian reminded him.

"Bastards," Fagerberg snarled. His eyes had begun to water.

"Sir, they're our men."

He eyed Bogosian and Grassmick suspiciously. "You never know."

Grassmick offered an innocent countenance, but Bogosian shifted uneasily in his chair and studied the calendar on the wall behind the desk, wondering if A.S.A.C. Fagerberg suspected that he had been sleeping with his, Fagerberg's, wife on Tuesday afternoons at the Mark Hopkins Hotel and charging the room to the Bureau as the Rainbow Three surveillance location. Fagerberg had seemed particularly paranoid recently.

"So where's the girl with the five grand?" he said. "And the unidentified male?"

Bogosian exhaled a sigh of relief. "Unknown."

Fagerberg noticed that the hold light on his desk phone was flashing. "Hang on a minute, boys. Let me talk to L.A. about this gal—what's her name again?" He looked at the file and smiled with relish. "McGovern. Muncie's gonna shit his pants when he hears we've got a bead on her."

• • •

Redondo Beach

It was not time for a coffee break, but Gordon Blackmon dropped by Design Room Six to visit Arthur Reuhl anyway. Arthur was trying to make sense of the schematics spread on the high table at which he was perched.

Gordon leaned over his colleague's shoulder. "So, Art, I was thinking it'd be a blast to decorate Elliot's house. When they get back from Hawaii they can, uh. . . . What am I trying to say?"

"Appreciate our friendship?" Arthur said, shifting his attention from the intractable schematics.

"Right."

"You'll have to do it yourself," Arthur said. He took off his glasses and rubbed his eyes. "I've got a real mess here. Why this burst of whimsy?"

Gordon shrugged. "We're the closest thing Elliot has to a best man. We should have thrown him a bachelor party."

"I don't think so. I mean, we're not the best man. Men."

"We're invited to the rehearsal luncheon," Gordon pointed out. "And we're standing up for him at the ceremony with Connie's brother."

Arthur put his glasses back on. "I suppose one of us'll have to offer a toast at the reception."

"Why I came down here is to see if you have a key to his place."

"Under the milk box."

"That doesn't seem very secure," Gordon said doubtfully.

Arthur cracked his knuckles. He was ready to get back to work. "You have to count me out on this one."

"Do you want us to pick up you and Marilyn on the way to the airport?"

"We'll be ready when you are."

"Good man. I'll call you." Gordon slapped his friend on the back and, shoving his hands in his pockets, passed back down the corridor, whistling a tune he had learned in the third grade in Manchester, New Hampshire.

• • •

San Francisco

There was not much left of the original Victorian splendor but the spacious rooms. In the bay-windowed parlor, people sprawled in various states of undress on mattresses, old sofas, an army cot, surrounded by a confusion of Chianti bottles, dope pipes, paperback books, dirty dishes, and desiccated houseplants. On the exfoliating plaster of the walls, someone had taped posters advertising local bands and nailed up an Asian tapestry that looked as if it had been used for target practice. Several antique firearms stood in a corner by a soot-streaked fireplace. From upstairs drifted the sound of a harpsichord.

Elliot struggled to consciousness. The raw morning light seemed excessively blue and granular. Through an open window came the sea-and-sourdough smell of the San Francisco dawn. He discovered that he was lying on a mattress. He wiggled his toes. He was not wearing shoes. Or socks. Or pants. He moved his hands and discovered that he was wrapped in the rain poncho Eli Tarr had given him. Morning Star's embroidered shoulder bag rested on his chest. He was not wearing a shirt.

Groaning, he pushed himself upright. Everything snapped and whirled, as if time itself were falling back into place, piece by piece. He looked at the crackled layers of paint on the window frame, the smudged panes. There were mourning doves on the telephone line high above the street. His eyes felt like two holes punched in his face. His teeth felt as if they had been shattered and stuffed down his throat and replaced with blocks of wood. He reeked of something that he dimly recognized as marijuana, and he itched all over.

When he had verified that his muscles were still attached to his bones, he looked around the room. Next to him on the floor were a naked man and three naked girls who resembled each other to such a degree that Elliot questioned whether he might be hallucinating. He closed his eyes, and when he opened them, the naked girls still looked like three versions of one person, dewy bodies, flossy pubic hair and sharp wings of hipbones, sleep-smeared features—yet somehow, in their nakedness, chaste, untouched. The naked man had red hair and a goatee and a corrugated ribcage. Next to the girls, he looked seven feet long. He was talking in his sleep or perhaps chewing on something.

Elliot labored to his feet. Slinging Morning Star's bag over his shoulder, he picked his way across the room, treading on the lifeless hand of someone buried under a pile of blankets, and nearly upsetting a chamber pot fashioned from a gasoline can. The woman who had given him the lump of stew in Panhandle Park was bivouacked on the army cot. In a corner by the stairs, one human being gruntingly straddled another.

He approached an open doorway and saw a kitchen. It was the filthiest room he had ever seen. Paint peeled from the cupboards, and the linoleum had worn through to the floorboards. Piles of dirty dishes stood on the counters and in the deep mossy stone sink. On the gas stove a dented percolator burbled. The smell of coffee suffused the air. At a splintered wooden table sat Frantz Campbell, wearing round blue-tinted sunglasses, a cigarette dangling from his lip. He was holding a box of Raisin Bran.

They stared at each other. The cigarette fell from Frantz's mouth. "Far out, man!"

Elliot blinked with surprise. "Frank?"

"Yeah, man. Only it's Frantz now. You know—Frantz Fanon, *Wretched of the Earth* and that whole poli-sci trip."

Elliot shuffled over and lowered himself carefully onto a chair.

Frantz plucked the burning cigarette from the tabletop and stubbed it on an old cantaloupe rind. "I can't believe this, man! What are you doing here?" He reached across the table and slapped Elliot's shoulder. "Connie's out of her mind over you. Where the hell've you been, man?"

"I'm not sure," Elliot said, testing his tongue. "My head feels like a dinosaur egg. Everything seems so. . . . I went to a place with this girl, and then it was. . . hilarious and fluctuating, and I could see through people, like they were ghosts. The wind told me secrets. It was like I'd pulled a thread and the whole world unraveled into pure information."

"Elliot, man, you were tripping!"

Thrusting aside the box of Raisin Bran, Frantz jumped up and grabbed a soiled dishtowel and picked up the percolator. He poured coffee into an old jelly jar and pushed it across the table.

Elliot reached out and touched the side of the jar. "It was like everybody in the world could hear my thoughts. It seemed like a problem, but it wasn't."

"It's Jungian," Frantz said excitedly, sliding back onto his chair. He grabbed a handful of cereal from the box and stuffed it into his mouth. "You and me," he continued crunchily, "in this kitchen at this moment in time. Worlds colliding, man."

Elliot could not comprehend how he had come to be sitting across from his future brother-in-law. "Where are we exactly?"

"Safe harbor, brother."

Elliot lifted the jelly jar and tasted the coffee with the tip of his tongue. "I was at the Avalon Ballroom," he remembered.

"Everybody was there, man."

"I fell through a door."

"Right down the rabbit hole. You must've been in a bona fide condition. You probably got scooped up by the freak-sweepers. Every night they go around picking up strays like you and bringing them home." He pointed at the parlor.

"Was there a woman with me?"

"I didn't even know *you* were here. Shit. Elliot Ames," Frantz marveled.

Elliot lifted himself off the chair and went to re-examine the front room. The copulating individuals had disappeared.

Frantz, lighting a fresh Pall Mall, followed.

"There's like six bedrooms upstairs," Frantz informed him. "You want to check and see if the chick is up there?"

"Her name is Morning Star." Elliot touched the embroidered bag depending from his shoulder. "This is hers. It's full of hashish."

Frantz's eyes lit up. Before he could pursue the matter, he noticed the naked red-haired man and the dewy triplets. He stepped over for a closer look. "Hey, man!" he whispered. "That's Stanley Stokely! This is way beyond my head."

"I don't believe it," Elliot said. He picked up the striped pants next to the mattress where the naked people were sleeping and began going through the pockets. He pulled out a wallet. His wallet. He looked inside. Empty. He put it back in the pocket and pulled the pants on. For a long moment, he looked down at Stanley Stokely and debated whether to disturb his slumber. After all, two violent thugs were looking to kill him. On the other hand, Stokely had spent all of his money, and for all Elliot knew, the man was a menace in his own right. It was best, he decided, to let the parties work out their grievances without his involvement.

Then he moved around the room, locating a discarded denim shirt and a pair of sandals that looked about his size. It was chilly wearing nothing but the rain poncho.

• • •

West Los Angeles

The FRANCO'S—FLOWERS WITH SOUL van was parked across the street from Elliot Ames's house, as conspicuous as a fire truck.

A car pulled up behind the van. A minute later, the rear doors swung open, and Special Agents Armbruster and Clegg squeezed in next to Hawk Fundy, who had been kept on the job for his electronics expertise. The van smelled of tape-head cleaner. Other than performing a few minutes of routine maintenance, Fundy had spent the night sleeping. Now he unscrewed the cap from a thermos and poured coffee into a red plastic cup. "Man, am I beat," he said and faked a yawn.

"Anything?" Armbruster asked. His mirrored shades were smeared with fingerprints. He was raddled and worn, having caught only an hour of sleep between getting home from Big Dean's bar, fighting with his wife, and going back in the field. Five sticks of wintergreen gum were stuffed into his right cheek.

"Not even a squirrel," Fundy told them. "You guys might be wrong about this one."

"Negative," Clegg declared. "What about the newspaper boy? I picked up the morning paper on the lawn."

"It must've been dark," Fundy mumbled.

Clegg made himself comfortable on the carpeted floor of the van, sitting cross-legged, like a Buddha in a gabardine suit, and unfolded the newspaper. He began to read aloud. In the Mediterranean, Israeli jets and torpedo boats had attacked the *USS Liberty* spy ship.

"It's a set-up," Armbruster responded. With a groan he arranged himself so that he was leaning against the equipment and shook his head like a dog. "LBJ's excuse for jumping into the war with Egypt."

Clegg turned the page. "They're still putting out the fires in Boston. Every day's another riot."

"Let it burn," Armbruster said grumpily, although he did not, in fact, have an opinion on the issue. He shifted the wad of gum to his other cheek.

Clegg turned the page. "Bedroom furniture's on sale at Bullock's. Think I should take the wife for a look-see?"

"It's always better in the ads," Armbruster said. "Nothing's as good in real life."

"You seem kinda depressed," Fundy observed.

"Hey, Armbruster." Clegg rattled the pages of the newspaper. "Our dead guy in the Valley made the morning edition. They're treating him like he really was a private investigator."

Armbruster grunted. "If that's what it says, then that's what the Agency wants it to say. Gimme the sports."

"When did you learn to read?" Clegg inquired.

Fundy snickered.

Armbruster looked hurt, and Clegg regretted chaffing him in front of the temporary help. He pulled out the sports section and handed it to his partner. "Dodgers got beat, 5-4," he noted conciliatorily. "Regan blew it in the ninth."

"Drysdale can't be happy about that," Armbruster said gruffly.

"He shoulda gone the whole game," Clegg said. "Helluva pitcher, Drysdale."

"Helluva handsome man," Armbruster said and rattled the pages.

• • •

Berkeley

It was late morning. Frantz's orange Volkswagen Beetle putt-putted gamely up the hill. Elliot slumped in the passenger seat, the vibrations from the engine passing through the floor and up his legs to his innards. He was wearing his future brother-in-law's blue-tinted sunglasses. His head was a wreck, his eyeballs burned, his joints hurt. He had a red, crusted scrape on his cheek, and he needed a shave. Morning Star's bag was strapped across the front of his poncho.

Frantz coaxed the underpowered vehicle around the final curve and pulled up in front of the Campbell house. Parked at the foot of the driveway behind Carl's and Connie's cars was a police cruiser, and along the curb were an official-looking sedan and a Berkeley Police Department van.

"What the hell's the fuzz doing?" Frantz wondered for the both of them; Elliot was still having trouble forming thoughts.

Curious neighbors had come out to see what was happening. Across the street a man was washing his car with a hose. Someone inched an empty baby carriage along the sidewalk.

As they climbed out of the Beetle, a station wagon with the logo *Golden State Messengers* emblazoned on the side nosed up behind them. A reedy, adenoidal voice called through the open passenger window, "Is this 1099 Moraga Drive?"

"Yeah. So what?" Frantz said and continued up the walk, anxious to find out what the authorities were doing at the house.

Elliot went over and squatted on the grassy verge so that the poncho ballooned around his ankles. He was not wearing socks with the borrowed sandals, and the grass felt unpleasantly damp on his bare toes. He peered into the car. "Sorry about him. We had a long night."

"Hey, no problem, playboy," said a mop-haired kid who looked no more than sixteen. He winked. "I've got a delivery for a party named Constance Campbell. Can you sign? I'm way behind and I don't wanna get outta the car."

Elliot reached through the window and took the ballpoint pen from the kid and signed the receipt on the clipboard.

The messenger handed him a fat manila envelope. Elliot examined it. On the front was a label with Connie's full name and address, but there was no information identifying the sender.

The messenger cleared his throat. "It's a long drive up here, brother."

Elliot gazed at him blankly through the blue-tinted sunglasses. The kid rubbed his thumb and first two fingers together and winked at him again.

"Oh." Elliot patted the rain poncho with his free hand. "I'm sorry, I don't have any cash on me."

"Maybe in the bag...."

"No," he said, pushing the shoulder bag to one side. "She wouldn't have any money."

The kid scowled. "Hippies," he huffed and, throwing the station wagon in reverse, backed down the hill at top speed.

Elliot stood up and shuffled toward the house. He met Sheilah Robinson, car keys in hand, descending the steps. Her earrings flashed in the morning light.

"What's going on?"

"You should know, you son of a bitch," she spat out and clipped down the walk.

He went through the open front door, dropping the manila envelope on the counter as he passed into the kitchen. In the living room, Connie, Carl, and Helen Campbell crowded around Frantz, all talking at once. Strips of torn bedsheets lay scattered on the carpet. A flashbulb went off. A two-man physical-evidence team was at work. They had spread their equipment across the coffee table. On the easy chairs sat two men in brown suits.

"I don't understand what's going on," Frantz was saying. "Why are the pigs in our house?"

Special Agents Grassmick and Bogosian exchanged looks. Mouths tightened; nostrils quivered. They rose in unison and crossed the room. "What was that?" Grassmick said in a dangerous voice.

The two agents had made the mistake of lingering in A.S.A.C. Fagerberg's office. When Fagerberg got L.A.'s request to visit a Constance Campbell in Berkeley, re national security, he tapped them for the task. "That idiot Muncie seems to think she's C.I.A. Connected to some dead operative in Van Nuys. He wants our take on it, see if we can share intel with the Agency. Remind me: is Van Nuys part of Los Angeles?"

"Why do we have to do L.A.'s work?" Grassmick complained.

"I don't like it any better than you do. On the other hand, you two aren't making much progress on the Stokely thing."

When they arrived at the house on Moraga Drive, they were displeased to find an active crime scene. The first thing Grassmick and Bogosian did was dismiss the Berkeley detectives. With the university still in session, the police were shorthanded and glad to shift the investigation onto federal shoulders. A female officer was left in the cruiser in the driveway to keep an eye on things. Lady cops were not part of the campus detail.

Connie glanced at the archway between the kitchen and the living room. "Elliot! Oh, thank God!" She rushed over and threw her arms around him.

"Look what they did to her!" Frantz cried, turning his mother by both shoulders so that Elliot could see. Helen's face was bruised, and there was an adhesive bandage on her chin.

"Someone came into our house under false pretenses," Carl Campbell said matter-of-factly. He was clutching a tumbler of scotch. The side of his head bore a nasty laceration. "He claimed he was an executive from Pacifidyne, and he was looking for you."

"He was *not* from Pacifidyne," Connie said, loosening her embrace.

"He said he was from Pacifidyne. He was wearing gloves, which seems strange now that I think about it."

"He broke my glasses," Helen said. "Then we were tied up on the floor. Right after I had my hair done!"

Connie fell back a step and looked accusingly at her fiancé. She sank her fingernails through the thin rain poncho into his arm. "It was awful. He rang the bell while we were eating dinner and said he had some papers for you to sign. Then he watched *Bewitched*. Right there!" She turned and pointed at the sofa.

"Let's not be melodramatic," Carl said.

"Why are you wearing those clothes?" Connie demanded, plucking at the poncho.

Elliot was once again having trouble making sense of his surroundings. Through the French doors, he could see a striped canopy, rows of wooden folding chairs, tiki torches, a pulpit covered with a tapestry. "He had papers?" he puzzled.

"He said they were from work. But he had a gun!"

She pushed him away and threw herself on the sofa and began making a sobbing sound. "This is all your fault," she wailed.

Carl eased himself onto one of the satin armchairs near the French doors. Helen did not like anyone to sit on them; they were antiques. He addressed Elliot: "Like Connie said, this fellow bound us, threatened us." He touched his wounded head. "Thank heavens Sheilah has a house key. That girl comes and goes like she lives here, and I'm damned glad of it."

Grassmick and Bogosian had had enough of family time. They broke off glaring at Frantz and turned their attention to Elliot. "I'm Special Agent Ed Grassmick, Federal Bureau of Investigation. This is Special Agent Russ Bogosian. When we arrived, Berkeley P.D. was on the scene. We had a request from the L.A. field office to pay Miss Campbell," nodding toward the sofa, "a visit, regarding a murder in the San Fernando Valley. Quite a coincidence."

"A murder!" Elliot exclaimed. "I don't understand. What would Connie know about a murder?"

"We don't have the details," Grassmick admitted. "We're not in the habit of doing L.A.'s legwork for them."

"They think I'm in the C.I.A.," Connie sobbed, lifting her head from the sofa, her tone of voice positioned between outrage and fear. Helen leaned down and patted her back.

"No, ma'am," Grassmick said. "I'm confident you are not in the C.I.A. This intruder—that's another story. We don't know how he fits."

"Not a coincidence," Bogosian said.

"He could be with the Agency."

"Or D.O.D.," said Bogosian.

"Right. He might be N.S.A. gone rogue."

"Should you be telling us this?" Carl Campbell asked. He clinked the ice in his glass.

Grassmick turned back to Elliot and examined him up and down. "What about you, fella? You look very familiar. How do you know these people?"

"We're supposed to get married. I mean, I'm supposed to marry one of these people tomorrow afternoon."

"Your name?"

"Elliot Ames."

"You got some identification on you?"

Elliot handed him the wallet he had recovered from Stanley Stokely's pants.

"What's in the bag?" Bogosian said, taking a step toward him.

"Nothing!" Elliot forced himself not to touch the shoulder bag. "Lunch."

"You sure you're getting married? You look like some kinda bum."

"Hey, now!" Carl Campbell bristled.

"Careful, Russ," Grassmick warned. "These seem like good people mostly."

Bogosian flushed and backed off.

"Just what I'd expect from the pigs," Frantz sneered.

Grassmick studied Elliot's driver's license and wrote in his notebook. "Los Angeles, huh? Whaddya do down there?"

"I work for Pacifidyne, in computers." Elliot shifted the bag full of hashish so that it was behind his back.

"A brainiac," Bogosian said in an uncomplimentary tone. "You have security clearance?"

"As a matter of fact, I do."

"Then we've got a file on you somewhere. We've got files on all you defense guys. Are we gonna find anything you need to disclose?"

"I can't imagine what," Elliot said. "Although you would not believe what happened yesterday afternoon. I was eating stew in the Panhandle with this girl I picked up—"

"What!" Connie yelped and sat up on the sofa.

"I told you on the phone that the car broke down. It's been a terrible, terrible experience. I was calling you from San Francisco, where we were—well, frankly, we were kidnapped and beaten by a man named Bobby Dobell. We were taken to this place called Astro Auto Body. Kidnapping is within the F.B.I.'s purview. Obviously, since you're here."

"We didn't know there had been a kidnapping at this location until we arrived," Grassmick said.

"But you investigate kidnappings, don't you?"

"Well, yeah. You said 'we were kidnapped.' Who was with you?"

"A woman from L.A. I don't know who she is. A UCLA student who used to work at the May Company."

"Did she have paint on her face?" Grassmick asked.

"As a matter of fact, she did."

"Does the name Mary Ellen McGovern mean anything?"

"I don't think so," Elliot said.

"And where is this woman now?"

"I'm not sure. I lost track of her."

Connie threw herself back on the sofa and resumed sobbing.

Grassmick leaned close to Bogosian's ear. "This guy's the civilian from the park. This is getting interesting."

Bogosian scrutinized the ragged, beaten, unwashed figure of Elliot Ames in his poncho and blue-tinted sunglasses. "You sure? He was kinda far away, and all these hippies look the same."

"The name Stanley Stokely mean anything to you?" Grassmick snapped at Elliot.

Elliot expressed surprise. "As a matter of fact, this Dobell character thought we knew where he was. That's why he and his man took us. It was something to do with his daughters running away with this Stokely person."

Grassmick and Bogosian exchanged looks.

"So where's Stokely?"

"He might be at a house in Haight-Ashbury."

"Address?"

"I don't know. I was there, but I don't know how I got there. Frank, do you remember the address?"

"I'm not saying shit to the pigs," Frantz said.

"If you're withholding information, fella," Grassmick said, "you're committing a federal crime."

Frantz laughed. "Let me put it another way: my memory's fried. See what drugs are doing to America's youth?"

"Very funny," Grassmick said. "We'll come back to you in a minute." He turned to Elliot: "Let's talk about your connection with Stanley Stokely."

"I've never met the man," Elliot said. "I saw him, that's all. I'm more concerned with what's happened here."

"That's right," Frantz said.

Connie sat up on the sofa and wiped her tears with a scatter-pillow. "The man who came here wanted to kill you, Elliot. He made me say I'd pick you up at the Avalon Ballroom, but that was just to find out where you were. Once he was sure he had you, he was going to come back and kill all of us, I know it!"

"That's terrible," Helen summarized.

"So who is this asshole?" Frantz demanded. "Why does he want to kill Elliot, and what the hell does it have to do with Stanley Stokely, and what're the damn pigs doing about it?"

"Now hold it right there, buddy," Bogosian instructed. "That's enough of that kind of talk."

The physical-evidence men began to gather their gear.

"Those are actually good questions," Grassmick said. He pointed at Elliot. "Why would someone come gunning for you? Who are you anyway? Who do work for, comrade?"

Elliot did not know what to say.

Connie had fully recovered her wits. She got up from the sofa. "Look what you've done, Elliot. Look what you've brought on this family. On me."

Elliot raised his hand to his cheek and felt the wound he had suffered when he hit the concrete floor of the auto-body shop. It had scabbed over, and it felt hard and rough. He ran his fingers through his tangled hair and wiggled his bare toes. "I don't know what to say, man."

· · ·

San Francisco

Fisherman's Wharf. It was nearly eleven o'clock. Much of the fishing fleet was out to sea, but not the *Sally Belle*. Although for appearances' sake she ventured periodically beyond the Golden Gate with a part-time crew, she always returned with an insubstantial catch. The *Sally Belle* was mainly used for nocturnal rendezvous with boats anchored in international waters. In the past decade she had been involved in the exchange of persons, firearms, communications equipment, gold bullion, and counterfeit currency. Pegasus, having coordinated these operations for two years before being reassigned to L.A., knew that the boat would not leave the marina between sundown Thursday and dawn on Monday, when the skipper, an ancient communist from Genoa, came on board to check the engine and head out with a skeleton crew to fish. Pegasus doubted that Sagittarius, who, he believed, had taken over his position at the *rezidentura* in Pacific Heights, had changed the routine; the man had eaten the same bread-and-cheese lunch every day of his life.

As soon as he had maneuvered the girl, high as a kite in her ludicrous purple hat, onto the boat, Pegasus had handcuffed her to an iron staple in the dank, stinking hold and stretched duct tape across her mouth. Then he hurried back to his rental car, which he had unwisely left in a restricted-parking zone. He was certain that after slipping through his fingers Canis

Minor would go to the house on Moraga Drive. He had, he complimented himself grimly, been prescient enough to keep the family alive, especially the bitchy young woman, until Canis was in his grasp.

Alternatively, if Canis Minor suspected he had been identified, he might go underground. It was possible he had rudimentary tactical training. Pegasus did not believe he would go to the *rezidentura*, not until he knew what was happening. Operations always involved cut-outs, and he doubted that Canis Minor had met his handler, whoever he was.

The rental car would not start.

Pegasus felt a band of frustration tighten across his forehead. After a minute, he got out and walked over to the Italian diner on the far side of the wharf. He sat down in the phone booth and located his Auto Club card in his wallet and called for an all-night mechanic. After an hour and a half, during which time Pegasus sat staring through the windshield, trying to keep warm in his thin windbreaker, the mechanic arrived and replaced the battery from the collection he carried in the back of the service truck. Pegasus hated having to provide Al Carpenter driver's license and Auto Club card, but the only other option was to steal a vehicle, which carried its own risks. In any case, he could not abandon a car rented in Al Carpenter's name and risk have it towed from the restricted-parking zone.

By the time he reached Moraga Drive, the eastern sky was petalled with pink light, and three Berkeley police cars were in front of the Campbell house. Following a milk truck, Pegasus assessed the situation and briefly regretted everything he had done or not done for the past seven years.

He returned to the marina.

* * *

Berkeley

Elliot sat on the front steps, his toes sticking out from under the edge of the poncho, which formed a tent over his knees. The sky was a high, milky blue. The sound of mourning doves on the power lines matched his low spirits. He examined how dismal he felt and discovered that he was suffocated by a tremendous sense that he was not in control of his actions and at the same time was responsible for the calamity that had befallen the Campbell household. He wanted to howl.

Grassmick and Bogosian came out of the house and stepped around him and descended the steps.

They paused.

"Berkeley P.D.'s gonna keep the patrol car up here in case your girlfriend's right and this creep comes back," Grassmick said to the top of Elliot's head. He glanced over at the policewoman sitting behind the wheel of the sedan.

Elliot nodded.

"The other girl, McGovern, is on our radar," Bogosian told him and prodded him with the toe of his shiny black shoe. "We're gonna talk to you, buddy, at greater length, soon as we contact L.A. and see what they have on you. Don't plan on leaving the area."

"We'll pay a visit to this Astro Auto Body," Grassmick said. "Maybe it'll yield something. Maybe not. There's something fishy about all this. You haven't been altogether honest with us. You have some kind of connection with Stanley Stokely."

"Maybe we should take this guy as a material witness," Bogosian said.

"I don't know. Fagerberg'll have our asses if we get a judge involved before we have a case."

"Right." Bogosian turned back to Elliot. "We're watching you, pal. You're on the radar."

Elliot tilted his head back and looked up through the blue-tinted sunglasses at their looming faces. He was on the radar. He closed his eyes. In a minute, there was the sound of car doors slamming and an engine starting up. He listened to the car speed away.

Elliot opened his eyes and lowered his head. A rabbit hopped across the lawn. It stopped and turned its large, liquid eyes on him questioningly. Its nose quivered. "I have no idea," Elliot told the rabbit.

. . .

San Francisco

Carrying a lighted propane lantern, Pegasus crossed the weathered deck and went down into the hold of the *Sally Belle*. He felt a flutter of weariness as he sat down on a wooden fish box. Missing a night's sleep was nothing, but the strain of beating and killing the fat man in Van Nuys, flying to Oakland, subduing the family in Berkeley, digesting the cheese fondue, and chasing the hell around the greater Bay Area was beginning to tell. Not to mention that he felt, as usual, a gonging urge to urinate.

He set the lantern on a second fish box and crossed his legs and appraised the girl sitting on the floor in a cold bath of foul water, her back against the bulkhead. Water dripped from his shoe.

She returned his gaze, blinking slowly. Her pupils were dilated, her lashes long and dark. He could not help contrasting them with Susan's pale eyelashes and pale blue eyes.

He reached over and pulled the duct tape off her mouth. "What's your name?"

She licked her ruined lips. The handcuffs fastening her to the iron staple checked her movement as she tried to raise a hand to her mouth. "Morning Star," she said.

Morning Star. A code name.

"What's *your* name?"

Pegasus thought. "Al," he said.

"Hi, Al." She gave the handcuffs a shake. "I appear to be enslaved. I mean, am I still tripping? This is some weird energy."

"I would not say you are enslaved. Restrained is more accurate. Shackled."

"Why are we on a boat, Al?"

"It's a good place to be right now," he told her.

The designs painted on Morning Star's face had flaked badly. By the light of the lantern, she looked as though she had a skin disease. Her eyes were red. Her clothes were wrinkled and soiled. The purple velvet hat with a blaring gold *S* on the crown tipped precariously on her head. Yet she seemed blithe, even cheerful. It was unsettling.

"Why aren't you scared?" Pegasus asked.

She thought it over. "Whatever is happening is a part of a bigger thing," she said. "That's nothing to be scared of."

"You believe that?"

"Probably. May I have some water? I'm really thirsty."

Pegasus climbed back onto the deck. Mounted on the roof of the wheelhouse was an old aluminum beer keg that was used for fresh water. He found the metal cup hanging on a hook and filled it and gulped down the water. It was warm and rusty. Then he went into the cabin to use the head.

When he was done, he refilled the metal cup and carried it down into the hold, his soft soles scritching on the metal stairs. He held the cup to Morning Star's dry lips. Then he sat on the fish box and tapped the empty cup on his knee.

What was her connection to Canis Minor? Why had they been together? Perhaps she was a floater, used and discarded. But then why the code name? And why her utter lack of alarm? Maybe the drugs had evacuated her of normal fear. Drugs could have been part of her training.

"I don't expect an answer," Pegasus said, "but I'll ask anyway. Who do you work for?"

"I don't work for anyone," Morning Star responded, puzzled. "I don't believe in the labor economy, at least not the exploitative form in which it's currently constituted. Like, I used to work for the May Company in L.A., but it was a monumental drag. Dig?"

"So you know Elliot Ames from your time in Los Angeles? Are you traveling with him?"

Her face brightened. "Elliot! Is he here?"

"I'm afraid not."

"That's too bad. We just met, but we have a real connection. He's a complicated man."

"He's not your boyfriend?"

"No way. I'm conflicted about the boyfriend-girlfriend paradigm. I mean, love wants to be free, right?"

"Why were you with him?"

"Why not? He's a gifted driver. I kind of flashed on him, and we were having a beautiful time." She frowned. "Except for the beating and kidnapping."

"You need to explain that," Pegasus said.

"Two evil dudes snatched us off the street and took us to an auto shop. They were quite threatening. They beat Elliot and tied us up. Then this cat,

Eli, found us." She chuckled. "Now I'm locked up all over again. I must be living wrong."

Pegasus struggled to integrate this peculiar information, which indicated that someone besides himself was after Canis Minor. But who? Surely not Sagittarius. Maybe the auto shop was an F.B.I. interrogation site.

"Where is this place?"

"Near the Haight, I think. We told them we didn't know anything about Stanley Stokely."

"Who's Stanley Stokely?" Pegasus added the name to the growing list of people involved in the situation.

"He gave me his hat!"

Pegasus reached over and plucked the purple velvet top hat from her head. He studied it, turning it in the light of the propane lantern and running his finger inside the sweatband. There was nothing hidden there.

"What was in the bag you passed to Elliot Ames at the Avalon Ballroom?" he said.

"Oh, that. I wanted to dance! Later on, I was hoping to connect with the Grateful Dead and hand it off. Everybody's desperate for Primo."

The terms "Grateful Dead" and "primo" were new to Pegasus.

"Where?" he said.

"At their place on Ashbury Street. Do you have an old lady?" Morning Star inquired.

Pegasus was not about to get drawn into a discussion of his personal life. There were dangers in conversing with a prisoner. "Dead," he muttered.

"Bummer. I need to pee."

Pegasus pointed at the fish-funky seawater in which she was sitting. "Your jeans are already wet."

"Oh, wow. You're right."

She closed her eyes. After a minute she opened them and said, "I feel better."

He held up the lantern between them, debating his next move.

"You're storing a lot of emotions in your muscles," Morning Star observed. "You're not living true."

"I'm not living true?"

"Yes."

The familiar band of frustration tightened on his forehead. He let out his breath slowly. "I don't know what your relationship is with Canis Minor, but—"

"Canis Minor?"

"Elliot Ames."

"He *is* a Canis!"

"I don't know what you and he have going. But I hope he cares about what happens to you."

Pegasus got to his feet and, carrying the purple top hat, went back on deck and closed the hatch.

He needed to use the pay phone at the Italian diner.

• • •

Berkeley

Elliot watched the rabbit nibble its way through a row of marigolds along the walk. He could not determine if he wanted to get up or remain seated on the front steps. Inside the Campbells' house the telephone was ringing. The third ring cut off, and in a moment Connie called to him through the open front door. Wearily, he got to his feet.

In the kitchen, cigarette in hand, recovered from the trauma of the night, Connie thrust the receiver at him. "It's for you," she sniffed. "He sounds familiar. It might be Arthur or Gordon, he didn't say."

Elliot turned his back on Connie and stretched the coils of the phone cord taut as he moved into the dining room, Connie following at his heels. "Hello?"

A man's voice, flat and pleasant, said, "Canis Minor?"

"Pardon?"

"Elliot Ames?"

"Who is this?"

"I have the girl, Canis."

"Who is this?"

"I have Morning Star."

"Morning Star! Thank God. Where is she?"

"Morning Star!" Connie exclaimed. "Is that the girl you picked up?"

Elliot tried to turn away. "Where are you? Who is this, please?"

"It doesn't matter. If the police are still on the premises, you need to take steps. We both have reasons for not wanting them to listen to this conversation."

"No one is listening."

"I suggest you make certain for your own sake. Given your position, I assume you do not want law enforcement involved."

"The only person here is my fiancée," Elliot said firmly. "There's a patrol car in the driveway, but no one is on the line." Through the dining room window, he could see the patrol car. "Why are you calling? I don't understand. Tell me where Morning Star is, and I'll come and get her."

Connie tugged on the poncho. "Elliot, who is that?"

He jerked away from her.

"You know why I'm calling," the man continued. "I want your key."

"What?"

"You will deliver the key, or the girl gets a bullet in her ear," the man said evenly.

"What do you mean, my 'key'?" Elliot panicked. He began to understand that he was not speaking to a Good Samaritan; he was speaking to the person who had come to the house on Moraga Drive, looking for him, and had terrorized the Campbell family. "Do you mean my car key? The key to my house? A computer key?"

"This is no time to play stupid, Canis. The code key."

"I don't understand."

"I know your directory. I want your designation. Your key."

Elliot tried to make sense of what was being asked of him. "I don't know what any of that is."

"Do you want your friend to die?"

Connie slapped at his shoulder.

"No, of course not! I can give you what you want. But I have to see her first. I have to know she's all right."

"I expected you to make that request. These are your instructions. Listen carefully."

"Wait!" Elliot rushed to the kitchen. He snatched up a ballpoint pen that was lying near the phone for taking messages and scribbled frantically on the manila envelope he had tossed on the counter, trying to get the ink to flow.

"At nine p.m., you will come to Fisherman's Wharf."

"How will I find you?" He finally got the pen to work.

"Stand at the fuel dock at Hyde Street. I know who you are. When I determine that there is no law enforcement on the scene, I'll contact you. You give me the code key, I'll give you the girl. If anyone accompanies you— a bullet in the ear. Do you understand?"

"She needs to be with you, where I can see her."

"Nine p.m. The fuel dock at Hyde Street. Do you understand?"

"Yes. What—?"

The line went dead. Elliot, pen trembling in his hand, looked stupidly at the telephone receiver.

Connie slapped his arm. "Who was that? Was he calling about the girl you were with?" Her eyebrows formed a churlish V, and her lips were pressed into a knot.

From the other room came the sound of Carl Campbell and Frantz arguing about how much respect was due to agents of the U.S. government.

What had happened last night? Where had Morning Star gone? Someone had taken her. The man had taken her. Who was he?

Elliot's panic grew.

Why did he want a key? A key to what? What did he mean by his 'designation'? What was his 'directory'?

"Elliot!" Connie tugged at the poncho. "Who's Morning Star?"

Elliot shook himself. "No one. I need to. . . ." He looked at the manila envelope on which he had written the instructions. "I need to see Amadeo Knizner."

"What's going on here? This is very upsetting."

Elliot went to the sink and put his mouth under the tap and gulped cold water.

"Elliot," Connie said sharply. "I demand that you tell me who was on the telephone. He sounded like the man who came here. Was that who it was? What does he have to do with this girl?" She gasped. "You're having an affair, aren't you? Is that her hippie bag? You have her bag! Oh my God, first I'm kidnapped, then I find out that my fiancé has been cheating on me, and now a killer is calling him on the phone!"

The sound of her voice scarcely registered. Elliot turned off the tap and wiped his mouth and chin with the dishtowel. He looked blankly at the instructions he had scrawled on the manila envelope. He slit the top of the envelope with the ballpoint pen he was still holding and pulled the contents onto the kitchen counter. *From the Office of Frederick Happ, Private Investigator*: black-and-white photographs, time logs, an expense accounting, a summary report.

Elliot was dumbfounded. He spread the material across the formica countertop, unsure what he was looking at. His name was on every page, his face in every photograph.

Connie tried to push him aside. "What is that?"

As she reached for the envelope, the significance of the contents came clear to both of them. He grabbed her wrist and pulled her around, hard, so that they were face to face. Connie tried to scoop the papers together with her free hand. "That's not for you!" she cried.

Elliot thrust her back and held her with one hand while he shuffled through the photographs, putting events in order.

"That's personal material, Elliot! You're hurting me!"

He released her wrist.

She began to cry. She stamped her foot.

He stared at her, confusion and anger condensing in his eyes. Who was this person, this duplicitous person, this woman he was going to marry?

With sudden decision he folded the empty manila envelope lengthwise and jammed it under his poncho into his back pocket. Then he strode across the kitchen. "Frank! I need your car keys."

Frantz materialized in the doorway.

Elliot snapped his fingers. "Come on, come on!"

In an instant, Frantz had sized up the situation. His future brother-in-law was still largely unknown, but he knew his sister well. Her tears of rage were all he needed. "In the ignition, my brother."

"I need money."

Frantz went to the cabinet over the kitchen sink and took down a Folger's coffee can.

Connie, crying, protesting, cursing, clung to Elliot. "Let me explain," she pleaded.

Frantz popped the plastic top and pulled out a roll of cash. Then he picked up Connie's purse from the counter and took out her red leather wallet and removed all the money that was in it.

Elliot pocketed the cash. "Give me your student i.d. I need to use the library."

Frantz fished out his wallet and found his identification card.

"And your watch. Somebody walked off with mine."

He unstrapped the watch on his wrist and handed it over.

"I appreciate this. I truly do," Elliot said, swatting Connie aside. He lifted Morning Star's embroidered bag over his head and handed it to Frantz. "Take it. It's yours."

Frantz opened the bag and pulled out one of the foil-and-plastic-wrapped bricks. He weighed it in his hand. "No sweat, man."

"What is that?" Helen Campbell said. She and Carl were peering through the archway from the living room.

"Not now, Helen," Carl said.

Frantz put the brick of hashish back in the bag. "This is some kind of real shit," he said.

Elliot nodded. "Stay near the phone. I might call you. Do you have a map of San Francisco in the car?"

"Glove compartment."

"Elliot, please!" Connie stamped her foot.

"Get away from me."

"I just wanted to be sure! Please, Elliot. I just needed to know."

Elliot adjusted his poncho. He looked at Connie. "Now you know," he said.

PART FOUR

Pasadena, August 5, 2020

While we're eating dinner, Talia says that if this story were a movie, she would make the following changes:

Carl and Helen Campbell are deadweight. Their scenes would eat up unnecessary minutes. Delete them from the narrative. Connie and Frantz are enough Campbells.

Elliot's acid-trip should continue for several pages. Imagine what a good special-effects designer could do with that.

After being tied up in the auto shop and threatened with violence, Elliot and Morning Star should be so delighted to regain their freedom that they have sex in the Avalon Ballroom bathroom.

If Morning Star's shoulder bag is meant to achieve totemic status (I'm not sure where she acquired this vocabulary) the viewer (or as I like to say, the reader) should be able to picture the unique patterns stitched on it. Maybe something about where she got it.

First, just because Talia thinks she knows all the tricks for keeping a person's eyes glued to a screen does not mean she has insight into the centuries-old expectation that authors offer their readers a chance to dwell in the text, *without the benefit of special effects*. One of the things I like about books is they don't have to shape themselves to the imperatives—the tyranny (yes, dear daughter, that's the word)—of visual narrative. I like television shows and movies and YouTube videos. I don't criticize them for failing to be books, and I don't think she should criticize a book for failing to be a movie.

Second, an author has only so much latitude when weaving together history and fiction, especially when loved ones are involved.

Third, why does anyone want to have sex in a public bathroom? I know it happens a lot on cable shows, but what's so thrilling about committing carnal acts in a place where people piss and shit and spit in the sinks? (Don't pretend you're being sex-positive, Talia.)

Finally: totemic status?

She wonders, peevishly, why I bother to ask for her opinion. Don't I have any damn friends I can call? Or maybe I could make an effort to meet someone online; obviously, I'm sexually frustrated, yuck, and computer algorithms can be pretty amazing when it comes to putting people in bed together.

I ask that she kindly not change the subject.

This discussion turns into a meandering quarrel. If Talia had her driver's license, she would storm out and drive around for a while. But she doesn't have her license, and the August heat is punishing, and she doesn't feel like walking around in it. So instead of storming out, she goes to her room to watch baseball played in an empty stadium accompanied by the ersatz sound of last year's crowd, and I settle on the couch with my virtual red pen and try to decide if she's right. She often is.

• • •

Berkeley, June 9, 1967

Amadeo Knizner had never mastered chopsticks. Despite years of careful practice, he could not find the proper position for his fingers. Chunks of fried pork fell in his lap, rice scattered across the tabletop, bok choy ended up on other diners' plates. Inevitably, he had to abandon the chopsticks in favor of the fork wrapped in a red paper napkin the waitresses offered to the American customers without their requesting it. It vexed him that he, who loved Chinese food, Chinese art, and Chinese wisdom literature could not figure out how to eat like a Chinese person. It also vexed him that the music they played in his favorite restaurant was the local pop radio, strident and inane. He would have preferred something authentically Asian, although the family that owned the restaurant had lived in the East Bay for several generations and were in a better position to judge their customers' musical tastes than Knizner, who was, in fact, a naturalized citizen.

He scowled and picked up his fork.

The restaurant was crowded with office workers, graduate students, and a smattering of undergrads, including, in one corner, Jojo, who was sipping tea and contributing to the acrid haze of cigarette smoke that filled the room. Through a plate-glass window painted with a brutish dragon stepping into an enormous bowl of rice, Jojo watched a Chevy Impala cruise along the street. It was a good-looking car, dark red with white pinstripes, and he liked it, although he wouldn't be caught dead driving such a vehicle. In the distance a crowd was milling about in the soft spring air. Some women were chatting with the Berkeley cops standing along the edge of the campus.

Elliot slid into the booth across from Knizner. He laid the creased manila envelope on the table, next to the professor's open copy of the *I Ching*, on which rested the three square-holed oracle coins. Knizner had been recording the results of his tosses in a spiral notebook while waiting for his lunch. Elliot pulled his wallet from his back pocket and dropped it next to the envelope. Then he remembered what had happened the last time he put down his wallet, and he slipped it back into his pocket. He pushed his sunglasses up into his disorderly hair.

Knizner looked up, surprised, then pleased. "Elliot Ames—how marvelous [*ahem*]!"

"Your departmental secretary said you'd be here."

"Like clockwork [*ahem*]. I am a creature of habit [*ahem*]."

He examined Elliot more closely, taking in the wild eyes, the disheveled hair, the poncho flung over one shoulder, the denim shirtsleeves too short for his arms.

"I know," Elliot said, divining his thoughts. "I've had a rough twenty-four hours. I'm sorry I missed your seminar after I promised to sit in. I wanted to discuss some problems we've been tackling down in L.A."

"It would have been instructive for the students [*ahem*]," Knizner acknowledged. He waggled his fork dismissively. "Don't give it another thought [*ahem*]. You're busy with your nuptials, I suppose [*ahem*]." He offered a yellow-toothed smile. "Operation Matchmaker, wasn't it [*ahem*]? Not as trivial as it sounds [*ahem*]."

"Yes." Elliot decided to say nothing about Connie's betrayal.

"Did you track me down just to apologize for the seminar [*ahem*]?"

Elliot shook his head. "I need your professional expertise. Someone's life depends on my understanding something I don't understand."

Knizner gestured to the plate of pork and bok choy in front of him, but Elliot shook his head. He was too distressed to eat.

Knizner impaled a chunk of meat, dipped it in a little bowl of candy-red sauce, and brought it to his lips. "Most of life depends on things we don't understand [*ahem*]." Pleased to have devised this apothegm, he pulled the meat from the fork with his teeth and smacked his lips. "Would you like some meat [*ahem*]?"

"No, thank you. I'll have your ice-water if you don't mind." Elliot lifted the glass and drained it in a migraine-inducing gulp. "You're a code man," he said, massaging his temples. "You worked on Venona during the war."

"Did I [*ahem*]?"

"And you were at N.S.A."

"Was I [*ahem*]?"

"You understand the methods."

"As I recall, Elliot, you were in counterintelligence in Germany not so long ago [*ahem*]."

"I spent a year cleaning up radio signals, that's all."

Knizner continued to eat. "What do you need from me, my friend [*ahem*]?"

Elliot stopped rubbing his temples. "Don't Sleep in the Subway" rained from the speakers in the ceiling. The bell over the door tinkled as new customers arrived. In the corner a table full of doctoral students erupted in obscene guffaws. Managing to gather his roiling thoughts, he took the ballpoint pen from his shirt pocket and uncapped it and cleared his placemat so that he had something to write on. "Tell me about decryption keys. Assuming some kind of blind network in which the sender and the receiver are unknown, or only partially known, to each other, what kind of code would you use?"

Knizner's eyes sharpened. He laid down his fork and arranged his face in a pedantic attitude. "It does not matter whether the network is blind [*ahem*]. You use a Vernam cipher [*ahem*]. The one-time pad is virtually unbreakable [*ahem*]. Unbreakable but not absolutely secure [*ahem*]."

Elliot nodded. "Refresh my memory. I'm out of my field."

"Basically, what Vernam proposed in 1917 was an additive polyalphabetic stream cipher using a Boolean exclusive-or function [*ahem*]. Basic mathematics [*ahem*]."

"Right."

"The combining function he specified applied to the individual bits used in the Baudot code [*ahem*]. Shortly thereafter, Mauborgne suggested that the paper-tape key should contain random information to create an automatic one-time pad [*ahem*]. Shannon—you remember him—at Bell Labs showed that this system creates an unbreakable code, as long as the key is as large as the plaintext message, is never reused, and is kept secret [*ahem*]."

Knizner tore a sheet from his spiral notebook and began to write: $Pr [M=m \mid C=c] = Pr [M=m]$.

"You've seen this [*ahem*]?"

"Yes. The a posteriori probability that the message is equal to M conditioned on the observed ciphertext being equal to C is exactly equal to the a priori probability—."

"The problem," Knizner interrupted, "with using cipher machines for this business is that they have to involve mathematics to achieve their ends, and mathematics by definition is not random [*ahem*]. That's why you can't make your IBM machine generate a true random-number key, although it seems like a perfect task for a computer [*ahem*]. Otto Lieberich has demonstrated the superiority of pen and paper—at least for now [*ahem*]. No doubt our computers will manage it someday [*ahem*]. Developing secure ciphers is going to be essential for networked computers, when we get to that point [*ahem*]."

"I have a smart guy named Stefan Blicks. He would know about the problem."

"Why don't you call him [*ahem*]?"

"Time is of the essence, as is confidentiality. I know you, Amadeo. Besides, you know these problems from the inside."

"Do I [*ahem*]?"

"How do the users transmit the message?"

"Steganographically, hidden in plain sight [*ahem*]. You don't conceal the fact of the cipher-text communication [*ahem*]. If it's unbreakably encoded, meaning the key is generated randomly, it doesn't matter who sees it [*ahem*]. Perhaps you've heard of this notion—Kerckoff's Principle [*ahem*]. You send the message through the newspaper classified ads or via a shortwave numbers station [*ahem*]."

"There's a numbers station I monitor to help me sleep. I think it broadcasts from Eastern Europe." He thought of the ding DONG ding DONG sign-on tone, the "Ready? Ready?" query, the soporific effect of the woman's voice reading the sequences.

"So you keep your hand in [*ahem*]."

Knizner picked up one of the oracle coins lying on the open pages of the *I Ching* and began flipping it as he spoke.

"So: the one-time pad depends on a cryptographically secure random-numbers generator [*ahem*]. There are several methods, including, for example," tapping the book, "tossing these three coins and converting the resulting hexagrams to binary [*ahem*]. The randomness of the coin-flipping comes from atmospheric micro-disturbances and the imperfection of the musculature of the human hand [*ahem*]."

He turned the book so that Elliot could see the illustrations of the hexagrams. Elliot shifted restlessly on the booth; he was sick with worry about Morning Star.

"If we assign a value of 'two' to 'heads' and a value of 'three' to 'tails,' we can achieve a hexagram in six tosses [*ahem*]. Every solid line represents a 'one,' every broken line a 'zero' [*ahem*]. Thus we achieve random binary strings [*ahem*]. With randomness we have a chance at achieving perfect secrecy [*ahem*]."

"So how does this translate into practice?"

Knizner stopped flipping the coin. "The block cipher consists of two paired algorithms, one for encryption, the other for decryption [*ahem*].

Both algorithms accept two inputs, a block of size n bits and a key of size k bits, and both yield an n-bit output block [*ahem*]. The decryption algorithm D is the inverse function of encryption [*ahem*]."

Knizner continued describing the substitution-permutation network for some minutes, while Elliot scribbled notes on the red paper placemat, then, when he ran out of space, on the front of the manila envelope.

"The goal," Knizner concluded, "is to make it impossible to recover the cipher's internal state from the keystream [*ahem*]."

"What's the decryption key?" Elliot asked. It was all he really wanted to know, all that the unknown man had demanded of him.

Knizner poured a cup of tea from a porcelain pot and shrugged. "If it's a one-time pad, it would be printed and distributed [*ahem*]. Even if we design computers that can attack encrypted communication, they will not be able to break a one-time-pad communication [*ahem*]. It's crucial that the user not lose the key or get caught with it, or, God forbid, turn it over to an adversary [*ahem*]. That possibility is what makes an unbreakable one-time pad problematic [*ahem*]. A public book code is, in that sense, safer [*ahem*]."

"I don't have to be a cryptographer to understand how a common book code could be cracked through guesswork and pencil lead." Elliot tipped ice cubes from the water glass into his mouth.

A waitress appeared. "More tea for you?"

"No, thank you [*ahem*]. Just the check [*ahem*]."

Knizner turned back to Elliot and said, "So, my friend, tell me what this is all about [*ahem*]."

Elliot did not know how to explain his situation to Professor Knizner, because he was not sure what it entailed. He said, "Somebody—I don't know who, although I can make a reasonable guess—thinks that I have the key to a code. At least that's what I *think* he thinks. Or what he *wants* me to think. In any case, he's a very dangerous man."

"Why would someone believe you have a cryptographic key [*ahem*]?"

Elliot sucked in his breath and let it out slowly. "I don't know. I don't know what the code is. I don't know how it's delivered, and I don't know what the key is. I don't know why this person would think that I have the key with me, given what you've said about the dangers of losing it or being caught with it. But given my position at Pacifidyne, I assume it has to do with the work we're doing for ARPA. To be frank, this is a matter of life and death. You haven't been contacted in the last twelve hours, have you?"

"I have not [*ahem*]." Knizner's eyes roamed worriedly around the room. A light sweat broke out on his brow. He forced a laugh. "I'm glad the semester is over [*ahem*]. I might be leaving for Copenhagen on Monday [*ahem*]. Maybe sooner [*ahem*]. Almost certainly [*ahem*]."

"Who else besides the people at Defense would be interested in computer networking? The Russians, I suppose."

Knizner's unease increased. "God forbid they infiltrate the ARPA-net [*ahem*]. Perhaps it's the phone company [*ahem*]," he said, trying to make a joke of it.

On the other side of the room, Jojo lit a cigarette and cast glances at Elliot and Knizner. His body language suggested that he hankered to insert himself into the conversation, maybe cozy up to the professor before final grades went to the registrar's office, find out if the Computer Center needed a research assistant over the summer—anything to juice his G.P.A. and maintain his draft deferment, not to mention supplementing the $150-a-month stipend he was earning from the F.B.I. to keep tabs on campus radicals.

The waitress slid a lacquered tray onto the table. From habit, Elliot picked up one of the fortune cookies and tore the cellophane. He broke the cookie in half and read the message. He had seen this one before: *You will find peace in labor.*

Elliot put the strip of paper in his shirt pocket. He stood up and folded the placemat and put it in the manila envelope. Then, with the rain poncho thrown over his shoulder, he lowered the blue-tinted sunglasses over his eyes. "Thank you, Professor. I need to think now."

"Of course [*ahem*]." Knizner made a half-hearted effort to rise. "Best wishes for your honeymoon, my friend [*ahem*]."

On his way out, Elliot collected two more fortune cookies that had been abandoned among the dirty dishes on another table. As he passed, Jojo slunk out of the booth where he was lurking and sidled toward Knizner, who was again engrossed in tossing the oracle coins and writing in the spiral notebook.

• • • •

Los Angeles

"Henry! What's shakin', you old son of a gun?" A.S.A.C. Muncie offered Armbruster and Clegg a comic grimace and leaned back in his chair with the phone against his ear.

He listened.

"Izzat right?" His face grew serious. Dark. Darker. "I'll be in touch."

Flushing purple, he slammed the receiver into the cradle. "Do you know what Fagerberg wants? He wants us to check out a character named Elliot Ames. Pull his jacket. Toss his house. Official request to follow."

"Ames!" Clegg sat up straighter. "Why is San Francisco involved?"

"No idea. Son of a bitch never gives you anything."

"Let 'em do their own work," Armbruster said.

"You got that right," Muncie agreed. "Of course, we'll have to keep surveillance on his place, see if he surfaces. Goddammit, Fagerberg always gets what he wants."

• • • •

San Francisco

Bobby Dobell slumped on the wire café chair, weeping disconsolately. A half-dozen Hells Angels, stinking of beer and grass, scraped their boots uneasily on the concrete and gazed in various directions. A man's tears called for violent scorn, but the outlaw bikers' loyalty to—and financial dependence on—the chop shop left them confused and passive.

Rowdy Gomez put a tentative hand on his boss's shoulder. "It's all right, Bobby. It's just a hangover."

"It is!" Dobell wailed, quivering like an animal. "I'm drinking too much. Motherfucking Stokely!"

"Also, you know, the stress of life. It discombobulates a person."

Dobell was wracked with shameless sobs.

"You're upset, Bobby. Who wouldn't be?" Gomez jerked his chin in the direction of the old library chairs to which Elliot and Morning Star had been tied. The severed ropes lay on the floor. "The guy must've had a knife on him."

"You should've searched that motherfucker!" Dobell bawled.

"He looked like a civilian," Gomez defended himself. "It's okay to be upset. Any father would be if his little daughters had scampered. But let's focus on the future. Okay?"

"Okay." Dobell wiped his eyes.

"I'm on your side, brother."

"Thanks, Rowdy," Dobell snuffled. "You're a good friend."

"Rowdy's right," ventured one of the Hells Angels, a three-hundred-pound boulder who went by the name Half Pint and wore an Iron Cross on a chain over his rotting t-shirt. "We gotta think about the future. Maybe it's time to let this Stokely thing go." None of the bikers wanted to lose their supply of Stokely acid, which guaranteed an easier source of riding-around money than piecing out stolen auto parts; the chemist wouldn't be of much use if Bobby Dobell killed him.

Dobell rose slowly to his feet. He wiped his nose on his shirtsleeve, shook himself all over, and moved toward Half Pint until they were belly to belly in the center of the shop, ringed by the tattery crew. The moment hung.

"What did you say?"

Half Pint shifted uncomfortably. "I mean, the important thing is getting your girls back," he explained. "We got patrols all over the damn Bay. But offing Stokely, man, that makes problems. If you take him out, you're gonna knock over the whole. . . ." He could not think of the word he wanted.

"Economy," Gomez filled in.

"That's right. The whole economy."

There was a murmur of agreement which, in the thick throats of the outlaw bikers, sounded like elephants approaching through tall grass.

Through tear-swollen lids Dobell looked at the big man. Nodded slowly. Reached into the pocket of his khaki trousers. In a flash, the screwdriver swept around and plunged into Half Pint's abdomen. A thick layer of fat saved him from instant death. Half Pint yelped and grabbed furiously for Dobell, who kicked him in the crotch. The biker went down. Dobell leaned his weight on Half Pint's massive chest and seized a broken timing chain from a nearby trolley. He flailed the chain, delivering a half-dozen lacerating blows and reducing Half Pint's face to a gummy crush of flesh and bone, before Rowdy Gomez could act. Wrapping his arms around his boss, Gomez wrestled him away from the ruined heap that was Half Pint.

The other bikers began drifting through the customer-service door. Half Pint had spoken out of turn. He was only a prospect; he was not going to earn his patch.

By the time the Angels melted away, Dobell had calmed to his usual slow boil. He bent down and pulled the screwdriver out of Half Pint's side and wiped it on a rag and slid it back into his pocket. Half Pint moaned. Dobell breathed deeply through his nose. The glint returned to his eye. "That did me a world of good, Rowdy. Grab the shotgun and let's go find my babies."

Gomez retrieved the shotgun from the workbench and hopped over to raise the door of the garage. The rolling clash of twenty-two-gauge steel masked the sound of the City of San Francisco tow truck that was backing in from the street, piloted by the man responsible for both freeing the captives and introducing Dobell's teenage daughters to the rawboned ex-professor who had whisked them away. A familiar Ford Mustang dangled from the boom.

"Hey, boss!" Gomez called over his shoulder. "It's Eli."

Eli Tarr, catching sight of Gomez and Dobell in the side mirror, threw the truck out of gear and set the brake. The Hells Angels who were scattered on their choppers in front of the bar next door watched with dispassionate expressions. Several surprisingly clean-scrubbed women had joined them and were hanging on their old men's shoulders or sitting in their laps.

Gomez stood on his toes and leaned into the open passenger window. "Where you been, man?"

"Around," Eli mumbled. He scanned the street, checked his clipboard, glanced in the side mirror. "Around."

With a threatening glare at the outlaw bikers, Dobell approached the truck. He looked over the top of Gomez's head. "Excellent wheels, Eli. When you get her unhooked, see if you can do something about that pile of donkey dung in there." He jerked his thumb at Half Pint's oozing form.

Eli twisted to look over his shoulder. "Uh uh. No way. I do not need that kind of hairy trouble."

He released the parking brake with a thump.

"He ain't even bleeding that much," Dobell scoffed.

"Nope. Uh-uh."

"Well, goddammit, leave the motherfucking car."

"I'll come back at a better time," Eli said, looking straight ahead through the windshield.

"You leave that motherfucking car, Eli, or don't fucking come 'round here again."

"Then I'll say sayonara." He put the truck in gear.

Gomez jumped back and saluted with the shotgun. "Take care, brother!"

Dobell smacked the back of his head. "Don't you know how to use that thing?"

"I ain't gonna draw down on Eli. He's my friend." Gomez looked hurt. He waved again as the tow truck pulled onto the street.

"Let's go," Dobell said.

"What about Half Pint?"

"Forget it. One of their old ladies is probably a nurse. Leave the door open."

. . .

From the sedan parked at the end of the block, Grassmick and Bogosian had a clear view of Astro Auto Body. The agents had stripped off their suit jackets and loosened their neckties. Perspiration soaked through their shirts. Their foreheads gleamed. They looked like businessmen who had lingered too long in the cocktail lounge.

During the past few minutes, several grimy bikers with blurry tattoos on their forearms had exited the garage and were now sprawled on their motorcycles with their ladies, drinking beer and soaking up the sun. Their presence suggested, at least to Grassmick, that the aerospace guy was not entirely off the rails about this Dobell character and his auto-body business.

Then a city tow truck had wheezed stertorously up to the shop, pulling a Ford Mustang, and backed toward the garage with admirable precision. The door had rolled up, and the truck had stopped while the driver spoke with someone hidden from view. Grassmick wondered out loud why a city vehicle was making a delivery. He took the camera from the hardshell leather case that rested between his thighs.

Bogosian peered through his binoculars. He expressed his opinion that unless the Mustang was stuffed full of explosives or dead bodies, the matter was not F.B.I. business.

The two-way radio under the dashboard squawked and muttered obscurely.

Grassmick raised the camera and pressed the shutter release. "How do you know it's not?" he asked.

"Not what?"

"Stuffed full of explosives and dead bodies."

"We never have that kind of luck. Everybody else, it falls in their laps, but not us," Bogosian complained without lowering the binoculars. "I'm hungry. If I don't eat, I get stomach acid."

Grassmick thumbed the film-advance lever, but it wouldn't move; he had reached the end of the roll. He stowed the camera in the case. He was tired of hearing about Bogosian's stomach. "You don't eat a good breakfast is your problem. Then you bitch and moan about it until noon. Then you skip lunch, and you're a wreck for the rest of the day. Why don't you make a schedule?"

The tow truck suddenly jerked forward, belching exhaust, and headed away from them, exposing the men who had been talking to the driver. Grassmick started. He recognized the one brandishing the shotgun. It was the guy who had snatched the McGovern girl and the aerospace hippie, Elliot Ames.

The two miscreants waited for a delivery truck to pass, then crossed the street and climbed into a burgundy Chevy Impala.

"That's the car, Russ," Grassmick said excitedly. "That's the one from yesterday when they grabbed our target."

"You think she's in the building?"

"Could be."

"We should check. I mean, kidnapping and all, not to mention she's on the radar in L.A."

"Forget about L.A. Screw 'em."

"I also need to use the bathroom."

Down the block, the Impala's engine roared to life.

"C'mon, Ed." Bogosian reached into his armpit for his service weapon. "Let's take 'em right here, right now."

Grassmick restrained his partner. "Better idea. We follow these jokers, see if they connect up with Stokely. That aerospace guy said he's still in the Haight. If we miss another shot, Fagerberg'll put us on the desk. Then it's so long Tuesdays at the Mark Hopkins Hotel, huh?"

Bogosian chewed his lip. A car passed, going in the other direction. "Yeah. Bye bye, Rainbow Three. I can't afford to screw around on my own dime. Still, we should call in the location. If the McGovern girl's in there, we can score twice."

He fumbled under the dashboard for the radio.

"Better mention those bikers," Grassmick said.

The gleaming Impala surged away from the curb and headed towards them. A salvo of beer bottles from the Hells Angels exploded on the street behind the car.

"Down!"

The agents pressed themselves below window level. The Impala growled past like a prehistoric raptor, sending tremors through the sedan's occupants, and faded around the corner.

Grassmick sat up and started the car and performed a picture-perfect three-point turn.

Bogosian lifted his head. "How about stopping for some Rolaids?"

"Maybe they'll meet up at a drugstore, just to accommodate you," Grassmick said sarcastically; he did not want to talk about Bogosian's digestion.

• • •

Berkeley

Elliot sat at a long walnut table in the reading room of the Doe Memorial Library. A soft light came through the high windows. Despite the fact that the university was still in session, examinations loomed, and final papers remained unwritten, the library was deserted, as silent as a church. He was surrounded by piles of cryptography books, the pages of which were dense with mathematical formulae. He leaned over an open volume illuminated by an oiled bronze reading lamp. Next to his folded rain poncho rested the sunglasses and his wallet. Habit.

What to do?

He tore the flyleaf from *Cryptanalysis: A Study of Ciphers and Their Solutions* and began to write a list of questions and answers:

Q: Why does Mr. X want to meet at the fuel dock at Hyde Street?

A: He is familiar with the location. Public place. Easy for me to find. Has Morning Star nearby in case he needs to produce her.

Q: Where is nearby?

A: Probably a boat.

Q: Why does he have a boat?

A: Irrelevant.

Q: Is Morning Star alive?

A: Irrelevant. He believes I must act as if she is alive.

Q: Why didn't Mr. X put her on the phone when he called? Proof of life.

A: No phone there. He had to use a payphone. Supports boat theory.

Q: Why didn't he kill the Campbells?

A: He believed he needed them to reach me. (May have been correct.)

Q: Why does he put himself in a situation where he will be easily apprehended if I call the police?

A: He does not believe I will call the police.

Q: Why not?

A [Elliot thought for a while.]: He thinks I'm also afraid of the police.

Q: Why?

A: He believes I'm someone I'm not. Someone like him.

Q: Since I'm not who he thinks I am, why shouldn't I call the police?

A: He might have an alternative plan. He might behave unpredictably. Risk is too high.

Q: Why does he believe I have a code key with me?

A: Unknown.

Q: Why does he need the key right now? Why not wait until I'm at home to approach me?

A: Unknown.

Q: If I give him what he wants, will he kill me anyway?

A: Unknown but seems likely.

Q: How can he coerce me into giving him what he wants?

A: Torture M.S. Torture me—assuming he can get me off the dock.

Q: Why not tell me to come directly to the boat?

A: He's afraid I won't come. He's afraid M.S. is not important enough.

Q: What if I indicate that she is not important to me?

A: He will kill her.

Q: Does he believe I know who he is and what he wants?

A: Yes.

Q: What is his endgame?

A: Unknown.

After half an hour, Elliot stopped writing and leaned back. His mind turned and turned again. The reading room, in its stillness, seemed to tick.

Absently, he fished one of the fortune cookies from his shirt pocket. He tore off the cellophane, broke the cookie in half, and began crunching. The fortune read: *A wise person seeks limited ends.*

He slipped the strip of paper into his shirt pocket and began making notes again, trying to spur inspiration. He had no time. He felt sick. He felt guilty, terribly guilty, but he did not know why. He had done nothing to put

Morning Star in danger, nothing to create this situation; she had been the one motivating the strange events of the previous twenty-four hours, involving him when he did not want to be involved, stealing from him, drugging him. Yet he could not help feeling that he was responsible for her.

He tore the cellophane from another fortune cookie and broke it open. *Our days are preludes to nothing.*

He slipped the paper into his shirt pocket; but the words bothered him, and after a moment he pulled it out again, along with the fortune about the wise person and the fortune he had, out of habit, pocketed at the restaurant. He laid the three slips of paper one above the other on the varnished tabletop and studied the texts. Each of the fortunes was cast in exactly six words. It seemed a minor matter, a trivial coincidence, yet Elliot could not help feeling that the word-count conveyed something he should understand.

He picked up the torn cellophane wrapper and examined it: *Happy Smile Cookie Company, Las Vegas, Nevada*, in uneven green ink.

"Las Vegas?" he said out loud, his voice echoing through the somber room. "Really?"

The chair scraped loudly as he got up. He hastened to the circulation desk and pushed one of the ten-dollar bills from Connie's purse across the glass top. A student worker was perched on a stool, studying a book of nineteenth-century French nudes.

"I need change," Elliot said. "Quarters."

"Sorry, man." The student worker kept his eyes glued to a sybaritic painting by Delacroix. "We're not allowed to make change unless you're paying an overdue fine."

"Look, I badly need to make a phone call."

"Those're the rules," the student worker said.

Elliot thought fast. "Fuck the rules! Right? Fuck 'em! The rules are dead."

The student worker raised his head, brightening, and beheld the madman before him.

"Right on, man!" He gave a power salute. "Fuck the rules."

A minute later, Elliot was wedged into a phone booth in the basement, feeding quarters into the box.

. . .

Redondo Beach

Arthur Reuhl hunched over his table in Design Room Six, trying to figure out how his team had managed to come up with such half-baked solutions to a thermal-isolation problem in the new-gen ballistic missiles. There seemed always to be a gap between theory and execution which he could attribute to nothing except malice and sabotage. Maybe the men were drinking too much at lunch.

The telephone on his table rang.

"God *damn* it." He slammed down his slide-rule and reached over to scoop up the receiver. "Yeah?. . . Well, hey, Elliot! Aren't you supposed to be pawing through wedding presents or getting drunk or something?. . . Yes. . . What the hell? So the whole thing's off?. . . I'll tell Gordon and the wives. They'll be disappointed. . . Sure, I can do that. . . If it can't wait, it can't wait. I'll go right now. Hey! Did you hear about Percy Wu? Shot a guy trying to rob the restaurant. . . No kidding. . . Okay, I'm on it."

He stood up, knocking a pile of *Aviation Week* magazines to the floor, and lifted the sport coat hanging on the back of his chair.

Slipping into his coat, he went down the hall, through the clattering secretarial bullpen, and into the Wing, moving along the glass-walled corridor where managers paced like caged animals and murmured into their telephones, until he reached the computer lab. Elliot's team members, clumped around the room, were engrossed in matters that Arthur, as a mechanical engineer, did not fully understand. The punk who manned the console of the enormous computer—Stefan somebody—gave him a suspicious look.

As Arthur stepped into Elliot's doorless office, the telephone on the desk rang.

He picked up the receiver. "Yeah. I'm here."

Parking himself on the desk chair, he swiveled to face the corkboard on which his pal had fastened in chronological order the fortune-slips from hundreds of Peking Palace lunches.

"This'll take a while, Elliot. Got a pencil?"

He paused to light a cigarette. Then, beginning in the upper-left corner, he started reading the messages aloud: "*Expect water as you ask for wine. . . Rivers need spring. . . If you are afraid to throw dice you will never throw a six. . . Open your heart, open your mind. . . .*"

• • •

West Los Angeles

Although the van was parked in the shade of the sycamores, it was hot inside. The afternoon had been marked by excruciating monotony, broken only when some kids on roller skates had pounded perfunctorily on the side of the van as they clacked by. Clegg and Armbruster read the newspaper, played hearts, played gin rummy, played five-card stud. Clegg rejected Armbruster's proposal to turn on the radio for fear of running down the battery. Elliot Ames had not returned to his house.

"You ever feel like you want to tear your skin off?" Armbruster said.

"What do you mean?"

"I mean, your bones are jumping and grinding, and you can't get relief. Like your teeth are gonna pop out. Like you're turning inside out."

"You mean frustration?"

"I don't know," Armbruster said miserably. "Like you want to empty your service weapon into. . . ." His hand crept toward his underarm holster. "A watermelon or something. Sorry to lay this on you, Don. The wife doesn't want to hear about it."

"Well, I mean, why would she? Try taking her to the movies. *The Dirty Dozen*'s opening next week at the El Capitan."

"Yeah? Lee Marvin?"

"And Charles Bronson. I saw the billboard on the Strip."

• • •

Berkeley

On the long library table Elliot had stacked as many Yellow Page directories as he could carry from the reference section. The afternoon was dwindling.

The flyleaves of the cryptography books were filled with notations, front and back. Copying from the directory in front of him, he squeezed in another few lines.

He was looking for Chinese restaurants. There were few listings in some of the directories, but he found enough to give him what he needed.

He got up and went out to the phone bank and dialed a number in Torrance and waited for the long-distance operator to tell him how many quarters he needed to feed into the box.

There was far-off ringing on the line.

"Yes?"

"Hello? Is this the New Canton Palace?"

"Who is this please?"

"Are you the manager?"

"Who is calling please?"

"I have a question for the manager," Elliot pressed.

"I'm the manager."

"This might seem strange, but could you tell me which company supplies your fortune cookies?"

"You want to order some fortune cookies?"

"No. I want to know which company supplies them to you."

"You only get cookies if you order food. They are free."

"I understand," Elliot said impatiently. "Look, I only eat fortune cookies from the Happy Smile Cookie Company. Before I order anything, I need to know if you get your cookies from the Happy Smile company."

"One moment please."

There was the sound of dishes crashing and a woman yelling, then a long murmurous period, then the sound of breaking glass. Finally, the manager came back on the line. "Yes, Happy Smile fortune cookies. You want to order now?"

"Thank you very much," Elliot said. "Another time."

He hung up.

At the circulation desk he persuaded the radicalized student worker, who was drawing dirty pictures in a Krishnamurti book, to change another ten-dollar bill.

Back in the phone booth, he dialed 0.

"Operator."

"Yes, I'm looking for a Las Vegas number. The Happy Smile Cookie Company."

Pause.

"I'm not showing a number, sir."

"Is the number unlisted?"

"I'm not showing a number, sir."

• • •

Berkeley

From the den, where he was seated at the card table, playing Scrabble with himself, Carl Campbell could hear his daughter, his wife, and Sheilah Robinson talking in the dining room. He had last seen them ranged around the table with a pitcher of sangria. The tone of their conversation betokened a deepening disenchantment with men. Carl thought it best to keep to himself. His head hurt like hell where the maniac had slugged him; he thought he might have a concussion.

"I don't see how this is my fault," Connie said. She expelled a plume of smoke and stubbed her cigarette in an aluminum ashtray.

"Of course it's not your fault," Sheilah said. "Not all your fault. It's bad luck, bad timing. Mostly."

Helen sipped her drink. "The important thing now is to contact the guests."

"It's a train wreck," Sheilah declared.

"It's not too late to call Elliot's mother," Helen said. "I suppose it's his responsibility, though. And, of course, Reverend Ross. I hope he can find something else to do tomorrow night."

"You'll have to cancel the rehearsal luncheon," Sheilah said. "I'll take care of the caterer and the cake as soon as we finish the pitcher."

"If Frank lets you use the phone," Connie complained. "He's been hogging it all day. I feel like screaming."

Helen refilled her daughter's glass. She could not help thinking that Connie had maybe brought this on herself. It all had something to do with the documents that had come in the manila envelope.

At the kitchen counter, Frantz sat listening to the unhappy voices and guarding the telephone in anticipation of Elliot's call. While he waited, he marked his sister's brand-new copy of *The Naked Ape* with a ballpoint pen. The book was spread open on the bricks of hashish. Several calls had come for Connie regarding the wedding, and Frantz had told the callers to forget it, the whole thing was off, and hung up. Occasionally, he glanced out the window. Shortly after Elliot had left, the Berkeley patrol car had gone on its way.

The telephone rang. Frantz lifted the receiver. "Campbell residence."

"Hey, my brother, what's the story?"

"Jojo, my man. I can't tie up the line right now, brother."

"That's cool. Listen, man, I'll be grading exams for Knizner tonight, so if you fill out a blue book with your signature and i.d. number, I'll slip it in the pile."

"That's terrific! You're saving my ass." As Frantz was about to hang up, he had an inspiration. "Listen, man, I have a proposition for you. What's a kilo of Primo going for?. . . Know anybody with the bread?"

• • •

Berkeley

When Elliot returned to the reading room, he found some students sitting in a circle on the floor with a fifth of vodka. Class notes and purple-streaked mimeographed pages layered the spaces between them. As the students passed around the bottle, they seemed to be waiting for a signal to begin studying. Someone lit a joss stick.

Elliot laid the *Los Angeles Herald Examiner*, hanging from a long wooden rod, on the table. He had noticed it on a rack with other newspapers from across the nation. The front page featured the below-the-fold headline A SIDE OF LEAD: ROBBER KILLED AT RESTAURANT.

As Arthur had reported, Percy Wu had shot a robber at the Peking Palace. Elliot followed the "continued on" pointer to page six, where he was surprised to find a story about a private investigator named Frederick Happ, who had been beaten and shot in his office in Van Nuys—the same Frederick Happ who had sent the manila envelope in his hip pocket. He remembered that the F.B.I. agents had mentioned something about Connie and a murder in the San Fernando Valley. He was surprised by the coincidence.

Then he was not surprised. In a flash he understood that whoever had taken Morning Star prisoner had also killed Frederick Happ. He did not know how he knew this. But after the events of the previous night, which had shattered his sense of normal order and scattered his senses to the wind, he knew it was true. This had been a day of revelations.

He stood and gathered his papers, an idea of what he needed to do next taking shape in his mind.

· · ·

San Francisco
Stanley Stokely, strolling along Fisherman's Wharf in a personal atmosphere of grooviness, nibbled honey-glazed donut holes from a bag. Surrounded by the Dobell sisters, he moved like an emaciated prophet, like a column of bayou air, over the paper scraps and cigarette butts that sullied the waterfront. His mustard-yellow corduroy suit with a floral-print shirt and a black bowler hat matched his attitude of cosmic hipness. The triplets were attired in silk-crepe tunics, spangled shorts, and white sandals with flowers on the straps. The quartet moved through the scattering of sightseers and fishermen, who turned, one and all, to watch them go by. They could not have been more conspicuous.

As they neared the marina, where the white and green Monterey clippers, prows raised like a lesson in geometry, bobbed at their berths, Stokely began to discourse: "You see, my dears, if we are to attend the festival next weekend, we must needs obtain certain substances. I have a hankering for a potent tetrahydrocannabinol. To my chagrin, I have yet to discover a way to synthesize the effects of Mother Nature's product. The secondary metabolites are extraordinarily complex. Nothing on earth mellows Papa's buzz like a pungent bowl of resin. Unfortunately, our fair city is experiencing a shortage of quality hashish. But a little birdie tells me that my dear friends Terence and Andre are due from Mexico with a load of blonde Lebanese. For my part, I have a delightful batch of STP I'm yearning to release into the culture. If we can locate their craft, Papa is ready to do some horse-tradin'."

The rock cod and halibut highliners had come back long ago, along with the salmon boats, which ranged up the line to Fort Bragg. The crews going after sable and Dover sole were preparing to venture out. Snatches of guttural third-generation Italian could be heard on the decks. Seagulls fought over a pile of garbage. Nearby, someone was grilling chicken, and the aroma blended with the stench of the fish houses on Leavenworth Street.

Moving royally around stacks of crab pots and draped nets drying in the creosote-scented air, Stanley Stokely paused to examine the name painted on the stern of each boat, bending formally at the waist, as if inspecting sarcophagi at the British Museum. The Dobell sisters whispered among themselves and inclined their bud-like faces towards the sea lions poking their noses through the surface of the lustrous green water.

In the belly of the *Sally Belle*, Morning Star's hearing had become acute. She detected the lapping of water and muted voices, the faint scrape of boots and the fainter sound of three pairs of sandals, accompanied by the tap of a walking stick on the planks, once for every four steps.

. . .

Berkeley

According to the phone directory, the nearest RadioShack was on University Avenue. Elliot tore out the page and folded it into his pocket.

Then he telephoned the Campbell house. Frantz answered, and Elliot asked if he would meet him at the store. "I'm sorry I had to take your car," he said.

"No sweat. My man Jojo's over here doing some business. He can drop me down there."

When he got to the RadioShack, Elliot parked the Beetle in the loading zone, risking a ticket or a tow. He hoped the City of Berkeley policed its curbs more leniently than did San Francisco. Then he had second thoughts and drove around, feeling precious minutes slip by, until he found a legal parking spot two blocks away.

A few customers—serious men, pipe-smokers, tinkerers—were picking through the racks of packaged capacitors and transistors, relays and rectifiers, occasionally exclaiming over their finds. The parts were plentiful. The cheap, private-label gadgets on the back shelves seemed perfectly designed for modification by the amateur science-fair crowd and were more than sufficient for Elliot's needs.

Moving systematically through the cramped and cluttered aisles, he gathered into his folded poncho batteries, a portable shortwave-radio receiver, a coil of #18 insulated copper wire, an assortment pack of other wire, two sets of three-watt walkie-talkies, a Realistic-brand portable tape-recorder, a half-dozen three-inch reels of tape, headphones, a Phillips screwdriver, two straight screwdrivers of differing sizes, a wire cutter, a needle-nose pliers, a battery-powered soldering iron, rosin-core solder, capacitors, resistors, an ohm meter, a wristwatch ("for the Man-on-the-Go"), and a roll of masking tape. He dumped the goods on the sales counter.

A clerk with a flattop haircut examined the gear through half-glasses. He tapped the shortwave receiver. "You'll have to wrap some copper wire around the whip. These devices have crappy reception, pardon my phrasing."

"They certainly do," Elliot agreed. "Where can I find an Army-Navy store? I need binoculars and some parts you don't carry here."

"Try San Pablo Street," said one of the other customers, who had wandered over to inspect Elliot's purchases. "I'm sure you've seen it."

"Then I wouldn't need to ask," Elliot said shortly, glancing through the front window to see if Frantz had arrived.

The clerk picked up the portable shortwave radio and turned it over. "Do you ever listen to the Latin-language news broadcast out of Belgium? Sundays? Five p.m.?"

"Haven't heard it."

The clerk appealed to the other customer. "Do you know the Latin news show on Sundays? I can't remember the frequency."

"I'm sure I could locate it," Elliot said.

"It's pretty remarkable. Of course, you have to understand Latin," the cashier said smugly and tugged on his red vest. "If you're interested, you might want to invest in a higher-quality device and maybe a hundred-forty-foot wire. This model won't do the job." He tapped the receiver. "Sundays, five p.m. That's Pacific Time."

"Thanks for the recommendation," Elliot said curtly.

"You'll probably want a higher-quality device. You should buy an Eddystone."

Elliot dug some money out of his pants and slapped it on the counter. "I'm not looking for high sensitivity. And I don't want to worry about intermodulation. I'm buying a portable unit because I'm specifically not at home with my Eddystone."

"You're going to get a lot of interference," stuck in the customer.

"Maybe you could modify this model with some kind of preselector," the cashier said. "Better yet, buy a Blaupunkt. Or a Grundig. We don't carry those." He burped into his hand.

"Can I pay now, please?" Elliot said.

"Suit yourself." The clerk adjusted his eyeglasses and, carefully re-examining each item, began to ring up the sale. By the time he was done, Frantz had arrived.

. . .

San Francisco
Bobby Dobell and Rowdy Gomez had been, it seemed, up and down every hill in the city. Hunger gnawed. Near the Panhandle they recognized a

luncheonette where they sometimes met Eli Tarr with a list of makes and models to prowl for. The place had terrific meatloaf.

"Haven't seen you boys in a while," said the waitress without a trace of interest. She was a musty middle-aged woman with a stack of orange hair and a crust of makeup. She pulled her order pad from the pocket of her polyester uniform.

"Two meatloaf specials," Dobell said.

"And two iced teas," Gomez added.

"And two slices of banana-cream pie."

While they waited for their food, Dobell leaned back in the booth and stared moodily out the flyspecked window. A dark sedan—an unmarked cop car if ever he saw one—crept by. At the corner, the sedan stopped, and a sweaty-looking individual in a suit climbed out of the passenger side and pushed his way through the mass of freaks and hippies swirling around the intersection. All over the city, it seemed to Dobell, parades of new arrivals— stoned, boisterous, dressed like extras from a mishmash of movie epics— clogged the sidewalks and barnacled the stoops and bus benches. Their presence made it difficult to spot his daughters and the acid-slinging freak in the purple hat who had enticed them from home.

Although the sidewalks were crowded, only a few old-timers in buttoned-up raincoats ventured into the diner. The red-and-white-checked curtains were faded and moldering, the linoleum floor gray with neglect. Hard lumps of chewed gum studded the undersides of the tables. Strips of flypaper festooned the ceiling. Even the hippies, Dobell mused, wouldn't set foot in the dump. He loved the privacy.

The waitress, wheezing, returned with a tray of meatloaf, mashed potatoes, and green beans on heavy china plates. She set down a plastic basket of sliced bread and two age-clouded glasses of iced tea in which floated shriveled slices of lemon.

Gomez began to eat as if he were demolishing an old jalopy.

Dobell looked at him and shook his head. As he tasted his food, he glanced again through the window and spied a familiar figure hobbling down the street: Little Pete. His jaw was swollen, and the skin around his eyes was bruised and ugly. His left arm was in a sling.

"Hey, Rowdy, look who's coming."

Gomez stopped eating and looked out the window. "Well now."

Dobell rapped his knuckles on the plate glass. Little Pete turned, terror flashing across his battered face. Dobell motioned for him, and to his surprise, Little Pete came into the diner. He looked around at the elderly patrons and pulled up a chair from another table. Trembling, he lowered himself carefully onto the seat.

"You see my dentist?" Dobell inquired.

"Soon as I lose this hardware," Little Pete said through clenched teeth. He spread his lips with his fingers to reveal a mouthful of metal.

"Are you high? You're shaking like a motherfucker."

"Naw, man."

"I guess you haven't heard from Stokely," Dobell said. "We're still tryna run that butthole to ground."

"That's the thing," Little Pete said, his voice cracking with excitement. "He's down to the marina. There's a boat comin' with some quality hash, and I'll bet my ass he's looking to trade for it. He can't manufacture Lebanese blond in his basement."

Dobell laid down his fork. His eyes were bright and dangerous. "Are my girls with him?"

"Most definitely. I saw them on Jefferson. The boat ain't there yet, but Stokely'll go back. He wants to use that shit to get in with the Grateful Dead."

"What time?"

"I don't know. After dark, I think."

Dobell pushed out of the booth. "Let's move, rough stuff," he said to Gomez.

"I'm not done eating," Gomez protested.

"Get up. I want to go home and catch a nap before dark." He pulled out a handful of money and tossed a few bills on the table. Then he leaned over and tucked a twenty-dollar note into Little Pete's shirt pocket. "No hard feelings, guy." He patted him on the shoulder and pointed at their half-consumed dinners. "All yours. There's pie coming."

• • • • •

Little Pete fidgeted, morosely eyeing the unfinished meatloaf and green beans he could not open his mouth to eat. He had moved into the booth so that he could look out the window. Sipping Rowdy Gomez's iced tea through a paper straw, he read the mimeographed page he had found in the gutter on his way from one place to another:

San Francisco Open Your Golden Gate for the Sons and Daughters of America / Be Yourself in Golden Gate Park / Soulstice Release of Inhibitions Leading to a Long Overdue Communal Orgasm / Begin the Foreplay Now / Loosen Up / June 21.

As the glass emptied, the straw made a stuttering slurp.

A man in a limp suit slid into the booth across from Little Pete and slapped a leather wallet on the tabletop. He flipped it open to reveal his credentials.

"Oh, man," Little Pete said and pushed away the empty glass. "Federal pigs."

"Watch your mouth," Bogosian said.

"What d'you want, man?"

"The two guys who just left. One of them was named Bobby Dobell. Who was the other one?"

"Why should I tell you shit?"

Bogosian's hand shot across the table and clamped onto Little Pete's injured arm.

He yelped.

"Because if you don't," Bogosian said, "I'm going to take you to a dark place and fuck up your other arm and both your legs and maybe finish off what's left of your teeth. Then I'm going to arrest you. You don't want to look all ugly when you go to court, do you?"

"Rowdy Gomez," Little Pete managed. "He's some kinda demolition-derby champ."

Bogosian released Little Pete's arm, and Little Pete grasped it with his right hand and whimpered.

The waitress came over and put down two plates of banana-cream pie. She looked at the two men, started to say something and shook her head, sweeping up the money Dobell had left. She moved off toward the register.

Bogosian licked his lips. He picked up a fork and began to eat.

The bell over the door sounded and a moment later, Special Agent Grassmick dropped onto the chair formerly occupied by Little Pete. "I couldn't find parking anywhere," he complained. He plucked a paper napkin from the plastic holder and wiped his face. "Now we've lost Dobell, goddammit."

Little Pete made a move to stand. "I gotta book, man."

Bogosian, his mouth full of meringue, rapped the table with his knuckles. He swallowed. "Right here until I say otherwise."

Little Pete eased back onto the booth.

Bogosian turned to his partner. "This little fuck—. What did you say your name was?"

"Pete."

"This little fuck was just about to tell me about Bobby Dobell."

"Where's he going?" Grassmick said.

"The hell I know?"

"You know. They took off like bats outta hell. Are they meeting Stanley Stokely?"

"You know about that?" Little Pete exclaimed, looking from one agent to the other.

Grassmick smiled.

"Just let me get on with my day, man," Little Pete moaned.

Grassmick started in on the other slice of pie, and Bogosian took over. "Where are they meeting?"

"I don't need this hassle, man. I ain't even sure you pigs have jurisdiction."

"What did I say about taking you to a dark place?" Bogosian reminded him.

Grassmick laid down his fork, leaned over, and blew a hot gust of gingival air in Little Pete's face. "Let's not make a scene." He put his hand on the back of Little Pete's head and sucked in his breath for another go.

"Okay, okay! Jesus. What do I care about that psycho? Bobby and Rowdy went to take a nap. Then they're goin' to Fisherman's Wharf. Stokely's hangin' around there with Bobby's girls."

"The girls. We know about them," Grassmick said. "Where exactly?"

Little Pete shrugged. "They're waitin' for a boat."

Bogosian put down his fork and leaned back. "So that's it," he said. "That seals it. They're bringing in firepower."

"That's it," Grassmick agreed.

"Right under our noses."

• • •

Eli Tarr hummed an aimless tune as the tow truck trundled along the street. He was trying to accumulate some overtime hours with the city; it might be some time before he was back in Bobby Dobell's good graces. At the corner he spotted a dark sedan parked at a hydrant. His humming rose a couple of decibels. He pulled into the intersection and then backed the truck toward the sedan. When he climbed out and peered into the car, he saw a two-way radio under the dashboard. A cop car. Grinning, he ambled back, in his loose-hinged way, to lower the hook.

• • •

Pegasus lay on the floor of the wheelhouse of the *Sally Belle* and pulled a blanket over himself. He needed to rest.

• • •

West Los Angeles
"Where the heck is Fundy?" Bert Armbruster complained. "I gotta get outta here. My kid's got Little League tonight."

"Oh, yeah?" Clegg said noncommittally. "How's their record?"

"I don't know," Armbruster admitted. "I only go so I don't have to go home. All I get at the house is an earful of you know what. She counts my beers, out loud."

Clegg leaned over the seat of the van and peered through his binoculars. Elliot Ames's place made him envious. In the back yard, he could see the brick barbecue pit and the coping of the swimming pool. He wished he had a swimming pool and a barbecue pit. And a high-end stereo system. He suspected that Hawk Fundy had walked off with Ames's stereo after they had told him not to, but he did not want to attract more attention from the nosy neighbors by going into the house to confirm his suspicions.

After a hot, smothering hour-long silence, a yellow Pontiac pulled into the driveway.

"Who's this now?" Clegg murmured.

Armbruster crawled up beside him and peered through the windshield.

Someone got out and opened the trunk and took out a cardboard box that appeared to be filled with party decorations. He was dressed in a short-sleeved white shirt and olive-green gabardine slacks. His horn-rimmed glasses reminded Clegg where he had seen him: "That's one of the Pacifidyne guys that hang around the China One location."

"Do we have a name?"

"Search me."

With the box under his arm, the man strolled up the walk and stooped to retrieve the key from under the milk box. He went into the house and shut the door.

In the dining room Gordon Blackmon set the cardboard box on the table and began pulling out rolls of silver and gold streamers. He took out a banner that, when unfurled, spelled out CONGRATULATIONS NEWLYWEDS, and a series of humorous pasteboard panels featuring a bewitching bride and a panicked-looking bridegroom in advancing stages of undress. He had left work at lunchtime—the Peking Palace was closed—to visit a novelty store on Sawtelle. Elliot and Connie were going to get a real kick out of the decorations when they got back from Hawaii.

"What do you think?" Armbruster said.

"He knew where to find the key."

"Anybody could find it. We found it."

"Yeah."

"It's not like we can just go inside."

"Yeah."

"Maybe he knows where Ames is."

"Probably."

"I say we move on it."

Clegg grabbed his suit coat. "What about your kid's game?"

Armbruster, half-standing, duck-walked toward the rear of the van. "It's Little League. Nobody cares."

. . .

San Francisco

The boat rose and fell on gentle swells. A ghostly creaking and squealing of mooring lines swept along the pier. On the floor of the wheelhouse, Pegasus came abruptly awake. He kicked his legs free of the blanket and stood with care, looking through the dirty window and contemplating the bay. He felt as if he had been fighting wild dogs.

By now Canis Minor must have a clear idea of what was happening. What was the next move? It was still possible that Canis would try to contact the *rezidentura*, although Pegasus was certain that Sagittarius and Ursa Major would not risk getting involved. Canis would come, and he would come prepared; he would suspect he was walking into a death trap. If he showed any reluctance to reveal himself, the girl might have to be brought out. It was unclear what she meant to him. Pegasus was almost sure she was not involved in operations; she was a bystander, a civilian. She was a bargaining chip.

At some point he would have to kill her. If he could lure Canis Minor onto the boat, he could dispose of both of them at the same time. Ideally, he would take the Monterey clipper out to sea, but since he had no nautical skills, he would have to settle for dumping the bodies overboard after dark.

If the *rezidentura* connected the bodies to the *Sally Belle*, the axe, Pegasus hoped, would fall on Sagittarius.

By the time he finished with this business, it would be too late to catch a flight back to Burbank. That meant taking a motel room, with all the germs and bedbugs and revolting epidermal shedding of previous occupants. He felt his stomach turn.

In a few minutes his queasiness passed, and he secured the hatch and headed for the Italian diner.

. . .

The narrow back seat of the Beetle was strewn with stripped wires and electronic parts, and there was the smell of rosin-core solder. As they reached the exit from the Bay Bridge, Frantz, who was driving, cast a curious glance at Elliot. "You explained what's happening with all the gear, but you never told me where you were all afternoon."

Elliot turned his head slowly from the window. "What?"

"Where were you before the RadioShack?"

"Oh," Elliot said. He blinked rapidly and shook his head. "Sorry, I was thinking about something. This person who called—this person who has the girl I told you about—

"Morning Star."

"Yes. He demanded that I give him a code key."

"What's that?"

"A key used to decipher coded messages."

"Like spy codes?"

"So I suspect. After this fellow called, I went to see a friend of mine who knows more about codes than I do. He told me about random-number ciphers, the kind someone might use in the line of work my—my adversary is in. Then I went to the library. To be frank, I was panicking. These kinds of things don't ordinarily happen to me, and I was still experiencing the effects of the drugs."

"No doubt."

"Once I started reading and thinking about random-number ciphers, the flipping of oracle coins, ciphers and their solutions, patterns emerged. At least they seemed to emerge. I started clutching at interpretations. That's the thing about the human mind: it's a meaning-making machine. The computers I work with can *uncover* patterns, but human beings *make* patterns out of almost nothing. I started seeing weird similarities in the messages in fortune cookies. Did you know that this week, every paper fortune I've seen has exactly six words? Between twenty-four and twenty-nine characters, if you count the spaces between words. I called my colleague at Pacifidyne to check. I pin those silly slips of paper on the bulletin board in my office. It turns out the character-counts are different every week. Twenty-nine characters and six words this week. Eighteen characters and five words last week. Thirty-nine and nine the week before that, with some permutations thrown in."

"That blows my mind!" Frantz drummed his palms against the steering wheel. By now they were driving along the Embarcadero toward North Beach.

"Mine too. While I was talking to my colleague, I noticed the yellow-pages directory in the phone booth, and it gave me another idea. I went to the room where they keep the national directories and started looking through the phone listings for defense contractors on the West Coast. Every single aerospace, electronics, and communications company or research institution I know about in California or Washington State—Teledyne, Lockheed, Pacifidyne, Aerojet, McDonnell, Honeywell Marine, RAND, Northrop, Douglas, Rockwell, Pacific Semiconductor—is within four blocks of a Chinese restaurant where, I can guess, a significant number of employees eat. I thought, Ah ha! Each restaurant is a node in a communications network in which the sender and the receiver are unknown to each other. The fortunes from the cookies distributed by the Happy Smile Cookie Company in Las Vegas are redundant message blocks used in conjunction with radio messages, either as authentication signals or as a kind of packet-delivery system. The owners of the restaurants have no idea that they are being used. The Peking Palace in Redondo Beach, where I eat every day, along with a couple hundred Pacifidyne employees, was part of a blind distributed network. Potentially robust."

"Far out!" Frantz said.

"But, of course," Elliot went on, "my theory was utterly absurd. My mind was grasping at straws. Who would bother with a scheme like that? It was a kludge."

"Oh." Frantz looked disappointed. "I don't know what a kludge is."

"An ill-assorted collection of parts. The scheme was too complicated. A code—a communication system—needs to be complex, not complicated."

"So did you figure it out?" Frantz said. "I mean, is everything cool?"

"Yes. Go east here. We need to start scouting locations."

Frantz piloted the Volkswagen along North Point, down Hyde, back along Beach Street, and north on Jones, circling the area three times in the early twilight, until Elliot was satisfied. He directed him to the curb. Frantz set the brake.

"You remember what to do?"

Frantz nodded.

Elliot handed him one of the walkie-talkies he had purchased. A piece of masking tape with the word *Frantz* was stuck to the top. "I'll call you on this one. Stay with the car until 8:50 or until you hear from me."

"Got it."

He handed him a second walkie-talkie. The masking tape read *Contact*. "This one goes to the man, Mr. X. He'll probably be at the fuel dock. We'll have to see. All you need to do with the rest of the equipment is turn it on, just like I showed you. He'll find you quickly enough."

"This is some kind of spy stuff."

Elliot nodded. "Some kind."

He climbed out, leaving Morning Star's embroidered bag, which was now filled with gear, with Frantz. He began moving down the street, carrying the rain poncho and his own pair of walkie-talkies in a paper RadioShack bag. Around his neck hung the binoculars from the Army-Navy surplus store.

· · ·

Inside the Italian diner, Pegasus pushed away his bowl of cioppino. He had no appetite. He never did these days. By his elbow on the counter rested the purple top hat. Binoculars hung around his neck. He picked up the hat and carried his check to the register and politely paid his bill without removing his gloves and exited the restaurant, slapping the hat against his thigh as he moved to a position to the west where he could observe the wide sweep of the wharf. He assumed Canis Minor would arrive early to reconnoiter. He might already be here.

He doubted that Elliot Ames would have enlisted confederates; his would necessarily be a solo operation. But the years had taught him to be wary. Eyes were always watching. Even when he was certain they were not, they were.

Pegasus removed the binoculars from around his neck. They were not the high-quality Swiss model he preferred—he had found them on the fishing boat: an ancient Manon product—but they were sufficient to the task. He scanned the wharf, following the progress of a tall man in a colorful suit and three girls in matching outfits as they sauntered from the fishing boats towards the Italian diner. They went inside. Through the front window, he could see the girls, talking all at once, arrange themselves in a booth while the man made his way toward the restroom at the back.

Pegasus swept the binoculars back across the wharf. The person he recognized as Elliot Ames—despite the striped pants, work shirt, and disheveled appearance—was coming down Hyde Street. He was carrying a paper bag. He turned east, mingling with the early evening crowd of fishermen, tourists, hippies, and neighborhood people, and disappeared from view behind the diner.

• • •

As Elliot climbed onto a trash bin and reached for the rusted iron ladder that led to the roof, the evening sun painted him in liquid gold. He swung a leg up and gained a foothold. Clutching the RadioShack bag under one arm, he made his way to the top. The location could not have been better.

He crossed the roof through the fishy steam pouring from the ventilators and positioned himself behind a low parapet at the front of the diner. There was the sound of a transistor radio playing in the crowd of sightseers below. A happy dog barked. Elliot put down the paper bag and took out the rain poncho and folded it twice to make a pad to protect his elbows. Stretching flat on the gull droppings, he lifted his head above the parapet and raised the binoculars. He assumed that the person he was meeting would arrive early to ensure the location had not been compromised. He also assumed that his adversary had not enlisted confederates. His was almost certainly a solo operation. Then again, his adversary would assume, wrongly, the same about him.

It was 8:28.

Shifting on his elbows, he focused the binoculars on the fishing boats that had settled in for the night. Here and there sat gulls, quiet and drowsy, and some of the fishermen loitered on their boats. He did not see anyone who looked prepared to kill him.

• • •

This trip was not turning out as expected. In the cold, dark, wet hold of the boat, Morning Star wondered if she was experiencing some kind of karmic punishment. She remembered a mantra Dr. Malcolm had given her during an all-night therapy session and began to repeat it as best she could with the tape over her mouth: *shuba, shuba, shuba.* Barbs of hunger shot through her belly. Her tongue felt as dry as cardboard. Her mind undulated with the residual effects of the LSD. In some respects the last twenty-four hours had been the adventure she had imagined while sitting through endless anthropology lectures or shadowing executives with wandering hands at the May Company, although her daydreams had not included so much physical discomfort. On the other hand, she reminded herself as she slipped in and out of consciousness, she'd never heard of anyone being kidnapped twice in one day. Surely, it meant something.

• • •

Streetlamps spangled the shimmering hillsides. People moved lazily about the wharf in the lingering blue of the June dusk, watching the fishing crews tend to their gear, content to be together with one another. The sounds of the day had receded, and in their place came the lapping of water and the distant moan of foghorns. A boy with a classical guitar sat cross-legged at the edge of the pier and began to play, as skillful as Segovia. Next to him, a woman skipped rope.

At 8:57, Elliot had not spotted anyone who might be his man. At 8:59, he lifted the walkie-talkie that had *Frantz* written on a piece of masking tape on the top.

"Turn on the shortwave. Over."

"Copy that."

A half-minute later, from where Frantz was sauntering along the wharf, came a faint, familiar four-note musical chime: ding DONG ding DONG. Then: "Ready? Ready?" and the woman's monotonous voice. "One two three nine... zero two nine one... five four two two... eight four zero one...."

Elliot spoke into the walkie-talkie: "Move along the perimeter toward the fuel dock. Stay near people. Stay in sight of the diner."

Elliot watched Frantz, a cigarette between his lips, cross the open area between the Italian diner and the fuel dock. He moved casually, Morning Star's bag on his shoulder, the walkie-talkie in one hand and the shortwave radio in the other, a hippie among hippies, digging the scene.

As he approached the fuel dock, a nondescript man with thin, light hair, dressed in slacks and a windbreaker, moved to intercept him. His gait was stiff, like that of someone who has banged his shin. He carried a familiar purple hat.

The man met Frantz before he reached the hut on the dock. He spoke. Frantz turned off the droning shortwave and put it in the shoulder bag and took out the second walkie-talkie, the one marked *Contact*. He handed it to the man and turned on his heel, joining a convivial band of Friday-night revelers moving across the wharf.

Through the binoculars, Elliot watched Mr. X watch Frantz go into the diner. Although he appeared sturdy enough, the man gave the impression of occupying very little space. He stepped back into the shadows under the eaves of the hut and lifted the walkie-talkie.

"Canis Minor?" The signal was clear and present.

Elliot had thought the matter over and had decided to leave this misunderstanding of his identity unchallenged. Let Mr. X think he feared the law, that he was duplicitous, a traitor; let him think he was a problem. He pushed the talk button. "This is Elliot Ames. You recognized the numbers station. It means I have you pegged. Over."

The walkie-talkie crackled.

"Very good, Canis. Where are you?"

"On the roof of the diner. You lost track of me from your position."

The man on the fuel dock lifted his binoculars.

Elliot stood. Nobody who was milling about on the wharf noticed him. He squatted again behind the parapet. The walkie-talkie squawked.

"I didn't expect you to have an associate, Canis."

"I might have several," Elliot replied.

"We both know you're a solo operator. That's how it works."

"Okay. Let's say I am. But I don't recommend coming onto the roof. I'm armed. So is my associate."

"I don't think so." A testy note had crept into the man's voice.

"Can you risk finding out?"

"Can you risk trying me? If you shoot me now, you'll never find the girl."

There was nothing more to say on the subject.

"What's your name?" Elliot said.

"You don't expect me to answer that."

"What difference does it make? You've identified me—Canis Minor."

Pause.

"Pegasus."

"Good. Who are you, Pegasus?"

"I check your signals and recover the material from the drop site. Your payments come through me."

"As I suspected." A light burst of static.

"You don't know me," Pegasus said.

"I think I do. I did enough work in counterintelligence with the Army in '59 to have some idea what I'm talking about. In your organization you occupy a position of middling importance. You're a utility man, a fixer. Not a case officer. Not even a recruiter. In fact, you don't have any direct access to your assets on the ground nor to your superiors. They contact you, and you handle routine day-to-day matters, picking up sensitive material that is passed up through the ranks. Once in a while, something big happens, and you take care of it. I know for a fact that you've killed at least one person, but I suspect you've killed more. You're like a crab. You never move up in the organization, just side to side if you're lucky, operating blindly most of the time, given barely enough information to do your cruel, boring, cynical, unrewarding job." He paused. "Eventually, the crab gets thrown in a kettle of boiling water. Over."

"What's your designation, Canis?"

"Ah, yes. This business about the code key and my designation was your signal to me, just like the shortwave broadcast was my signal to you. You believed I'd recognize what you wanted, who you were to me, and you could flush me out and kill me. You think I'm a threat to your organization and that the threat is an immediate one. You were counting on my caring about the girl enough to play along with your ploy. And I did. Here I am. Over."

"Here you are. So?"

"The funny thing is, I think you really do need the key—not just my designation but the whole thing. To have arrived at your conclusions about me, you must be operating in the dark. Maybe no one has provided you with the new decoding scheme. Maybe you have a new personnel designation nobody bothered to tell you about. There might be logistical problems, or it might be a matter of bureaucratic incompetence. Maybe you're being cut out. Those are all reasonable conclusions. Otherwise, getting the key has nothing to do with eliminating me as a threat to your security. You're simply hoping to kill two birds with one stone. Over."

"You seem to know a lot."

"You made a big mistake, Pegasus. You concluded I was a threat. I wasn't. But I am now, because I know how the code works, and I know what the key is. It would give American intelligence a fix on your network in the U.S. and, probably, abroad. That's the kind of information that would make your operations vulnerable. All that's needed is for one of your assets to give up his designation code to American intelligence. Such information would immensely help a person like you, Pegasus, if you chose to defect. And I have a strong suspicion you will need to do that one of these days, maybe even today. Too bad you're missing your personal designation. As I said, the kettle is always boiling. Over."

"I don't believe you."

"I can prove it. Release the girl."

"Not yet."

"I don't even know that you have her."

"I have her," Pegasus said.

"She's on one of these boats. That's why we're meeting here, in case you need to produce her. You need to produce her."

There was a pause. "Here's a token."

He stepped from the shadows under the eaves on the fueling dock and held out the purple velvet top hat so that Elliot could see it through the binoculars.

He stepped back.

Elliot depressed the talk-button. "That doesn't prove she's alive."

"This is attracting too much attention. I'll take you to her."

"I'm not going on board with you. I won't come back, and neither will she."

"I have a confederate," came the reply. "Just like you. He's on the boat with the girl, waiting for my signal. He can either bring her to you or put a bullet in her head. Play it smart, Canis."

"You're working alone."

"You can't know."

It was true; he could not risk finding out if Pegasus had a confederate. "So. What now?"

In the silence that followed Elliot could sense Pegasus' frustration over failing to dislodge him from the roof. He decided to prolong it. He wanted Pegasus to talk, to commit himself.

After a moment the walkie-talkie crackled: "I showed you the hat. It's enough."

"I want you to listen to me," Elliot said. "I'm going to tell you what I know so that you can make the right move."

"The right move?"

"Whatever that is for you. My only interest is seeing Morning Star—the girl—returned alive."

"What difference does it make to you?" Pegasus' frustration was growing; Elliot could hear it, even in the thin voice on the walkie-talkie.

There was a burst of interference, and he momentarily lost the signal. "Are you there, Pegasus?"

"I'm here."

"Good. Let me tell you what I know. During what was probably a routine surveillance of the Peking Palace in Redondo Beach, you noticed a private detective named Frederick Happ paying attention to me. This had been going on for some time, raising your suspicions. I suspect you were aware of some kind of law-enforcement activity and had reason to be alert. In any case, having stumbled across him on your rounds, you concluded that Happ was an intelligence agent or contractor, hiding in plain sight as a private investigator. Why not? After all, the Peking Palace was your connection to your asset in Pacifidyne. It was a hot spot. Once you started down this path, you concluded that I—a man whose real name you didn't know—was the target of an investigation and was, therefore, your man Canis Minor. You didn't know what to do about me. If I were arrested, I might talk. I imagine you have a pretty good life here. You don't want to end up in prison. If you were to save your operation and yourself, you had to take control. That's why you went to Happ's office in Van Nuys, hoping to discover something that would identify me. When you had what you needed, you killed him. Then you came after me. There was nowhere for you to lurk around the Pacifidyne parking structure, waiting to tail me home at four-thirty when two thousand other cars were heading onto the street, not unless you had several days and a lot of luck. So I'm guessing you went to my house, but I wasn't there." Elliot paused. "Am I right?"

"Essentially."

"Now it's your turn. Go get the girl."

"Are you really in a position to make demands? Tell me about the code key, and we'll negotiate."

"Since you persist, I'll share what I know," Elliot said. "The numbers station provides the code. You monitor it, obviously. Anyone with a shortwave receiver can listen. Every listener knows the numbers mean something, but nobody knows what." He paused. "Over."

Crackle of static. "Tell me something I can use."

Without lowering either the binoculars or the walkie-talkie, Elliot shifted his weight to relieve the pressure on his elbows. "The numbers are keyed to a Vernam cipher. Any operative in this country—in the world— could, if provided, use a one-time pad for decoding the messages. You yourself use one, or at least you did until recently. Problem: once you've used up the pages on the pad, someone has to smuggle a new one into the country and deliver it. Problem: if you are caught with the pad or lose it, the whole system falls apart for everybody. Problem: a one-time pad shared among a dozen operatives multiplies the risk a dozen-fold. If any agent turns into a security risk, the code has to be abandoned. Stop me if I'm wrong."

"Go on."

"I suspect that someone changed the way your numerical designation works. I assumed all the sequences were four digits long to correspond to entries on a one-time pad, but now I know that's not the case. This afternoon, I was looking through some phone directories at the library. I remembered that you used the word 'directory' when you called me in Berkeley. Suddenly, it clicked. My mind expanded, and I knew what you were talking about. I realized that the white-page directories, with their columns of telephone numbers, would yield a random distribution of sequences if you eliminated the first three digits, which are assigned to geographic areas. In fact, the last four digits of phone numbers could be used as Vernam-cipher keys, tailored to individual users across the country. Maybe even across the world. I'm not sure how phone numbers are assigned in Britain or South Africa. In any case, somebody has to provide copies of the pages to whoever encodes the communications. Somebody like you spends his afternoons in the bathroom at the public library, maybe right here in San Francisco, photographing the White Pages from all over the country—L.A., Seattle, Oakland, Washington, New York, Arlington, Detroit. Any good library carries the current directories. Better yet, the agent could simply steal the phone books he wanted. The books or the microfilms of the books make their way back to the Soviet Union, probably in diplomatic pouches, and are distributed for broadcast. The radio announcer conveys the starting page number of the appropriate local directory each time a new message is transmitted. There's probably some sort of simple permutation code, secondary to the main code, in the first digits after a particular agent's call numbers are announced. Then it's a matter of using the first twenty-six number sequences to represent the letters of the Latin alphabet, then the next twenty-six, and so on, to prevent patterns from developing. Or maybe you use the thirty-two letters of the Russian alphabet. It doesn't matter. New phone directories are issued every year, so the problem of running out of pages is moot. Each operative uses his local phone directory as a personal code book. Furthermore, any operative whose home is searched will never be caught with a one-time pad. Everybody has a phone book at home or the office. Where do you live, Pegasus?"

No reply.

"Where do you live?"

"North Hollywood."

"Then that's the directory you use. Am I right?"

"Yes."

"But nobody's given you the new start sequences."

"Yes."

"For me, the West L.A. phone directory would be used."

"Would be used?"

"If I were Canis Minor. I'm not."

"You are."

"I really am not," Elliot said. "I don't have a designation. I have nothing to give you but a scheme you already know."

"If that's true, I have no reason to release the girl. Yet you came here anyway. Are you that foolish?"

Elliot smiled. Pegasus had said enough.

"Canis, are you there? Over."

"Copy that, Pegasus. I wanted everything on the record."

"The record?"

"I'm very skillful when it comes to improvising electronics. As I mentioned, I have military training and, conveniently, there's an Army-

Navy surplus store in Berkeley with all kinds of specialized parts. If you point your binoculars through the front window of the diner, you'll see the bearded gentleman who handed you the two-way radio. He should be sitting in the phone booth, wearing a set of headphones. In his bag is a tape recorder. The tape recorder is wired to this particular communication channel. Everything we're saying is going on tape. If you attempt to hurt me or the girl, or if you make a move toward the diner, he will call the police. Over."

Elliot depressed the talk button on the second walkie-talkie. "Hold up the tape recorder. Over."

"You got it."

"He's holding up the machine," Elliot said into the first walkie-talkie. "Do you see it, Pegasus?"

There was a long pause. Elliot, patient, listened to the sounds of the evening, letting Pegasus think the matter through. Finally the walkie-talkie crackled:

"What do you want me to do?"

"You can't kill me. Not here, not ever. In the event of my death, my associate has instructions to deliver copies of our taped conversation to the F.B.I., the Soviet embassy in Washington, and the Soviet consulate here in San Francisco. Your superiors will be furious. There will be significant political consequences. You don't know the identity of my associate, so you won't be able to track him down."

This time the pause lingered.

"She's on the *Sally Belle*. I'm telling you because I hope you'll give me a head start. I need to make some decisions."

"Yes, you do. If she's dead, everyone receives copies of the tapes within hours. At that point, your life will be a short one. If she's alive, you still have the opportunity to defect and save yourself. If not, you'd better run like hell. In either case, you're finished. Take out your gun and throw it in the water."

To reach his pistol with a free hand, Pegasus put the purple velvet top hat on his head. He threw the gun in the bay.

"Good."

Through the binoculars, Elliot saw that his adversary had raised his eyes to the rooftop of the diner. Pegasus pushed the talk button: "All this for the girl?"

"All this for the girl."

"You're a smart fellow, Canis."

"You're damn right I am. Now throw your walkie-talkie in the water."

Pegasus turned and flipped the walkie-talkie into the dark water.

As he stepped off the fuel dock, he wondered what Susan was doing. Had anyone called to ask about him? Had she told them he had gone to Guadalajara? Of course she had; she was devoted. She would come with him now that the old life was over. He made a mental note to cancel the dental appointment he had on Monday.

The first shotgun blast hit him in the shoulder and spun him around.

"Stokely! You motherfucking son of a bitch!"

The second shot caught him full in the head, shredding the purple hat and taking off most of his skull. He slammed face-down onto the wharf. Bobby Dobell pumped the shotgun as Rowdy Gomez sprinted up with a baseball bat in his hand.

An instant later, Special Agent Russell Bogosian shouted, "Drop the weapon!"

He and Grassmick were crouched fifteen yards away, service revolvers drawn. People screamed and scattered.

Dobell swung the shotgun in their direction, and Bogosian shot him once in the hip and twice in the abdomen.

Gomez dropped the bat and threw his hands in the air. "Don't shoot, man!" But Grassmick shot him anyway, three times, taking off his left ear and winging him in the neck before drilling him through the heart.

Grassmick and Bogosian rushed up and stood over Dobell, who was thrashing in pain. Grassmick kicked the shotgun out of his reach. Gomez sprawled on his back, a dark stain spreading on his chest.

There were screams, and the people on the wharf scrambled in confusion away from the fuel dock. Then, like crows resettling on the branches, they moved back toward the scene of carnage, joined by curious customers from the Italian diner.

Frantz spotted Elliot, smeared with roof tar, as he came around the side of the restaurant. He held up the tape recorder and grinned. "Now what?"

"Get to the car before the police arrive," Elliot instructed. "I'll need the tapes in the unlikely case someone comes for me in the future."

"You got it. I'll wait for you."

"It might take some time. I have to make a phone call about the *Sally Belle*, and I want to stick around to make sure Morning Star is okay when they find her."

"What about those feds?"

"I'll hang back. It won't do me much good to get involved with the F.B.I. again. Without specific designation codes tied to geographical areas, the directory cipher won't be of much use. I might not even be right about it. They'll have to figure out who Pegasus is on their own."

Stanley Stokely and the Dobell sisters, unaware that it was their father who had been shot by the F.B.I., circled behind the crowd at a leisurely pace, for once attracting not the slightest attention. As sirens rose in the distance, they slipped down Jefferson and vanished into the gloaming.

. . .

Berkeley

The Computer Center was dark, but the CDC 6400 went about its unceasing business. The alarm clock on Professor Amadeo Knizner's desk ticked off the seconds, and at irregular intervals the telephone rang, insistent and shrill. On the seminar table, illuminated by a forty-watt desk lamp, lay Knizner's copy of the *I Ching* and a sheaf of blank computer paper. His eyes shone, as if with an undiagnosed fever. Across from him sat Jojo, a red pencil in his hand and a stack of blue exam books at his elbow.

Knizner tossed the three oracle coins. They fell with the faintest sound on a green blotter he had laid out for his work. With a pen, he made lines on the computer paper, constructing a hexagram, boosting or demolishing the G.P.A.s of the deserving and the undeserving, determining the fates of his students.

"Fascinating [*ahem*]. Gèn Kǎn [*ahem*]," Knizner murmured, finding the hexagram in the book. "That warrants a C-plus [*ahem*]."

Jojo marked a large red C-plus on the blue book and set it on the pile of graded exams.

"Next [*ahem*]?"

"Jesperson, David."

Knizner tossed the coins and, murmuring to himself, began limning the new hexagram.

Jojo slanted his eyes toward the stack of ungraded exam books. He ran his thumb through them until he found his own and slipped it out of the pile. On the cover, he marked a large red *A*.

• • •

San Francisco, June 12, 1967

Communicating by glances, shrugs, and murmurs, Sagittarius, Ursa Major, and the consul-general in Pacific Heights worked over the wording of the report. They finally decided to say that "Pegasus," facing apprehension by the American authorities—there was some question about whether it was the F.B.I. or the C.I.A.; they settled on the A.T.F.—had committed suicide. Shot himself in the head and chest in such a way that his weapon ended up in San Francisco Bay. He had been on a boat. An informant's boat. A stranger's boat.

• • •

Pacing around his office, Assistant Special Agent in Charge Henry Fagerberg, Jr., with input from Special Agents Grassmick and Bogosian, formulated his report. The victim, identified as Albert Carpenter of North Hollywood, California, had been shot and killed at Fisherman's Wharf by Robert J. Dobell and Ruben "Rowdy" Gomez in an apparent case of mistaken identity. Dobell and Gomez were known criminals and close associates of F.B.I. target Stanley Stokely. The shooters had in turn been shot by Special Agents Eduardo Grassmick and Russell Bogosian. [No mention was made of having to find their way to the wharf after their car was towed from the Panhandle during their encounter with Little Pete.] Gomez died on the scene. Dobell was in custody on murder charges for killing Albert Carpenter and attempted-murder charges for stabbing Julius "Half Pint" Gronkowski with a screwdriver. The agents had followed protocol.

Found on Robert Dobell's person were ten thousand [after an argument they reduced the number to a reasonable one thousand] doses of LSD-25, and [after another argument over numbers] almost two thousand dollars in a money belt. It had been documented. Dobell was believed to be the primary liaison between Stanley Stokely, the Hells Angels motorcycle club, and the revolutionary underground in Oakland, using money from the sale of LSD to finance the purchase of illegal weapons. [Fagerberg made a note to investigate this hypothesis.]

In addition, based on an anonymous phone call to the S.F.P.D., the agents had discovered a kidnapping victim in the hold of a fishing boat, the *Sally Belle*, moored at the marina. Investigation into the ownership of the boat was ongoing. The victim, Mary Ellen McGovern, had identified Albert Carpenter as her kidnapper but was unable to provide an explanation for the crime nor any insight into his killing by Robert Dobell, whom she identified as the perpetrator of an earlier kidnapping. The McGovern girl had been observed in the company of Stanley Stokely, as well as Ruben Gomez, but her connection to the two remained ambiguous. She had told such a wild story that A.S.A.C. Fagerberg doubted her sanity. There had been mention of an aerospace engineer named Elliot Ames, encountered earlier in the day at the scene of a home invasion in Berkeley. The whole thing was looking like a case of botched surveillance and poor investigative technique. It made the Bureau look incompetent, and Fagerberg did not need another chewing out from the Special Agent in Charge.

Grassmick reminded him that the McGovern girl was wanted in Los Angeles for grand theft; but as far as Fagerberg was concerned, that son of a bitch Muncie could do his own work, why was the Bureau messing around in an L.A.P.D. matter, and anyway what did the L.A. field office ever do for San Francisco?

She disappeared from the report.

• • •

Los Angeles

Standing at his window, observing the sluggish passage of cars in the street below, Assistant Special Agent in Charge Roderick Muncie, the back of his neck swollen and red from a fresh beekeeping incident at his place in Simi Valley, dictated that the apprehension of Gordon Blackmon (code name Canis Minor), a senior design engineer at Pacifidyne Corporation in Redondo Beach, had resulted from the long-term surveillance of the target's daily movements, establishing a pattern of suspicious behavior, and culminating in a visit to a residence in West Los Angeles believed to be associated with active espionage. Don Clegg, seated next to Muncie's desk tapped out the report on a sticky Royal typewriter. Discarded wads of paper littered the floor. Bert Armbruster slouched indecently at his elbow, aviator shades pulled over stale eyes, his left foot juddering with chemical energy.

Upon being approached at the residence by Special Agents Donald Clegg and Robert Armbruster [here Muncie turned to give his men a crabby look], Blackmon had attempted to flee and was apprehended after a short—make that a prolonged—chase. Clegg stopped typing. He pointed out that when Blackmon had caught sight of their badges, he'd fainted dead away and was transported to St. John's Hospital. Quite by accident he and Armbruster had found a pilfered set of blueprints in the box of decorations Blackmon was carrying and a trove of classified material in his car. Muncie told him that accidents didn't matter; results mattered, goddammit.

When they searched Blackmon's home in Hawthorne, they discovered the micro-photography equipment and the shortwave radio, which was sitting, for some reason, on a tall stack of old phone directories in his garage. The wife had been distraught. Blackmon was cooperating with F.B.I. interrogators and was expected to provide valuable information about

Soviet operations in the aerospace, electronics, and communications industries on the West Coast. [Up yours, San Francisco.]

Since Blackmon had so far failed to implicate other Pacifidyne employees, Muncie decided to strike Elliot Ames's name from the report. It appeared he was nothing more than one of Canis Minor's lunch buddies. Why had Clegg and Armbruster bothered to bring him to the Bureau's attention?

· · ·

San Francisco

After several hours at various city offices, Elliot managed to track his MG convertible to the impound lot where it had been deposited the previous Thursday afternoon. Dressed in slacks and a button-down checked shirt from the Roos Brothers store, he looked like a new man. Morning Star and Frantz, wearing matching leather headbands, accompanied him on the rounds of municipal authority, trying to keep his spirit light in the face of bureaucratic indifference. Between offices, the two of them shared rank-smelling joints rolled in yellow paper.

Now they were crammed into the passenger's seat of the MG, giggling and attempting to construct a fresh doobie. The convertible top was down; the air was soft and promising.

"At least my luggage is still in the trunk," Elliot said, climbing into the car. "Too bad about your duffel bag, Morning Star."

"I hope somebody's making good use of it."

"Maybe you should hold off on that." He nodded at their four-handed dope-rolling endeavor. "This is city property."

"We have enough for everybody!" Morning Star said.

The engine refused to turn over. "I don't know why I expected that to work," Elliot said. He got out and walked over to the yard office.

"Is it too late to get a mechanic out here?" he said to the attendant.

"Maybe." The attendant stuck his hands in the pockets of his coveralls and looked at the space above Elliot's head.

"Maybe I can use your phone?" he said amiably.

"Nope."

Elliot drew a deep breath. "Can I make a contribution to your vacation fund?"

The attendant raised his eyes higher to the heavens. "I could use forty dollars."

"You gotta be kidding."

"Suit yourself." The attendant turned away.

Just then, a City of San Francisco tow truck dragging a sleek black Italian automobile turned into the lot. A familiar face was behind the wheel.

"Elliot, it's Eli!" Morning Star called excitedly. "Hi, Eli!"

Leaving the engine running, Eli Tarr climbed out of the cab. He ambled over to the convertible. "I have something of yours." Elliot grinned. "I never thought I'd see you again!"

"Likewise," Eli said, not quite grinning back. "You can keep that old poncho."

"Thanks, I will. I suppose you heard about Dobell and Gomez."

"That was a bad scene," Eli said, scanning the impound yard. He wiped his palms on his pants. "For ever'body. This thing with Bobby is gonna take a bite outta my income. Top a that, the F.B.I.'s really on Stanley Stokely's ass now, so no more a that cosmic sunshine for my people in L.A. I'll be eating beans in the near future. Looks like you're healing up though."

"Would this help?" Morning Star reached into her soiled shoulder bag and produced a brick of Afghan hashish. Jojo had bought the other one for a thousand dollars. She beamed. "It's supposed to go to the Grateful Dead. But they never, you know, saved our lives."

Eli leaned over and took the brick. He hefted it, held it to his nose, and inhaled. Sighed.

"You are an angel. An absolute angel."

"This is my friend Frantz."

"Frantz. Dig it."

"Like Frantz Fanon," Frantz said, raising his fist in an international sign of solidarity and spilling the rest of the grass on his lap.

"Right on," Eli said. "Where're you all headed?"

"Wherever the road takes us," Morning Star responded. "We might make it to Big Sur. Right, Elliot?"

"Maybe," Elliot affirmed. "I'm open to possibility."

"He said 'maybe'! He's so responsible with his language. Isn't that sad?"

"I said I was open," Elliot insisted.

"Also, I want to witness the music festival at Monterey," Morning Star said to Eli.

"We're not going anywhere if we can't get the car moving. The starter's defunct." Elliot slid back into the driver's seat and tried the ignition to prove his point.

Eli stroked his chin. "It doesn't sound like a starter problem." He lifted the hood and disappeared under it. After a moment, he looked around the edge. "Your starter's pristine, man. You got a loose battery cable is all."

"Oh," Elliot said, leaning around so that he could see him from the front seat. "I must have missed that class in high school. These last few days have revealed several holes in my knowledge."

Eli pulled an adjustable wrench out of his pocket. A few seconds later he slammed the hood. "You're good to go. Let's hear it."

Elliot turned the key and hit the gas. The engine snarled like a tiger and settled into a satisfying purr.

As the convertible pulled past the tow truck and through the gate, Morning Star braced herself on Frantz's shoulder and rose to wave. "See you in another dream, Eli!"

She pulled up her blouse and held it until the impound yard was out of sight.

.   .   .

Monterey, June 17, 1967

Promenading along the grassy fringes of the crowd, waiting for the band to take the stage, Stanley Stokely puffed on a meerschaum pipe which contained a chunk of hash the size of a thumb, while the triplets—Astrid, Angela, and Alice—slurped on slices of watermelon. A butterfly alighted on Stokely's beet-colored Borsalino. Exhaling a killer cloud, he continued a monologue begun several hours before. "My goodness, Papa likes his resin." His large Adam's apple bobbed. "What a great inconvenience that the Coast Guard intercepted Terence and Andre before they could reach harbor. Fortunately, an intimate of mine—you girls have met him: Jojo—managed to locate this delectable product. After the show, we will visit backstage with the Grateful Dead, who have agreed to take the rest of the brick off my hands for a very tidy profit, if I do say so, not to mention my stash of STP. Papa needs to raise funds and close accounts." He patted the leather satchel slung over his shoulder and puffed on his pipe.

In the crowd, which in the long shadows of the afternoon looked as if it had been translated *in toto* from Golden Gate Park, Frantz was also firing up a smoke. He passed the fat joint to Morning Star, and she sent it on down the row of folding chairs. At the end of the row, a group of Hells Angels in full colors received the burnt roach with open dissatisfaction. But the spirit of the festival had infected them, and they shrugged off their disappointment and went back to smoking their inferior kif and killing time reading the newspapers. Sparrows darted around them.

Morning Star could not believe she was going to see Moby Grape, not to mention. . . . "Who else is scheduled tonight?"

"Oh, man," Frantz mumbled. He had been toking steadily all afternoon. He reached under the serape he was wearing and handed her the handbill. She unfolded it and studied the list printed in magenta on a yellow field beneath an Art Nouveau drawing of a whale in a swimming pool. "Oh, boy! Otis Redding!"

Morning Star gazed at the handbill, mesmerized, luxuriating in the summer air, the odor of patchouli and hot dogs, the carnivalesque rippling of the crowd, sixty-thousand souls connected to universal consciousness, plugged into the cosmic groove, sizzling, the buzz expanding, amplifying, filling the world. Ten days ago, she had severed ties with her past and jumped onto the spinning wheel of freakish fortune, ready for whatever the world had to offer, ruthless chance or benignant fate. And now she was totally here.

She squeezed Frantz's arm. "Do you think anyone cares if I take off my shirt?"

"Oh, baby," he said. He held up a glassine envelope with two orange tablets in it. "Look what I found in my pocket. My man Jojo laid it on me last week."

Unnoticed by Frantz and Morning Star, the creator of this chemical treasure continued to address the triplets as they sauntered along the margins. "So you see, my dears, it behooves me to decamp to friendlier climes, namely the south of France. Papa's dear companion Philip has discovered a fabulous abode in Villefranche-sur-Mer where we will live in splendor until this business with Uncle Sam blows over."

Astrid, Angela, and Alice Dobell, their faces sticky with watermelon juice, exchanged worried glances.

"Now, now, my darlings," Stokely drawled, "Papa has not forgotten about you. With your dear father facing an indefinite period of incarceration, you will need to be provided for. You will be our guests. Philip adores you, particularly for your deep understanding of mathematical principles, my little geniuses. There is, of course, the obstacle known as the Mann Act, under which our relationship might be wrongly interpreted as impertinent, immoral, and illegal. Technically, we will be crossing state lines on our way out of the country. But as you know, Papa has no interest in sexual gratification with females, even ones as utterly delicious as you, my sweets. With all due respect to Dr. Leary, lysergic acid diethylamide has not cured Papa of his so-called deviancy." He drew a business envelope from his nehru jacket and handed it to Alice or Angela or Astrid. "Inside you will find the phone number of Papa's superlative travel agent, Miss Sheilah Robinson, and a detailed map to the villa from the airport in Nice." Stokely patted the satchel. "Upon connecting with the Grateful Dead, I will provide three thousand dollars cash for your immediate upkeep, whether you choose to remain in San Francisco or, heaven willing, journey to France."

As the foursome meandered back the way they had come, Tommy Smothers strolled onto the stage, blissfully bewildered, and stood before the microphone to cheers and rising waves of applause. He leaned in. The shimmering crowd inhaled its collective breath and held it. "The first group, Moby Grape, we're very, uh, happy to have," he stammered, "because nobody else wanted to go first."

. . .

Los Angeles

As the FRANCO'S—FLOWERS WITH SOUL van labored up Coldwater Canyon, the radio tuned to KFWB, the only station they could pick up, a grumpy pair of F.B.I. special agents munched on stale Clark Bars and drank from bottles of Dr. Pepper they had bought at a gas station on Sunset Boulevard. The d.j. announced that they were listening to the new single from Moby Grape. Clegg's and Armbruster's plan had been to celebrate the arrest of the Pacifidyne engineer by going fishing in the Sierras for a week, but A.S.A.C. Muncie had made a big deal about the wild-goose chase in West L.A. and the attention the D.A. was lavishing on the illegal bugs at the China One location, and he had put them on a new surveillance detail: some dump in Pacoima that was believed to shelter a bomb-making cadre connected to the Hells Angels motorcycle club in Oakland. Even though they had plugged the Pacifidyne security leak, here they were, chugging toward the north Valley as Saturday drew to a close, without alcohol, air-conditioning, or gratitude for a job well done.

Clegg, behind the wheel, glanced at his partner. "I still think that Ames creep is involved in this mess. I mean, what was Blackmon doing at his house anyway? Decorating? Give me a break. He was delivering classified material. Mark my words, sooner or later, he'll crack."

"Whaddya mean 'crack'? The guy's already confessing like he's on his deathbed. America doesn't have a thing to worry about if that's the kinda bastard the commies are recruiting."

"I still think Ames is involved. All those electronics in his back room."

"What difference does it make? Nothing turns out like it should." Armbruster drained his bottle and threw it out the window into the bushes rushing by.

They lapsed into silence. The engine strained on the incline.

As they reached Mulholland Drive, Armbruster suddenly straightened in his seat. "Stop the van!" he shouted.

"Whaddya mean, stop the van?"

"Pull over, goddammit. Stop the van!"

Clegg took his foot off the accelerator and let the van roll through the intersection and drift to a shivering halt on the gravel shoulder. The car that had been trailing them up the canyon burst past, kicking up yellow dust which drifted through the open window. Clegg sneezed. Below them, the

San Fernando Valley simmered in a broth of hot smog. The air was thick with the odor of sage and eucalyptus.

Armbruster leaped out of the van and plunged into the Spanish broom growing along the road. Clegg watched his brown-suited figure disappear into the brush. This behavior was becoming disturbingly usual. Armbruster never planned ahead. He should have used the restroom at the gas station.

Clegg released an irritable sigh and wished he hadn't drunk the bottle of Dr. Pepper. Now he'd spend the whole night on the stake-out having to take a piss. Maybe he should make a quick trip to the bushes himself.

Before he could act, Armbruster, wild-eyed and fouled with twiggy debris, stumbled back through the Spanish broom and barged into the van. In his arms he clutched a large orange tabby cat wearing a blue collar with a name tooled on it. Shreds of eucalyptus bark clung to its fur, and fresh blood stained its lips and nostrils. Dinner, Clegg supposed. Disgusting. The cat had enormous green eyes that looked at him without blinking—indeed, without any recognition of him as a sentient being.

"What the hell is that?" Clegg said.

"I spotted him in the bushes and figured I had to grab him."

"What for, for Christ's sake? You plan to shoot it?"

"Shoot it!" Armbruster exclaimed. "Good Lord, man. I'm gonna take him home. I need something to love."

Armbruster hugged the cat, which began to purr. He nuzzled its neck. His heart felt swollen, fated and swollen.

• • •

Pasadena, August 21, 2020
De facto if not *de jure*, we remain locked down, constrained by the pandemic, frustrated, racked by superstition, mourning the loss of mobility, eager to believe, in our lust for conspiracies, that this period of national delirium is somehow not the result of random events beyond our comprehension and control.

On Tuesday night Talia, after watching the Dodgers lose to the Padres, announced that she'd had enough of this bullshit. Online summer classes sucked, she was lonely for physical company, I was so not what she had in mind for a desert-island companion. "I could really use a road trip before school starts," she said. "Have some *fun* for a change. Of course, I'd rather go by myself, but since I haven't taken the driving test, I guess you'll have to come."

Tomorrow, we're heading to Sonoma County. The day will be almost exactly fifty-three years from the day my parents, Elliot Ames and Constance Campbell, having made peace—with themselves more than with each other—formalized the inevitable at the Alameda County Clerk-Recorder's Office. We will be visiting my Uncle Frank and his partner, Mary Ellen, who have lived since 1970 on three acres near Sebastopol, where they raised chickens, grapes, and two daughters, my cousins Janis and Carla, who both work for the City of Santa Rosa. So far Frantz and Morning Star have resisted the temptation to sell their little Eden to Silicon Valley weekenders at an ungodly profit. Their place is isolated enough to provide a quarantine bubble for a few days, although the wildfires burning through Sonoma might wipe out the farmhouse before we arrive.

My parents also owned a place in Sonoma for a while, a clapboard vacation house nestled in the vineyards. It was a long drive from L.A., and rural life never suited them. In 1979 my father left his job at Pacifidyne for a research position at UCLA, aiming to develop computers that could be "shocked" into reconfiguring their neural architecture. He retired in 2002. Now he is dead, passed into another dream.

Back at the turn of the century, when digital storage had not yet replaced analog tape, he recorded several hours of personal history on his beloved Teac. I have listened to a few of the tapes labeled *1967* and have been reminded that, contrary to formula and popular belief, the chance encounter of rom-com characters—or the people they often resemble—does not inevitably lead to love; traumatic experiences don't always bind those who suffer them; revelations do not always alter character; betrayals can be forgiven and mostly forgotten; people may be suited to each other at some fundamental level no human can understand.

While I was playing the second of the small reel-to-reel tapes that my Uncle Frank recorded that fateful night on Fisherman's Wharf, the Teac caught fire. I haven't managed to find a company that can transfer the other tapes to digital format. You would think someone in L.A. had the equipment. It doesn't matter. I don't need to hear them.

THE END

ABOUT THE AUTHOR

Eric Sean Rawson lives in Pasadena and teaches at the University of Southern California. He is the author of the novel *Banana Republic*, two poetry collections, and a rhetoric reader, *American Subcultures*. When he isn't writing or teaching, he dedicates himself to Dodgers baseball, mid-century California art, and street photography.

NOTE FROM THE AUTHOR

Word-of-mouth is crucial for any author to succeed. If you enjoyed *Any Better Than This*, please leave a review online—anywhere you are able. Even if it's just a sentence or two. It would make all the difference and would be very much appreciated.

Thanks!
Eric Sean Rawson

We hope you enjoyed reading this title from:

BLACK❀ROSE
writing™

www.blackrosewriting.com

Subscribe to our mailing list – *The Rosevine* – and receive **FREE** books, daily deals, and stay current with news about upcoming releases and our hottest authors.
Scan the QR code below to sign up.

Already a subscriber? Please accept a sincere thank you for being a fan of Black Rose Writing authors.

View other Black Rose Writing titles at www.blackrosewriting.com/books and use promo code **PRINT** to receive a **20% discount** when purchasing.

www.ingramcontent.com/pod-product-compliance
Lightning Source LLC
Chambersburg PA
CBHW010734100726
47899CB00009B/3047